The DEVIL
SHE KNOWS

The DEVIL SHE KNOWS

DIANE WHITESIDE

BRAVA

KENSINGTON PUBLISHING CORP.

www.kensingtonbooks.com

BRAVA BOOKS are published by

Kensington Publishing Corp.
119 West 40th Street
New York, NY 10018

All Kensington titles, imprints, and distributed lines are available at special quantity discounts for bulk purchases for sales promotion, premiums, fund-raising, educational or institutional use. Special book excerpts or customized printings can also be created to fit specific needs. For details, write or phone the office of the Kensington Special Sales Manager: Kensington Publishing Corp., 119 West 40th Street, New York, NY 10018. Attn. Special Sales Department. Phone: 1-800-221-2647.

Brava and the B logo Reg. U.S. Pat. & TM Off.

ISBN-13: 978-0-7582-2517-7
ISBN-10: 0-7582-2517-2

First Kensington Trade Paperback Printing: June 2010

10 9 8 7 6 5 4 3 2 1

Printed in the United States of America

Chapter One

Arizona Territory, north of Tucson, September 1878

The two stagecoaches raced onward into the setting sun, hurling dust into the sky like profligate gamblers. A covey of rifle-toting braves could have hidden in their wake's sandstorm, or their future hosts' few fences.

Gareth Lowell scanned their back trail using the best spyglass available within a day's ride from Job's Wells. Lady Luck had favored him enough at the card tables to give him this expensive piece of optics; he never bothered to look for the fickle wench anywhere else and simply went prepared for the worst.

Apaches were somewhere in this barren valley, but farther than his rifle and pair of Colt Peacemakers could reach. At least the fine bowie knife Portia Townsend had given him couldn't sink into any enemies at the moment.

He'd ridden all night from Prescott to meet this stagecoach at the dying station. He'd have fought Cochise's entire band for the chance to slog through hell, if William Donovan had asked him to.

He simply needed a few more minutes until he could escape Job's Wells.

Built atop an old Indian ruin, the stagecoach station's lone building was sunk halfway into the ground and no wall stood more than four feet high. Its pale stones melted and blurred at the corners like their builders' ghosts. Only a few, dark brown splatters survived to hint at why those inhabitants had departed, with deep gouges beside once crimson stains.

A single circle of stones rising in the center courtyard stood stalwart below its wooden arch, silent witness to this outpost's long purpose. A well was priceless in this wilderness of sand and thorns, carved by mountain ranges like coiled rattlesnakes. Reaching the next drink of sweet water meant riding hard for at least one day, while a man's skin twitched every time a breeze blew lest it be an Apache death blow.

Five horses fretted in the rickety excuse for a paddock, swishing their tails and warily assessing their surroundings. Four of them were saddled, while the fifth was a fully loaded pack horse. The two best saddle horses came from the Donovan & Sons stable, of course, something which reassured Gareth at a level so deep he merely had to glance at them and his heartbeat would ease.

Now the trailing stagecoach was close enough to count the rifles bristling from every window and the roof. Either the journey through Red Rock Pass had been nastier than usual or this crew was more determined than most of their kind to show how they'd protect the leader at all costs.

Gareth was hoping for the second reason. A smart man would put his money on the first.

"Any sign of Apaches?" asked Baylor. Like Gareth, his rifle rested against the wall beside him but a row of cartridge boxes, like substitutes for absent reinforcements, were lined up before him. His unkempt terrier Tornado paced beside his feet, a ragged ear alertly cocked.

"Nothing on the stages' back trail, in the east and north," Gareth answered.

Kenly grunted, the single sound indicating full understanding of everything either the younger man or Tornado hadn't said. The dog would have sounded the loudest alarm, if he'd found enemies coming in.

As rail-thin as Baylor was barrel-chested, the two had never been seen far apart during the years Gareth had known them. But each other's company was all they clung to—certainly not steady jobs or a single place.

"Nor where they're going." Baylor slung his rifle over his shoulder and rapidly stuffed the ammunition back into his pockets, with the dexterous movements of a poker shark readying himself for a new game.

The first stagecoach turned for the station, still moving so quickly that the ground shook slightly and the air trembled under the horses' tack's metallic ringing and the wheels' heavy rumble.

Baylor and Kenly promptly raced to fetch the previously prepared water for the horses, Tornado uttering small yips at their heels. Here and now, nothing was more important to them than waving the two stages goodbye.

Gareth waited on the yard's edge, rifle in hand, alert for any signs of attack. Five minutes from now and the visitors would be gone, having left behind the crucial package and its courier.

Then they would hit the trail together. Two armed men riding for Tucson these days had perhaps an even chance of making it there alive.

A door opened and a passenger burst out of the dusty coach.

"Gareth, my friend!" A well-dressed apparition hurtled toward him with no hint of his messenger. "Why are you here and not Uncle William?"

Portia Townsend held out her hands to him, her face shining with delight underneath a ribbon-bedecked hat. Her dancing feet sent her new and supposedly grownup skirts' hems twirling fast enough to kick up small dust devils.

Who the hell had dropped her skirts and put her in that adult dress? Didn't they know she was a child?

How old was she, anyway?

She'd been twelve when they met. No decent man lusted after a little girl, whether or not she was the boss's niece. Given how she missed her younger brothers, it was easier to think of her as a younger sister who needed a playmate.

But now?

When the devil had she grown enough curves to fill out a corset?

No, he would not consider her *that* way. This attire was another bit of her chicanery, designed to twist him around her finger and start another escapade.

He would never become obsessed with a child.

But her youth made it made worse for her to be here.

His stomach plummeted into an icy hell somewhere below his boots. He should have known the peace was too good to last. He'd have far rather heard hundreds of war cries erupting out of Victorio's army, than that single feminine whoop of joy.

If anything happened to her . . . Dear God in heaven, he couldn't let Portia end up like other victims of the murderous Apaches and similar bandits, bullet-ridden and burned like barbecued hogs because their murderers wouldn't let anyone leave a long-planned death trap.

The old, never-forgotten stench washed back over him again and his belly knotted like a rattlesnake ready to strike. He snapped his greeting at Portia like a lasso, cloaking his worry in a rough edge.

"What in the Sam Hill are you doing here?" he demanded. "Weren't you supposed to have started the fall term at the new fancy school by now?"

Portia's arms drooped back to her side, a fitting end for a journey which had begun badly before taking an appalling jog in the middle.

Dear heavens, a scorpion dumped out of a boot would have received a friendlier smile from him. She hadn't expected to be welcomed into Arizona. She'd barely hoped to see him so soon, since even rolling stones gathered more moss than Gareth did. But surely their past escapades had earned her more consideration from her oldest friend.

"Ah, yes." Her smile evaporated faster than drops of water on a sun-baked rock. She should have realized she'd have to confess immediately to the worst part.

She squared her shoulders. Gareth was the best man in the world and he'd never condone even the slightest falsehood. "I already did."

His eyes narrowed, in the typical start to a blistering inquisition.

At least with Gareth, once she'd told the truth—no matter how bad—he never stayed angry with her. So the sooner she told him why she was here, the faster she'd learn where Uncle William was now and the latest news about Aunt Viola. They'd taken Gareth under their wing since Uncle William hired him at age sixteen.

"Gentlemen, you may have five minutes to stretch your legs while the little lady visits her friend," one of the drivers shouted. "If you're late, we'll leave for California without you."

Gareth shot the stage company's senior official a glare promising retribution. He didn't need time to talk to her; he probably wanted help getting her back into that rolling lockbox.

The driver simply glanced significantly toward the western horizon, with its mountain pass leading to the next cavalry post, then checked his pocket watch. Any extra time for conversation was a gift, given how fast the lengthening shadows in that narrow route could conceal an ambush for the two coaches.

Genuine shock thudded through Portia but she didn't turn to see if the man had done anything additional to deserve Gareth's condemnation. Gareth always insisted ladies should be treated with the utmost consideration. So why was he objecting to the added courtesy of allowing her time for a visit with her old friend?

She managed a noncommittal smile, one of the few things she'd learned other than music from all those ridiculous schools.

Men stepped down from the stages, talking about the unexpected rest and comparing their guns. Gareth's two companions ran forward to start watering the horses.

Gareth nodded curt comprehension to the driver and headed over to the paddock where he and Portia could have a somewhat private conversation.

Portia cast her eyes down from underneath her new hat, the only one which matched her new, long dress. Her cheeks flushed appallingly hot.

Far too long experience with her gave him painfully fast understanding of the situation.

"Did you run away from there?" Gareth demanded and fixed his steel-gray eyes on her. "Or did you and that friend get into another scrape? Isn't Cynthia her name?"

"It wasn't Cynthia's fault; it was mine." She spread her hands, wishing she didn't want to hug him. Or kiss him. Or run off to join a circus with him. Life would be far easier if she could bamboozle him just a little, the way she could flummox her father. Of course, the amount of attention Father gave her was so limited that he might believe almost any nonsensical yarn, simply to get her out of his life. He'd never dealt well with his daughter, only his sons.

"Why did you leave this one, Portia?" Gareth sharpened his tone.

None of which meant telling the truth would be pleasant.

She huffed and brushed off her skirts before looking at him again. "My headmistress announced—to the entire school!—that all Irish and Papists are doomed to eternal damnation."

Gareth's fingers curled over his gun's butt. His face hardened until a bowie knife would have appeared friendlier. She'd seen that look before, when he'd faced down a drunken Barbary Coast mob to bring them home safe from seeing the bearded lady at the circus.

For the first time in almost a week, her stomach lost its roiling boil. Somebody else would have fought, too. Even staying close to her three brothers hadn't compared to avenging that insult.

"I knew you'd understand," she sighed, expressing a certainty she hadn't known needed to be put into words until she heard it echo to the world.

He rubbed his mouth. "What happened after that?"

"Well, I couldn't let her escape unharmed, could I? Not

when Uncle William is both Irish and a believer in Catholicism, and, and . . ." Her tongue stumbled below the tears glinting in her eyes.

"The best man either of us have ever met?" Gareth suggested gently.

"Exactly!" agreed Portia ferociously. "Not to mention how he and Aunt Viola adore each other."

He nodded agreement, probably remembering all the times Uncle William and Aunt Viola had shared the warmth of their loving home with him. She'd never asked him where his own family was and he didn't offer such news. The Code of the West insisted every man be accepted for what he was, not who he'd been, even if that meant leaving family behind.

His jaw tightened, until his lips stretched into their usual severe lines, as if holding back memories too painful to express.

Poor darling. Ever since she'd first met him, she'd longed to stroke his cheek and bring him comfort. Her news should help him.

Chapter Two

Several of the other passengers came back from using the station's meager facilities.

Were there any flashes of light or blurs of dust on the stages' back trail? No, no signs of anyone tracking those plump targets. But there were still a few hours of daylight left and Apaches were far too canny to let themselves be easily seen.

She needed to tell him about the message soon, so he could make arrangements for handling it.

"Better tell the boss man in Yuma to find another fool if he wants somebody here for next week's run," Baylor announced, his voice carrying clearly from beside one of the stages.

"You two won't stay? Guess I can't blame you for standing around and waiting for Apaches to plow you under." The second driver began to examine one of his wheelers' hooves. "Where shall I have the company send your pay?"

Baylor and Kenly silently queried each other over the horses' backs, while Tornado watched alertly.

"Denver," Kenly uttered at last.

"Colorado?" questioned the first driver. "But Tucson is only a few days' ride south."

"Past Victorio's band and every savage who wants to join up with him." The second driver dug a small stone out from his horses' hoof, then let it down. The bay gelding snorted and settled back into his traces, ready to finish the run.

"And the other heathen come out to murder and rob, no matter whether they call themselves Apaches or not." The first driver poured a ladleful of water over his head. "You're wise men, my friends."

Baylor spun a store-bought biscuit high into the air, more like a gambler making a bet than a stationmaster delivering rations. The four men snatched it and its brethren up then settled into eating with controlled haste.

"Where is your headmistress now?" Gareth looked at Portia sternly.

"Her love letters to and from the school's chief trustee were *accidentally* released to the press." Portia tilted her chin in the air, centuries of aristocratic breeding defying him to ask who was responsible.

Gareth grunted acknowledgement, undoubtedly biding his time until he asked her how she'd pulled the feat off. "And you left town."

"For California by the southern route. I thought the northern route would be watched by Father's men, even though the train is faster." Her voice was softer than the hoofbeats in the sand behind them, where horses stated their eagerness for the open trail.

Gareth pulled his hat off and slapped the dust off against his leg with unnecessary force.

She smoothed out her skirts, her heart melting yet again. Had there ever been two people more attuned to each other? She hadn't even explicitly mentioned her discomfort at seeing Father. Yet Gareth had reacted violently, smacking his leg as if it were an opponent.

She needed to exchange her news for his and finish up the Donovan & Sons' business quickly.

"What are you doing here?" He shoved his hat back on his head.

Now the nasty part—why she'd detoured south from the more direct, east-west route. Hours of riding in the dusty, dirty coach, her stomach wound tighter than a watchspring, while her fingers tensed and her skin shrank from every pebble spit out from under the wheels, lest it be an Apache bullet.

"Orrin—Uncle William's messenger?" she began in a soft, light voice. The small watch Gareth had given her, supposedly to help her be more punctual, nestled against her throat.

Gareth nodded brusquely, silently urging her to hurry.

"He came down with dysentery in Santa Fe. When I found him like that, I knew I had to bring the *package* myself. He said Uncle William needed it quickly and discreetly, not by the usual route," she added.

And when the owner of Donovan & Sons, one of the West's top freighting houses, needed something transported immediately for himself, arguments weren't wanted or needed. He and Aunt Viola had reared her after Mother's death and she knew how hard it was to deliver even the most ordinary goods. She'd never thought this item, clearly a trigger for far greater parcels, would be easy.

"How did you convince Orrin to share with you the details of a secret business journey?" Gareth demanded.

"He already knew I was Uncle William's niece. Besides, he was very ill." She shuddered at the memory of the dedicated courier's weakness. "I only did so because he was certain Uncle William was desperate for it."

Agreement flashed through Gareth's eyes for an instant.

"I have the package with me," she announced as quietly as possible.

Package? Gareth frowned, clearly unprepared for the full details.

She tapped her once slender waist significantly until leather thudded under her jacket.

"Gold?" he mouthed. He braced his thumbs into his gun belt.

She nodded, biting her lip. "Did I do well?" she whispered.

"You did right fine, honey. As well or better than any man." Nervous as he was of watchers, pride still blazed out of every inch in his body.

She allowed herself a few triumphant dance steps to push back her nagging fears for Uncle William and Aunt Viola.

Gareth shot a quick glance around them, checking for more watchers than the fretful horses. But the other passengers were tucked inside the stages, while the last guard was climbing back onboard.

Kenly whistled a quick warning at him.

"You have to hand it over now. Then you can leave for San Francisco." Gareth grabbed her elbow and started for the stationhouse, using the same move he'd employed during many of their escapades.

"No." She dug in her heels, rooting herself deeper than the walls around them. "Where is Uncle William? Orrin told me he'd meet him here."

For the first time, Gareth's expression grew harder than what she'd seen before and sent her stomach diving into her boots.

"Gareth, talk to me."

"It's the height of raiding season, Portia. You've got to leave."

"*What's wrong with Aunt Viola?*"

Silence whipped through the ruins faster than any sandstorm. Even the dog turned to stare at them.

"She had another miscarriage a few days ago." Gareth's voice was too harsh to belong to him. His hand fell away from Portia's arm like a broken manacle.

"How bad is she?" Portia grabbed Gareth by the lapels and dragged him down to look into her eyes. She and Gareth had always talked to each other, always told each other the truth, ever since she was twelve and he was twenty.

For him to lie to her now was far more terrifying than riding through Apache Pass with a squad of cavalry around her.

Gareth's silver eyes held no more hope than twilight's last rays. He wet his lips.

"Don't you dare try to lie to me now, Gareth Lowell." She rolled the cloth a little tighter around her knuckles, completely ignoring the crossed cartridge belts.

"When I left her two days ago, I went straight to the big

Catholic church and prayed I wouldn't find her in the church-yard when I returned." Gareth wrapped his big, warm hands around her very cold ones. "I'm sorry I can't tell you better news, honey. But you know she wouldn't want you to be in danger."

Portia rested her forehead against him, her heart shaking somewhere against her throat. Aunt Viola, who'd opened her home and her heart to a motherless child, who'd always supported and cherished her no matter what mischief she'd gotten into. Aunt Viola, the only mother she had now.

The road ahead was suddenly very clear.

"I must go help her." She shoved her sobs deep into her belly where they couldn't be heard and drew herself erect. "I'll take the package to Tucson with you."

"Have you gone mad, Portia? With Victorio's army on the loose, you want to ride across Arizona?"

"I must help save Aunt Viola's life, something neither you nor anybody else can do." If nothing else and the worst had happened, she could manage the household, while Uncle William dealt with his own ravaging grief. She bit her knuckle to force back a sob.

"Explain yourself, Portia." Steel would have been friendlier than his eyes.

"Neil and Brian are only little boys, who need somebody to look after them," Portia continued with barely a tremor in her voice, despite how she'd whitened after a look at his face. "Aunt Viola's maid can either tend to her or the boys, but not both. You know Uncle William has his hands full, running this branch of the business."

If she assumed—as she must—that Aunt Viola had improved since Gareth left. Portia was the only blood kin Viola had west of the Mississippi and she alone could ease the family's burden.

"But if I'm there, I can take care of Neil and Brian. So Aunt Viola will rest easily and recover more quickly," Portia finished, desperation leaking through her overly courteous tones.

"Aunt Viola?" Baylor questioned from a step behind Portia.

Kenly's long shadow, with the crisp rifle, flanked her on the other side.

"Miss Townsend is Mrs. Donovan's niece," Gareth announced bluntly.

The stationmaster's imperiousness immediately washed out of Baylor's face to be replaced by stunned horror.

Oh, dear God in heaven, Viola Donovan's condition was common knowledge. Gareth's fear wasn't a beloved foster son's nervous twitches but the frostbite from terror's wind.

Portia made a small, pitiful sound and staggered slightly before recovering herself. "I'm sure I can help Aunt Viola," she reiterated.

The three men regarded her with some sympathy but no gentleness. Sweet words and pretty gestures would solve nothing here.

Then Baylor and Kenly looked at Gareth, silently letting him carry the argument.

"This is one of the worst raiding seasons in years, Portia. Hundreds of savages roam those mountains, every one bent on murder and plunder."

"Of course, it's war time," she acknowledged with barely a tremor. Her jaw was sharp and tight above the ornate bow which steadied her hat.

"The only route from here to Tucson is a one, perhaps two day ride across those mountains. We'll be dodging savages every step of the way, especially when we stop for water."

"I'll manage." Her backbone was tall and straight, her blue eyes level. "Remember when we went hunting in the Sierra Nevadas and had to outride that blizzard? I'll do very well this time, just as I did then."

Yes, she had kept her head but blowing snow was almighty different than howling bullets. She crisply told her stomach to stop tying knots like objections.

"Will you hurry up? Daylight's wasting!" the lead driver hollered at them. "We've got to make it through the pass before dark."

"Do you truly understand, Portia?" Gareth stepped to within an inch of her. "Every one of those heathen will consider you a greater prize than any fancy horse or purse of gold. They will abuse you shamefully and pass you among their friends. You will pray for death."

She flinched but rallied, coming back to meet him toe to toe. "We'll have to ride fast."

He caught her chin in his hand.

"Remember how well I know you, Portia. I'd rather haul a box of cartridges through those canyons than you because they'd be of use, rather than a magnet for trouble. If you cause any disturbance, I swear to you on my mother's grave, that I will knock you out and carry you like those cartridges to keep you safe."

"You're being absurd." She sniffed and tried to jerk away. Baylor and Kenly came to attention and boxed her in like guardsmen, without touching her.

"Do you promise to behave?" Gareth demanded, his voice deepening to what he'd use with a man.

"That's not necessary." How dare he demand that sort of guarantee from her? Didn't he trust her after all the years they'd known each other and all the escapades they'd been on together? This ride would be to help Uncle William and Aunt Viola. Shouldn't that be enough?

"Do you swear?"

The three words hung in the hot air, quieting even the drivers.

"You have my word that I will always act as befits a lady." She gave him what she could. Her lips were a thin, furious line.

Gareth stared down into Portia's blue eyes, wondering what had triggered the switch from worried niece to angry teenager.

It was the best promise he could hope for. God willing it would be enough but his belly trusted it no more than rotgut whiskey.

"Thank you, Portia. You have fifteen minutes to change into whatever boys' clothing lurks in that carpetbag." He released

her and stepped back, while the erstwhile stationmasters returned to their previous relaxed alertness.

"Ten minutes," she retorted. She stamped her foot but quickly
turned the movement into a fast departure for the depot.

"Good luck, you fools!" one stagecoach driver shouted.

Gareth waved back, not bothering to disagree with his new
title.

"Yaw!" The two stages pulled out in a tumult of drumming
hooves, thundering wheels, and jangling harnesses. Dust stormed
over the tiny station, turning it once again into a ruin.

"We're coming with you," Kenly said quietly.

Gareth snapped his gaze back to the other man. "I thought
you two were heading north," he remarked.

"Bit late in the year for the high country."

"These old bones can certainly use some hot sun," Baylor
added. "Not to mention mountain riding wouldn't suit my favorite saddle horse."

"Thank you." Gareth inclined his head. The odds of taking
Portia safely through to Tucson had just increased from minis-
cule to barely possible.

"Can she truly be ready in ten minutes?" Baylor asked.

"Oh yes, since she said so. She never lies."

"Can she ride?" Kenly eyed the spare horse, saddled and
ready for the absent messenger.

"As well or better than most men." After he adjusted the
gear for her far shorter height, of course. "Plus, she shoots as
well as most men. Long gun preferably, though; she hasn't had
as much practice with a revolver."

"In that case, I'll loan her my old Henry."

"Thank you, Kenly." Gareth was genuinely touched. He didn't
have an extra gun to give Portia. But Baylor and Kenly could
afford more gear, since they traveled with an experienced pack-
horse.

"The last shot's for her, of course, should we be caught by
Apaches." Baylor's deep voice was as soft as the wind singing
over a cemetery.

"No matter which of us administers the coup de grace," Gareth agreed. No man wished that any woman he cared about—or even a female he loathed—should be taken alive by those savages. Mercy dictated a clean death, even if dealt by loved ones.

Without need for further words, the three men and one dog moved to make their final preparations. Daylight was fading faster than their chances of seeing Tucson while they were still alive.

Chapter Three

Three days later

Portia squirmed forward along the dusty ledge another half inch. Her heart drummed in her ears far louder than her boots shuffling against the hard rocks or her oversized shirt rubbing her skin. Her skin was the same reddish brown as the pebbles around them and her once-black hat now sagged into the murky shadows.

Gareth's hand locked onto her wrist and squeezed.

She immediately froze, her head hugging the ground to avoid any unfriendly notice.

A heartbeat later, his fingers glided back to grip his rifle again.

She relaxed slowly, letting her muscles ease her body into the ground until she was part of Mother Earth and completely invisible to any watchers.

But deep inside, her heart was rapturously caroling Beethoven's *Ode to Joy*. Perfectly rolling through every complicated harmony just as well as she'd arrived in position.

She, Portia Townsend, could sneak up a mountainside in Indian country better than most men. Gareth Lowell had first taught her how when she was twelve, so they could go fishing together on San Francisco Bay during the winter. He'd said she'd never crawl through mud to go fishing. He'd underestimated her hunger to spend time with him, not that she'd told him that, of course. Even then, she'd understood a lady didn't tell the object of her affections everything.

One day she'd lay this close to Gareth in their marriage bed. After she grew up enough so he could respectably pay his attentions to her, of course. She'd known ever since she first saw him that he was hers alone.

He had to feel the same way because he was always willing to take her about with him, whenever he visited Uncle William's house. Orphaned as he was and cursed with wanderlust, it was the only place he could call home.

Plus, he'd never walked out with any young ladies so she needn't fear any rivals. Not that other hussies didn't try to catch his eye.

He had black hair and silver-blue eyes set amid hard-edged angles and planes that could change into laughter at a moment's notice or lock into implacable silences. He was clean-limbed and corded with a muscle like a warhorse, not an effete poet such as her classmates swooned over. He was her boon companion, even if they rarely told each other many secrets.

Gareth's sleeve brushed her shoulder, bringing the rich scents of sweat and man and horse. But he said nothing, his attention totally fixed on the scene below and his rifle at his hand.

Portia hummed softly, almost drunk with intimacy.

She schooled her features into more sober lineaments. She should pay some heed to where they'd halt for dinner, instead of celebrating days adventuring with Gareth amid only the mild chaperonage provided by the former soldiers.

"How's Tornado?" Baylor asked softly from her other side.

"Guarding the horses as you ordered," Portia answered in a matching hoarse whisper. She doubted they could be heard from a yard away. "He'll sound the alarm if he spots anyone."

Baylor huffed his acceptance without looking at her, his attention entirely focused on the crags around them.

Portia allowed herself to shift a little closer to Gareth as a reward for doing so well. She'd obeyed his commands and stayed with the animals until she was sure they were settled. She'd even counted off the minutes, as he'd commanded, until she came forward to join the men, despite her dancing pulse.

Now she felt free to cautiously raise her head and see the first place where she'd have a long drink of water. Perhaps even wash her face, if Gareth would let them take some extra time to rest the horses.

The sun was setting in a violent haze of red and gold, sending purple and lavender shadows bursting across the mountains to her left. A box canyon spread below them, its steep walls permitting easy entry only from the north. Golden sands spilled across its broad base, while a few patches of silvery gray grass and trees bore witness to buried water.

They were lying on the southern cliff edge, in a hollow between giant boulders. The foothills' jagged shadows crept across the little basin like a natural cloak, changing men and rocks into the same shifting panorama. Few hunters, if any, could have spotted any prey there.

Portia strained up onto her elbows, eager to see more of what lay ahead. Gareth had always found the best vantage points for watching their pursuers blunder past during their adventures.

A single thick plume of smoke lurched up to the sky from the ranch house in the center.

Two figures writhed on the ground on opposite sides of the empty paddock. Their hands and feet had been tied down to stakes but their bellies were still free to flail about—except for the flaming torch driven through a loop of each man's intestines. Their outlines were brittle and ragged, charred from the fire which had taken their clothes and skin.

Portia drew breath to vent the scream ripping out her heart.

"Hush!" Gareth clamped his hand over her mouth faster than steel could strike sparks from flint. "It's a trap."

The scream faded but the horror remained branded into her very bones.

"But . . ." She shook her head but he tightened his grip.

A trap? It couldn't be; nobody was down there except for those pitiful beings.

Her stomach lurched and she jolted into Gareth's grasp once again. His silver eyes watched her, luminous as moonlight amid features harsher than a sword. A softer emotion flickered there briefly before his mouth twisted and settled back into its stern line.

One of the victims was whimpering, a broken little sound like a shattered violin.

Portia lay still, her heartbeat running faster than any sanity. Mother had been burned alive, her blackened skin tearing away anywhere and everywhere Portia touched her . . .

"Will you be quiet?" Gareth's tone was more powerful for its blade-like stillness.

She nodded, ancient panic seeping into her bones despite the sun-baked rocks, and he silently released her.

"But the Apaches must be long gone," she argued, trying not to look, or listen, or—dear God in heaven—smell anything from down below.

"This is a fresh attack, ma'am," Baylor said softly from her other side. "It'd be just like those savages to leave a few braves behind to kill anybody who comes riding in, whether for water or to help."

"More than one place to put an ambush," agreed Kenly.

"It shouldn't take too long to put the strongest man on my horse and the other one—"

"We're arguing about how many Indians are near us, Portia, not *if* they are here."

Stubbornness fired deep in her blood, the same fierce independence which had kept her going through all the bitter years in boarding school. Even if Gareth wouldn't listen to her, this time, as he had on all their previous adventures, she had to continue arguing for the correct course of action.

"Besides, ma'am, they're so close to death that they likely wouldn't last the journey." Baylor's voice, unlike Gareth's, was very gentle.

Even the best doctors couldn't help patients who'd been burned, except to give them laudanum until they slept their way into Death's arms.

She clenched her fists. There was one more deed they could do.

"We have enough water for the horses to reach Tucson," Baylor mused.

"Plus one extra canteen," Gareth agreed.

To take care of the fragile flower known as woman. Portia made up her mind.

"Or we can grant them a merciful end to their misery," she stated firmly.

"Portia, didn't you hear what I said?" Gareth lightly shook her by the shoulder. "There are Apaches here. Gunshots would surely summon them."

"You could use your knife," she suggested.

"I will not go down there and tell them we're here. Besides, leaving would cut down on your protection," he retorted.

"Ma'am, he's right." Kenly inserted himself into the argument.

Tornado growled softly in the distance.

"If those two were in any shape to talk," Baylor's voice was hoarser than the dust would account for, "they'd be the first to argue against risking your safety, ma'am. Above all else, we must keep you well."

Kenly silently rolled away, followed an instant later by Baylor. Only Gareth and she could help those two piteous wretches.

"I will shoot them myself." Her stomach lurched but she ignored it, together with any maidenly qualms which seemed to be making her pulse flutter like a frantic goose. She'd worry later about how to make Gareth once again amenable to her every suggestion. "We're far enough away that the Apaches won't know exactly where the bullets came from."

She gathered her feet under her, determined to get the hideous deed over with while she still had the nerve.

Tornado growled again, closer and a little louder.

"Portia, dammit!" Gareth lunged for her.

She yanked away and stood up in a patch of shadow behind them, ready to fetch her rifle from the horses.

One step—and she was in full sunlight again.

Second step—Something slammed into her head, simultaneously fiery hot, sharp, and unbearably solid. Stars somersaulted behind her eyes, bringing velvety blackness.

She collapsed, unconscious before she hit the dirt.

Chapter Four

Tucson, the next night

The house's big wooden door was as solid as its walls. Carved and reinforced with metal straps, it proudly proclaimed it could withstand as many sieges as the stucco bricks beside it. Golden light spilled from high barred windows, promising rest and safety within one of Tucson's finest neighborhoods.

Portia cast it a sour look but said nothing, granting it no more conversation than she'd offered her escort since the previous night. Finding herself lashed to a horse had inspired no friendliness in her bosom.

She'd been politer to Baylor and Kenly. They and Tornado had said goodbye a few minutes ago, off to become Donovan & Sons' latest employees. Their honest concern for her health had been far different from Gareth's high-handed superiority.

"How's your head?" Gareth asked, standing on the doorstep where he and Portia awaited an answer to his knock.

"I'm feeling entirely well, thank you," she stated firmly, in the same tones her stepmother used to discuss another woman's clothing or anything else of no interest at all.

As if she'd have told the brute anything different about her health, since he was the one who'd caused all the problems.

She sniffed loudly and refused to readjust her hat, despite the headache lurking at her temples. It would have served him right if she'd needed a massive bandage to hold back her blood-stained locks. She'd have liked to see him explain that away.

He cast a long, sweeping glance over her to measure her health as if she were a cow.

"What are you looking for?" she challenged. "You already checked my head this morning and didn't find a knot—after you untied me from the horse." *And ungagged me.*

"Your eyes are clear," he remarked. He took a step closer and her hands immediately came up, balled into fists and ready to fight, in the move he'd taught her years ago. Something distant and dark flashed through his eyes, half hidden in his hat's shadows.

"Thank you." She all but spat the words at him. To think she'd dreamed of one day hearing him praise her eyes' beauty.

She'd never wear his watch again, lest she carry another instrument for him to measure her by.

"And you still seem to have your wits about you, judging by how you can string words together."

She gaped at him, totally at a loss for words. How much thinking did it take to realize the man you loved didn't care—no, didn't give a *damn* about you? Proven when he hit you on the head with his Colt!

She started to throw a punch at that infuriating, handsome, all-too-memorable mouth.

Unfortunately, the door swung open first.

"Lowell? Sweet Jesus, you made good time!" Uncle William started to embrace his old friend. But Gareth sidestepped slightly and light from inside poured over Portia in a welcoming flood. Suddenly she wasn't dusty and chafed in her leather breeches and creased bandanna on a rutted street hundreds of miles from anywhere she knew.

She was a breath away from home.

Uncle William froze then leaped onto the threshold and swept her up. She wrapped her arms around his neck and clung, shaking, as if she were a little girl once again, back when she was always safe with her favorite uncle.

"Sweet Mother Mary," he muttered. They held onto each other for what seemed like an infinity, while her body ignored the contrast between itself and fresh clothing and clean skin, before he carried her inside.

"Viola, sweetheart," he crooned, "look what Lowell brought you for a birthday present."

He set Portia down carefully on a polished tile floor, covered with brilliant rugs. Soft white plaster walls reflected the golden lamps swinging from the ceiling and the fire crackling in a curved fireplace, until the large room seemed an oasis of warmth and love. Leather chairs and overstuffed sofas offered tempting places to rest.

But none of that mattered, next to the woman struggling to her feet.

"Portia, my love." Her mother's younger sister held out her arms, soft shawls falling toward the floor like autumn leaves at winter's first touch.

"Aunt Viola." Hot speech regarding Gareth's unjust treatment, rehearsed a thousand times over during the past day, died on Portia's lips.

Aunt Viola had never been hale and hearty like Aunt Rosalind, someone capable of playing tennis for hours. But her elfin beauty had always glowed with an inner joy, which made most men call her a beauty. Portia had always considered her healthy, although not extremely strong after her second son Brian was born.

But now? She could barely stand unaided and her skin was gray, more ashen than rose-petal. Dear Lord, she looked as if she was still close to death, yet the miscarriage had occurred almost a month ago.

Uncle William lightly squeezed Portia's shoulders.

She shook him off. She didn't need the warning to make sure she'd put her best beloved aunt first, in every way. She dropped her hat onto the nearest table and ran forward.

"Dearest, dearest aunt."

They hugged each other, scalding tears of joy blending on their cheeks.

Portia started to wrap herself closer, the way she'd always done but alarm rippled across her skin, edging her back. Aunt Viola was so very thin, far thinner than usual.

Portia shifted her grip slightly and held herself a little more cautiously, careful to keep her arms in a cradle rather than crush. She would keep the little hellions called her cousins out of harm's way, while she was here. That would give Aunt Viola time to rest and heal.

Aunt Viola stroked Portia's hair. Despite all her best resolutions, Portia leaned into the maternal reassurance.

Delicate fingers smoothed the lingering sore spot on her scalp. Portia yelped and flinched away.

"What happened to your head, dear? Did you take a fall?" Aunt Viola questioned. "Do we need to send for the doctor?"

Portia gritted her teeth, unable to form a polite answer.

"I'm sorry but I'm afraid I hit her, ma'am," Gareth answered.

"Why?" Uncle William shot the question at him like a cannonball.

"We stopped for water at Rio Perdido."

"Rio Perdido?" Aunt Viola sank back into her chair. "The final watering hole?"

"Yes. It was—" Portia started to interrupt.

"Yes, ma'am." Gareth's deeper voice drowned out hers. "The Apaches had arrived first, destroyed the ranch, and laid a trap."

"And?" Uncle William's expression was remote and contained, rather than furious. Portia wanted to box their ears for only paying attention to the professional fighter's story. Well, professional teamster and courier, which in Arizona was essentially the same thing.

"Portia was about to draw fire down upon us," Gareth announced.

Draw down fire? Portia desperately looked for something, anything to throw at him and shatter his appalling calm.

Did he have to describe her as if she was an idiotic child?

How many times had they gone adventuring together over the past four years? How many times had he told her that a man couldn't ride or shoot any better than she had?

If doing all that wasn't good enough to capture his, his damn attention, then it would serve him right if she went back East and became the most beautiful girl in New York. He'd know what he'd missed when he saw dozens of men begging for her attention.

"Knocking her out with the butt of my Colt—" Gareth continued.

"Was the fastest way to silence her." Her beloved uncle nodded in agreement.

"Uncle William!" Portia exploded and swung to face her kin. Couldn't she trust even him to stand up for her? Good heavens, if she stayed here, she'd probably be lectured on how badly she'd behaved at Rio Perdido.

Or required to be polite to Gareth, on the many occasions he frequented their house.

Disgust twisted her belly and her mouth for an instant.

"Does your head still hurt very badly, dear?" Aunt Viola asked softly.

"Just a small ache," Portia replied brusquely, more concerned with other matters. "But—"

"I'll have a room prepared for you here, Lowell," Uncle William announced, riding over Portia's voice.

She flung back her head involuntarily. Horror washed across her face before she could guard her expression again. How long did she have to be near her old playmate?

True, she had to remain until Aunt Viola was healthy again.

But after that? He was not someone who visited any place very often. Yet if he saw anyone regularly, it was William and Viola Donovan, who'd always treated him as a son.

Faugh!

Aunt Viola speared first Portia then Gareth with a searching glance but said nothing.

"No need, sir. I have to ride out immediately to Fort Lowell."

"At this hour?" protested the lady of the house, her Southern sense of hospitality obviously outraged. "Surely we can give you something to eat."

Portia sank into the closest chair, wishing she had a fan to shield herself. For the first time, she recognized the advantages of ladylike clothing as a prop to hide behind, rather than boys' clothing which left every emotion on display. Such as gagging at the mention of sharing a meal with an arrogant jackass.

"They promised an escort back to Rio Perdido, if we can leave before dawn." One of Gareth's shoulders lifted, then fell. "We'll probably arrive while at least one of the settlers is still alive."

"Thank you, Gareth." Aunt Viola limped over to him and kissed his forehead. He patted her back but said nothing more, his countenance offering little hope or gentleness.

"I'll have the cook pack a decent meal for you," Uncle William promised.

Gareth's eyes met Portia's. For a moment, something flickered in their depths. It was surely not an apology since he held himself too straight.

She inclined her head. If nothing else, she was grateful he'd bury those poor charred beasts once called men.

But she couldn't forgive him for proving exactly what category he placed her in. No man christened his beloved with the butt of his Colt.

No, she'd look elsewhere for her true love.

Chapter Five

New York, New York, October 1880

Portia paced in front of the upstairs drawing room's marble columns and closely watched herself in the mirror above the black marble mantel. The sun's dying rays plummeted through the stained glass transoms and slowly spilled crimson over the bronze maiden standing there.

A thousand lizards rioted in the void known as her stomach. She didn't want to think about them, the four hundred guests waiting at the church to see her married, or the clock ticking off the minutes till she, her father, and stepmother left for the ceremony. For one thing, they should have departed—she cast yet another glance at the curlicued bit of machinery facing the mantel—almost ten minutes ago.

But everything in this Manhattan town house moved at her father or stepmother's command. A year of expensive finishing school and another year touring Europe had shown her a broader palette of delights than the rigorous schools she'd attended earlier had taught her. She'd danced until she fell into bed exhausted at dawn, practiced notes backstage with opera stars, compared French poets to their Greek models in London drawing rooms, and more—always attired in the latest gowns from Paris.

And completely lacking Gareth Lowell's presence. She'd considered wearing his watch again, since the tiny enameled pendant could be hidden inside ballgowns and punctuality was an asset. But she needed no reminders of his autocratic ways, even if he was an honest man unlike most in her father's circle.

All those days and nights had also confirmed the advantages a matron enjoyed over a schoolgirl, such as not having to answer to anyone whenever she wished to say what she wanted or go where she pleased.

Only a few more minutes left until she headed her own establishment and set her own rules. Having her own house—no, houses—would be much better than living at her parents' beck and call. An enormous country estate, the proud horse farm which had been neglected for far too long, the town house which had been rented and abused. She could have all the books she wanted, sing for as long as she wanted. . . .

None of which mattered, since it wouldn't bring her Gareth.

She went back to what she could do for now: practice wearing her wedding dress.

Good, she wasn't tripping on the double lace flounce any longer. She was also moving so smoothly that the pearls holding down the rows of chenille fringe covering the skirt fluttered gracefully, rather than wrapping around each other.

Managing the yards of cloth was far trickier because she couldn't pick up her skirts. Instead she had to carry her mother's Bible, with its precious letter to her. The trustee of Mother's estate had delivered it that morning, too late for Portia to read it before the ceremony.

Glass shattered next door. "You clumsy idiot, how dare you curl my hair that way!" a woman screeched.

Portia grimaced, all too familiar bile rising in her throat. The new French maid, the third this year, had probably tried to make her mistress look attractive rather than fashionable.

"But, madame . . ."

Thud!

Babette yelped.

Portia wheeled for the door and rattled its knob. It was

locked as usual, unlike those at Aunt Viola's home. "Ma'am? Is everything alright?"

"Yes, of course," her stepmother answered. "But I'll need a few minutes longer than I expected." She ended the last syllables with a vicious snap.

"And Babette?" Portia queried. Usually there was more noise to her stepmother's rage than actual hitting. "Can she help me finish?"

"Don't be absurd; you're already dressed. Your father and I will come for you when I'm ready."

Portia mimed hurling a kick at the unresponsive door. But perhaps the mansion's mistress would behave better now, since she'd been reminded of the need for haste.

She went back to tramping through the drawing room. Once she had her own house, she'd be able to dictate little things, such as granting the Catholics the nearly unheard of benefit of hearing Mass every weekday. Of course, she'd have to give the Protestants something equivalent, like going to church as often or a few minutes of leave to walk in the garden.

She'd be a countess, with responsibilities and people dependent on her. She wouldn't be bored by endless conversations about the shape of a bustle or the latest color to be touted by Paris. She'd be part of a family which dated back centuries and spoke casually about matters of war and peace, while moving in the highest circles.

Focus on the dress, Portia. You gave your word to marry the man and Gareth Lowell would expect you to always keep your oath, no matter what.

She'd mastered the long train in order to be presented at the English court. It was a pity that her wedding day wouldn't feature any helpful footmen with rods to keep yards of ruffled brocade and tulle veils from tripping her.

She could barely breathe, of course, since Babette had laced her corset under the senior Townsend female's ambitious stare. But that had been happening for months now.

Portia reached the corner, pivoted, and kicked her train back into place behind her. Yards of brocade rustled smoothly over the oriental carpet.

She gave herself a jubilant thumbs up in the mirror. Something was going right, at least. Maybe she could succeed, instead of nervously looking over her shoulder for prying eyes calculating where her next flaw would appear.

"Portia."

The voice was deep, slow, and very western. Familiar—far too familiar, it resonated in her very bones.

"Gareth?"

She swung around and stared at more than six feet of abominably attractive masculinity. Her treacherous heart tumbled through in her chest.

"How did you get in here?" she demanded. Miraculously, her train piled up neatly at her heels like a cavalcade called to a sudden halt.

"Through the rear garden and over the balcony, of course." He raised a very black, superior eyebrow at her. "Why? Did you ask your father to post extra guards on the roof, the way Donovan would in Tucson?"

"No, of course not. He didn't consider it necessary." The presence of two presidents, plus two presidential candidates, on the guest list had galvanized New York's police chief into covering the streets with his finest men.

Gareth shook his head slowly, never taking his silver eyes off her. "In his shoes, I'd personally take some responsibility for the contents of the house, both material and human."

He wore a cutaway coat and striped trousers, the same extremely formal attire that every guest attending the ceremony would wear. He could have walked into the Court of St. James and been granted an audience with Queen Victoria.

She'd never seen him dressed like this. But somehow he looked just as comfortable as in scarred leather and canvas, bedecked with notched guns ready to spit fire.

Instinct, too deep to be denied, compelled her to take a step closer. Her fingers ached to touch him, but she pushed herself back. She was engaged. That was it, betrothed to another man.

Gareth himself would expect her to honor those vows.

"Why are you here?" She reached for composure and pulled herself even further into a lady's elegant upright posture, as polished and refined as for her presentation to the Queen of England.

Gareth's eyes flickered. For the first time ever, he truly looked at her from head to toe, her face and her throat, her shoulders and the curves down to her waist. He had to drag his gaze back up to her face. His chest was definitely rising and falling a little faster.

Something feminine deep inside her stretched its claws and purred. A flower which had set root in finishing school, budded in Paris and London during dances and flirtations, reached a little farther toward the light, ruffling her throat and lungs until speech—even thought—became an effort.

"Why are you here?" she asked more slowly, her vowels somehow falling into her mother's softer, slower Southern accent.

"To take you away." His tones were darker and rougher.

With him? Had he finally come to his senses? Oh please, dear God, let it be yes! Let the oldest dream finally come true.

But his face didn't betray any lover-like impatience and he wasn't holding out his hand to her. His eyes drifted over her with stunned fascination but he wasn't speaking enough of himself.

"Why?" Splintering hope cut an edge into her voice.

"You can't marry St. Arles."

"What are you talking about?" she fenced warily. *Please tell me more about why you want me.*

"I've been asking around about him." He frowned and pushed his hand through his hair, disarranging the heavy locks. "Donovan asked me to do so, since he couldn't arrive until yesterday."

Uncle William had started this, not Gareth? She flipped a handful of chenille fringe back into place on her thigh, wishing she could rearrange arrogant men as easily. Why couldn't she ever be someone unique to him, for himself, and not because of his close ties to William Donovan?

"So? My father did, also." As had every other wealthy American parent.

"What did he consider? Anything other than satisfying his wife's ambitions?" Gareth shot back.

Her jaw dropped in astonishment at his knowledge of her family's inner workings—and his willingness to discuss them.

"That's not kind," she retorted.

"Your British earl has more debts than the Army has mules."

"Yes, I know." She shrugged, wishing nothing more than to escape this dream-raddled debacle. "Uncle William made sure I knew who the London and New York fortune hunters were. But my father promised he'd make sure my dowry was well protected. And St. Arles considers my music and wit to be worthy of a diplomatic hostess."

"Do you honestly believe he loves you?"

Did he have to look as if he pitied her?

"Yes. My only doubts are my ability to be a good wife, a good English wife," she asserted and silently damned her old playmate for reigniting all her old qualms.

St. Arles was a charming conversationalist—but he sparkled most when the topic was himself or he was on duty, as a diplomat serving his queen. He somehow turned tariffs into a series of jokes about the strong devouring the weak and thereby drew even her father's most insular political cronies into his charmed circle. Yet he'd never exerted himself to discuss her family in detail. Instead he'd shared details about the run-down estates he'd inherited and his dreams of Britain's future glory.

Gareth's eyes narrowed, as if he were scouting a trail across very rocky terrain.

"Portia, I've asked the women of the town about him. The women of ill repute," he emphasized.

"Gareth!" she protested, appalled by his forcing such harpies into this day's solemnity. "Why are you telling me—"

"He treats them very poorly."

She gaped at him. Albinia Townsend might believe female ignorance was the best road to marital happiness but Viola Donovan had no such hesitations. Portia considered herself quite well informed about intimate matters between men and women. But what did a bachelor's wild oats have to do with her?

"Black eyes and split lips are the least of it. Two girls have suffered broken arms in the past—"

"No!" Portia flung up her hand. White ribbons fluttered from her mother's bible like an Indian's delicate amulets.

"One day, he'll handle you the same way. Your only hope is that he needs your healthy body to bear his sons."

"He calls me his princess and swears life will hold no meaning for him until I am his wife."

"Your father's gold doesn't drip from his fingers yet," Gareth said crudely. "Grow up, Portia, and start seeing the world the way it truly is, not a bonbon offered on a silver platter to you."

She slapped him. The few hopes she still cherished, that Gareth Lowell might one day see her as a lover, fled screaming from her memories' bleeding grasp. St. Arles might not be perfect but at least he wanted her, unlike Gareth.

He caught her wrist and held it, breathing just a little too fast. His eyes narrowed under their dark brows and she was fiercely glad she'd finally riled him up enough to shake his self-control.

"If you're marrying him because you want to hurt me—"

"Don't flatter yourself!"

A muscle twitched hard in his cheek before he inclined his head, silently agreeing with her.

Why did that make her want to hit him again? Couldn't he acknowledge at least a bond of friendship between them?

"At least remember William and Viola Donovan will always take you in. You need only turn to them, even when you stand at the altar."

"Are you mad? Do you know how much gossip that would cause?" Even her corset seemed to gasp in outrage.

Gareth released her as if dropping a scorpion. "Better a little chatter now than a lifetime of bitterness. But you can trust William and Viola to do—"

"What? The most notorious deed possible?" Walter Townsend's golden tones resonated through the drawing room, harbingers of the famous orator and backroom politician he was. His wife hovered at his shoulder, smugly certain of both her position and the situation's outcome.

Portia gulped unhappily. She could imagine several endings for this encounter, none of them gracious. She immediately caught her train up, ready to move in any direction.

"Why, everything possible for their niece, of course," Gareth said smoothly, betraying no discomfort whatsoever. "Excuse me, sir, I'm Gareth Lowell. You may not remember me but we were introduced at the Vanderbilts' horse race last week."

"Vanderbilts." Portia's father, patriarch of a far older lineage, sniffed loudly before fixing his gaze on his daughter. "My dear girl, you are not yet ready and society abhors tardiness."

She glanced down at herself, startled by the unjust description. Her stepmother chuckled and smoothed her dress over her ample hips, making her own bid for superiority in a blaze of over-corseted Parisian finery and clanking masses of rubies.

"And, you, young man, are an intruder." The master of the house looked Gareth over as if a servant had unaccountably left behind dead flowers. "Society's leaders are waiting at the church and I will not allow you to ruin our family's triumph."

Portia hesitated, uncertainty running like a spring storm through her veins. But staying near Gareth would only heat her father's ire higher.

She left the fireplace far too slowly.

"As a man of the world, sir, you must have heard the rumors about St. Arles." Gareth's demand for attention blazed like a knife fighter's blade in a dark alley.

Portia swung around, one step short of the doorway and her stepmother. The three Townsends faced the interloper in a single, united, hostile front.

"What of them? Idle chatter means little to me, except unnecessary delay to my wife's and daughter's dreams."

"St. Arles is no proper husband for any woman, let alone a beloved, innocent daughter." Gareth hurled the accusation at the household's senior members.

"So? My wife and child both desire an English title in the family, you fool, while I enjoy giving my friends a grand wedding—from which you will be excluded."

"He will harm her." Gareth's countenance carried the hardness of complete and utter certainty.

"Don't be absurd. He'd never cause a scandal or risk losing her dowry."

Father hadn't denied he knew St. Arles was capable of Gareth's accusations? Her stomach roiled, as if she'd returned to a swaying, pitching stagecoach, bound for a hellish, stifling journey through Apache country.

The leader of her family kept talking, sharp and disquieting as blasts from a guard's shotgun. "That's unlikely to become important. I have done my best for my daughter and you have no right to interfere."

Where could she go? What could she do? Surely she'd made her decision weeks ago, when she'd accepted St. Arles' offer.

"Except an old friend's worry." Gareth's tanned features were so saturnine as to be unreadable. "In that case, I will say farewell and simply ask Miss Townsend to remember my last words." The fear underlying his voice pulled her a half step forward but her dress's chenille fringe brushed her legs like silent sentries.

He was requesting her to leave her fiancé at the altar and run off to her aunt and uncle? How could she break her word of honor and do that?

She rocked back into immobility. Surely her engagement ring had never felt this heavy before.

He stared at her, his silver eyes as adamant as his silence—
and as desperate—about what he wanted her to do.

She glared back at him, equally stubborn.

"Of all the abominable pieces of impertinence," her stepmother burst out. "To break into my house and try to stop my
party! You—"

Gareth's hand shot out, palm up, and silenced her in mid-
tirade. He walked out, brushing past Portia without a backward glance.

His clean scent made her treacherous heart give a last, erratic thump. It had to be nothing more than silly, sentimental
claptrap over childhood memories.

"Coming, daughter?" Her father glanced at her from the
head of the stairs.

"Of course, sir." She locked her knees back into something
steady enough to move, and did her best to glide forward,
rather than stumble.

St. Arles wanted her and Gareth didn't. She'd given her pledge
to one man, but not another. What more did she need to know?

Chapter Six

Portia bowed her head one last time, grateful the interminable prayer had finally ended. The archbishop had seen fit to add additional prophets and evangelists' pleas for children to the standard wedding blessing. Now her head swam from the overpowering scent of massed roses, lilies, and freesias which swarmed up to the high altar and covered everything else they could reach.

They offered the only warmth in the enormous, gray church, since even all the swaying, wrought iron candelabras couldn't banish the cold chill seeping into every crevice from the heavy rainstorm.

She hadn't seen or smelled anything like these blooms, since she'd stood in the very small chapel when Mother was buried. The bitter winter that year had closed down travel, leaving only flowers to represent hundreds of friends and thousands of memories. Portia's head had spun until she wanted to sink into the stone vault with Mother's coffin.

Today, she gripped Mother's Bible until her fingers stamped her mark on the soft leather, then clambered onto her feet. Her heavy train tugged at her shoulders and she shook it impatiently back, to be caught and fussed over by her two stepsisters.

St. Arles observed her, too secure in his six feet of lionized British aristocracy and smug naval uniform to break society's conventions and offer assistance. A half smile toyed with his thin lips under his fashionable mustache.

Their audience leaned forward in a rustling slither of controlled anticipation. Her stepmother's crisp underskirts echoed like buckshot beside the aisle, while Portia could see from the corner of her eye Father smirking at an old social rival.

Uncle William, Aunt Viola, and their two young sons, Neil and Brian, sat in the following pew. Aunt Viola sniffled hard and briefly leaned her cheek against Uncle William's shoulder. He tilted his head toward hers, offering comfort and understanding so simply that Portia's heart twisted.

Uncle Hal and Aunt Rosalind, with their bevy of daughters and single son, her golden Lindsay cousins, Uncle Morgan and Aunt Jessamyn, and everyone else were a blur too distant to be distinguished as individuals.

Dear Cynthia stood behind her, both hands full with hers and Portia's bouquets. Cynthia's happy marriage to her gallant British army officer had helped persuade Portia she too could have a successful union to a foreign aristocrat.

Out of all that great assembly, only one man stood on his feet.

Gareth Lowell watched her from the side aisle, his silver eyes like beacons set deep in his hardened face.

Something deep down inside her leaned toward him yet again. She'd wanted him from the day they'd met, when she'd arrived in San Francisco after Mother's long, dreadful descent into death. He'd just come in from the storm, windblown and clean-smelling like the promise of a new beginning. He'd never reminded her of New York's gilded, cloying rituals.

Her two stepsisters finished their work and stepped back, leaving Portia isolated in front of the high altar.

"My wife." St. Arles's voice was clipped, British, and triumphant as brazen cymbals despite its quiet.

Her eyes widened to meet his. She blushed, thanking a merciful heaven she'd sighted Gareth over St. Arles's shoulder. No suspicion dwelt in his eyes when his forefinger brought her chin up.

Her husband. She'd sworn to forsake all others and cleave only unto him.

He was what she wanted, wasn't he?

She stilled, her skin drifting somewhere beyond the ability of her frantic pulse to warm.

He slowly lowered his head to hers, his black eyes glinting like a shotgun's muzzle.

What was he planning to do? He wasn't behaving like the groom at any wedding she'd ever attended.

She managed a welcoming smile, gentler than her clumsy fingers' frantic grip on her mother's Bible.

He very deliberately licked her lips, flicking his tongue across them like a rattlesnake tasting the air for prey. Again and again, never seeking to penetrate or seduce like those fumbling boys, but only taunt and brand her.

She wrenched herself away from him and staggered back, flinging her free hand up.

"No," she whispered. How could she yield her body to a man who treated her like that?

St. Arles chuckled too softly to be heard by anyone except the archbishop. Satisfaction flickered through her bridegroom's eyes, not some ridiculous prank.

Good God, he'd meant to frighten her.

Her blood ran colder than at her mother's funeral.

The audience surged onto its feet, filling the great church with a storm of dissonant questions and clashing fabrics.

She had to leave. But where could she go? She was married to St. Arles.

Her lungs fought to draw breath fast enough to fuel her irregular pulse.

To have and to hold, for better or worse . . . from this day forward.

Forever. She would be his wife for all of the days to come.

She lowered her hand as jerkily as a railroad engine stuttering to a halt. But she finished the motion and even added a half smile at the congregation, although she didn't dare look anyone in the eye.

Her father and stepmother erupted from their front pew and charged toward her.

St. Arles took her arm—and she permitted it. Her brain seemed to be somewhere distant from his touch, as if sheer terror had rescued all that was good and pure in her from him.

She glanced around the church, anywhere but at him, the man who'd kiss her again that night. Although she mustn't let anybody know what she thought of that.

She immediately and far too easily saw Gareth again. He jerked his head toward Uncle William and Aunt Viola, implacably demanding that she scandalously cast her husband aside and run off.

But he never gave any sign she should come to him.

Her husband drew her arm against his side.

Silence spread through the audience like the first flame in dry prairie grass.

"My dear daughter, let me be the first to congratulate you," her father gushed. "I will introduce you two to President Grant immediately."

The message in his eyes was as unmistakable as Gareth's: *You must pretend matters are proceeding well. You are married now, like it or not.*

A thousand people watched her, eager to see her next move. No matter what she did, there would be gossip. That'd be a minor penalty, though, for choosing the proper road.

Divorce? Impossible; she'd given her word to marry him— for better or for worse. After all, there had to be a future ahead for a woman who did her best to be a good wife.

She'd created more than one ruckus in her life but never the commotion that walking out on St. Arles now would cause.

What did any of that matter? Like it or not, she'd married him and she'd keep her vows.

Portia Townsend—no, *Vanneck*—wrapped herself in her best, well-bred smile and leaned very slightly on her new husband's arm. Her finishing school's deportment teacher would have been proud.

She deliberately did not look anywhere near Gareth Lowell.

But too much of her heart shattered when the side door slammed behind him.

Chapter Seven

The fire sparked and sizzled in the library's flamboyant, tiled fireplace. A flame leaped high toward the chimney and freedom until the log underneath cracked loudly then collapsed onto the hearth. Ashes billowed toward the room beyond like a small, deadly storm, dotted with ravenous sparks. They almost seemed angry they couldn't devour the wedding reception for a British earl and a New York debutante.

If William Donovan had any sense, he'd let those fiery devils seize the woolen carpet and burn down Walter Townsend's New York mansion. They would need far less than an hour and he'd easily have his family out of here long before they were done.

Richard Lindsay, Viola's father and Portia's doting grandfather, watched silently, brocade curtains spilling behind him like memories of the Barbary pirates he'd defeated as a naval officer decades ago. They'd drawn straws for who'd have the privilege of leading this conversation and William had won, illegally of course. Townsend was probably better off dealing with an Irish street rat than somebody who'd learned mercy in Tunisian slave pens.

Portia's father puffed another set of smoke rings at the paneled ceiling. He filled his leather easy chair like a toad on a lily pad, all corpulent self-satisfaction and disinterest in anyone else's condition.

Jesus, Mary, and Joseph, had the bastard no interest in his daughter's fate? Had he taken a single glance into Portia's eyes when she staggered away from her husband at the altar?

"Splendid ceremony, wasn't it, gentlemen? I fancy you won't see its like out west for many years to come," the poltroon commented and aimed a superior smile at his three companions. "People will be congratulating me for years on the bride's looks."

Hal Lindsay snapped his jaw shut with an almost audible click, his blue eyes hotter than the fire. Every blessed saint in heaven would be needed to protect somebody who spoke that callously of Hal's little girls.

Yet he locked down his anger, as if he tamped down his steamboat's boilers against an explosion, and took up station by the library door. A single fulminating glare warned his brother-in-law to hasten before he forgot their bargain and took action first.

"D'you think so, Townsend, my lad?" William inquired, sliding into a dark croon better suited for Dublin's back alleys than Manhattan's fancy mansions. "Or will people be talking for days about how your daughter cowered from her husband?"

"In God's holy church, too, no less," Richard contributed.

"Aye, a terrible thing that. Sure to increase the gossip," William mourned, eyeing his enemy's distorted appearance in the wineglass's facets. The grotesque countenance was probably an accurate rendition of the selfishness inside.

"Ridiculous!" The New Yorker slapped his hand down onto the table. "Did you see how many people came? She was simply overwhelmed by the occasion and started to feel faint." His voice rose, shedding its usual warm patina like a snake discarding its skin to escape predators. His eyes darted around the room and, for the first time, hunted for escape routes.

"I saw a girl jerk herself away from a man, like a filly fleeing a cruel spur." Even Hal's shortest syllable contained a deadly warning.

"Nonsense." Townsend stormed onto his feet, his watch

chain rattling across his over-fed gut. "Today was a great moment for the entire family. Portia will tell you the same, once I
speak to her."

"As soon as you tell her exactly what to say?" William asked,
rage ripping hot and wild through his blood. Did the bastard
consider his daughter an obedient doll, useful only for his ambitions?

"Of course! No matter what befalls her, Portia will do what
I command. She knows better than to argue with me." His jaw
jutted out, belligerent as the fire irons warding the hearth from
the room.

"You son of a bitch." William punched his brother-in-law
on the jaw and Townsend's eyes rolled back into his head. He
crumpled onto the carpet into a disheveled heap, like the shattered ruins of a false god.

Satisfaction spilled into William's belly, touching the few
edges left unoccupied by his terror for Portia. Jesus, Mary, and
Joseph, her skin couldn't have been any tighter over her jaw
when she left for her wedding night than if she'd sat next to a
cougar.

"Good blow," Hal commented from beside William's shoulder. "I wouldn't have been as polite."

The ambitious easterner stirred. He clambered onto his
knees and glared at them, his tiny eyes malevolent in the fireplace's baleful glow. "You had no right to do that. Girls were
meant to be obedient, not to be heard!"

"This is for sending *my granddaughter* away to the other
side of the ocean and separating her from her brothers."
Richard lashed out with his foot in a blow to make any vet-
eran saloon fighter proud. The kick sent Townsend onto his
back with a loud "oof!"

William watched grimly, wishing it had been that bastard,
St. Arles. Blessed Mother Mary, how he prayed Lowell would
find a way to help Portia.

"Come on, let's get him up," he ordered, hating the necessity to be civilized. "We need to find out if there's any way we can ease Portia out of that brute's clutches."

Hal helped him haul Townsend's flabby, elephantine weight upright. William brusquely cuffed him across the face, unwilling to waste time with extra words. The fool swayed in their iron grip, his eyes bleary.

"Lazy asshole." William slapped him again. "Listen to me."

Townsend blinked and tried to jerk away. Richard shoved him back into place.

"You're a pitiful excuse for a father but you're the only one Portia has," William snapped, more harshly than he'd ever spoken to a mule. "So we'll make the most of you, do you understand?"

Their ostensible host curled his lip and declined to answer—until Hal pricked his chin with needle sharp, cold steel. Townsend shrieked at the dirk and almost pulled out of William's grip, spilling a foul stench into the elegant room.

William cursed violently in Gaelic and yanked the fool forward by his vest. "Townsend."

The New Yorker trembled violently but didn't try to run this time. Hal's knife stroking his cheek undoubtedly aided his concentration.

"Will you be a good father to Portia?" Richard asked sternly.

"Yes," Townsend whispered hoarsely, his gray eyes flapping sideways toward Hal's blade. Sniveling easterner had definitely never seen a true threat before.

"A fine one, to be proud of?" William demanded.

"I swear it!" Blood trickled down his unhappy relative's throat and stained his collar.

"How much did St. Arles wring out of you for Portia?" Hal inquired, deadly as a coroner hurling questions over a corpse.

"A lump sum sufficient to pay off his father's and brother's debts." He tolled the words like an accountant recounting the loss of hard-won pennies to a bitter enemy.

"Good Lord!" Richard ejaculated. "Surely there were other

peers on the Marriage Mart you could have bought for that much?"

"Not of the same rank." Townsend shrugged pettishly, braver now that he could look away from the knife. "St. Arles was willing to take a far smaller annual income after the ceremony, if he received the bulk at the beginning. It was a better bargain all around."

"A half million?" Richard's tone indicated he named a larger than usual sum.

Townsend shook his head and jerked his thumb upward to indicate a far higher sum.

William's vision began to darken. He'd grown up on a seaport's streets and knew far too much about buying and selling flesh. But back there, the seller was always motivated by matters of life and death. Here, it was only to increase the feather bed comfort of a greedy fool's life—and risk destroying his own flesh and blood.

William's fingers tightened on the bastard's shoulder, grinding muscle and sinew against bone.

"Ahh!" The weakling's knees started to buckle and Hal ruthlessly yanked him completely upright.

"Did you tell St. Arles about Juliet's money?" Hal demanded in tones which would have cut steel.

William froze, a faint spark of hope warming his veins. Viola and Juliet, as the only granddaughters, had split Richard's mother's investments. Portia, Juliet's only daughter, had inherited all of her mother's share.

Surely Townsend would have told St. Arles about that family trust. But if he hadn't . . .

"Not yet. It's not a very sizable amount—is it?" He glanced around at the other men and read the answer in their implacable countenances. "A fortune? Good Lord, I must tell St. Arles immediately. He might refund me some of Portia's dowry!"

Hal kicked his greedy brother-in-law's feet out from him and sent him straight onto his knees with his face only inches from the fire.

"One more word like that," he warned, his immense sea-man's paw wrapped in his enemy's graying locks, "and your nose will start roasting. Do you understand me?"

Townsend's face and eyes turned the same pasty shade of gray. "You'd never do that to your brother—would you?"

"I'd gladly destroy anyone who threatened my niece." Hal's voice held the flat certainty of a butcher announcing the daily special. "Today you helped terrorize her. Why shouldn't I kill you?"

Townsend gulped for air, his lips fluttering like a dying fish's gills. He glanced wildly at William and Richard but found only cold silence, comfortless as the North Pole's icy reaches.

"Of course I'll keep the family secrets," he finally stuttered and climbed cautiously onto his feet. He swung his head back and forth, weighing the paths to the doors. Hal stepped in front of one, knife in hand, eyes joyous for any excuse for a fight.

Townsend recoiled and spun around.

William glared at him from the other side. If the easterner had an ounce of manhood, he'd draw a weapon—any weapon!—freeing William from his promise to Viola not to kill him. His darling thought their foster daughter needed to keep as much family as possible, given the hard times she sailed into.

Even so, William brought his dirk into the open fast and smooth so the arrogant beast opposite him would know the penalties.

Townsend squeaked, stammered, and flung up his hands.

"Good to know we're finally starting to understand each other." William bowed slightly, never taking his eyes off the other. "Let me reiterate our bargain one last time. You will never tell St. Arles of Portia's inheritance from her mother."

Because a trust's arcane rules just might keep the money away from her husband and thus give her a little independence.

Townsend nodded, a single bright spot of crimson burning on each cheek.

"You will be an excellent father to Portia, a veritable exam-ple to the world, no matter how great the effort."

"No," Townsend gasped. Horror blanched his cheeks even paler. "Surely, you cannot mean I'd have to approve all of her mad starts—"

"Or else her mother's family, the golden Lindsays, will enjoy increasing your punishment," purred the old commodore and twirled a hot poker like a sabre.

"Yes, yes, of course. My daughter's welfare will ever be—*is* always—my greatest concern," Townsend assured them, his eyes totally fixated on the iron's red-hot tip.

"And Portia will never know any of this," William reminded him.

"Certainly not!"

That at least held the ring of truth.

If only they could protect Portia herself as easily.

Chapter Eight

Silence assaulted Portia from all sides, dangerous as trackless sand dunes. Her finger rotated around and around her coffee cup's rim, every loop as meaningless as a politician's platitudes. If she set the china down, she might have to look at her wedding bed, here at their hotel.

She could barely see it in the shadows beyond her dressing table. The gaslight had been dimmed, except for two wall sconces. Not that there was much to see, despite the room's luxury. It could have been any small bedroom in a good hotel, meant to be occupied for a night and forgotten in the morning. She'd even seen its furniture a hundred times before, albeit in cheaper copies of century-old French originals.

Tomorrow she'd leave for London aboard one of Britain's fanciest liners. She wouldn't even have the comfort of honest American accents for a few extra days, no more than what she'd heard Gareth say in the church. Let alone actually speaking those very unsettling phrases in the note the hotel maid had slipped to her.

As if she would overturn her sworn oath to her husband now, no matter what the provocation! No, she would never run away from her husband tonight.

She shuddered slightly and swirled her cup to kick its dregs back into motion. Not much there, truly, but maybe enough to bring a little life into her cheeks. She'd always thought her wedding night would be different: an encouraging grin from Uncle William and a quick hug from Aunt Viola, then a wild rush into Gareth's arms.

Don't think about him now. Don't think about him ever again.

Her heart thumped disconsolately against her ribs, probably because she'd been alone for too long. Or maybe because she was so pale in this light. Blond hair and white skin didn't always display to their best advantage under spluttering gaslight.

Perhaps she should change. She wore a silver white satin peignoir with bands of embroidery and lace along the cuffs and lapels, over a matching nightgown cut high to her throat. Aunt Viola had argued against the shade, saying it faded Portia's coloring. But her stepmother had insisted, calling it virginal and irresistible to a man who'd been married before.

Now the cold threads skimmed over her bones like parchment wrapped around a trout, all decoration and no protection.

Surely everything would go well tonight. Surely her husband would approve of his new bride.

Portia wrapped both hands around her coffee cup and found another meaningless smile for the pale female facing her in the mirror.

A shadow blocked out the wall sconce behind her.

"My dear," St. Arles intoned with obvious anticipation, "be certain to keep your eyes on me while I instruct you. I married you for your reaction when you learned my true plans." Anticipation curved his mouth into a hyena's approximation of happiness.

Her cup rattled into the saucer.

"Clumsy child." St. Arles yanked her robe down her shoulders and over her arms, then ruthlessly, brutally tightened it around her elbows. Her peignoir's lapels bit into her night-gown. Lace, meant to be enticing, instead became a burning brand searing her breasts.

She yelped and tried to squirm away. But she couldn't get out of it, could barely even shrug her shoulders. She stared at him through the mirror, appalled and frightened, her heart beating faster than when she'd watched for Apaches.

"That's it, my lady, that's it. That's exactly how I want you to always behave when we're alone in bed." Bright satisfaction marched through his eyes.

"What do you mean?" She tried to pull away from him but his grip tightened. Could she even move her arms?

He dangled his white silk scarf beside her cheek and she shrank away from its dreadful softness. "Let me go!"

He chuckled, the sound glittering with evil. An instant later, he whipped it around her neck like a cravat and tightened his fist in it.

She shook, darkness clawing at her vision, and fought to stand up. She couldn't scream.

"No," she croaked, the sound harsher than duty.

"This is your first lesson in how to please me, my dear." Evil smiled at her through the glass.

"I enjoy my pleasure mixed with pain," he informed her, his words echoing with far too much prior experience. "After all, orgasm is called the Little Death. I merely prefer my partners gasping on the edge of death. I find it provides both of us a far larger jolt into climax."

"You're joking." The dreadful silk eased just enough to let her speak. Aunt Viola had never mentioned anyone could do something like this.

She pushed against the vanity to stand up but he shoved her back into place, the casual blow slamming her face against the unyielding wood. Tears started in her eyes, burning harsher than her throat.

How would she survive tonight? Or all the nights and years

to come? If he consummated the marriage, she could never have an annulment and she'd be tied to this living hell forever.

"Not at all." He licked his lips, his eyes crawling over her like tarantulas. "My first wife was a widow and she'd been poorly trained by her previous husband. But you're a virgin so you've nothing to unlearn. You're absolutely perfect."

"Noo . . ." She looked around desperately for an escape.

A door or the window, from which she could summon Gareth? She'd been such a fool when she sent him away. Could she reach it with her arms bound?

An iron bar locked around her throat and linen rasped her jaw. Her husband—heaven help her, her husband—dragged his teeth along her ear like a saw testing a log.

Blood dripped onto her cheek, hot and wet as the tears she fought back.

"I'll mount you the instant you start to lose consciousness," he whispered like Satan's wind against her hair.

His grip loosened slightly on the robe. She twisted sideways and slammed her elbow into his groin, barely missing his privates.

"You wretch!" he shouted and jerked away from her.

But she had no time to savor her triumph, let alone use it.

An instant later, the silk rope closed abruptly around her neck and the world went black around her.

"By God, I'll show you who's master here," were the last words Portia heard on her wedding night.

Dawn slunk into the rain-soaked alley behind the hotel, its fitful glow useless as a broken sword on a battlefield. Cobblestones gleamed clean and fresh for once, thanks to the night's deluge. A cat prowled past, secure in the knowledge he could either outfight or outrun any attacker in the long, narrow space.

Gareth flipped his knife, the blade Portia had given him,

end over end, as he'd done since before midnight. His throat was drier than if he'd walked across the Mojave.

Inside, the rooms were warm and dry, glowing with crimson velvet and oak. Here, the walls were chipped brick and plain iron fixtures, good enough for working folks. Fancy brocade curtains in the windows overhead screened the paying customers from any uncomfortable glimpses.

A beat cop yawned and warmed himself with more coffee from the hotel's stock. Two doormen leaned against the hotel wall, their uniforms brighter than any intelligence in their eyes.

Gareth tossed his knife again. Ten inches of California-made steel whirled like a galaxy through the mist.

Portia was a grown woman. How could he forget that, the way she looked in her wedding dress?

Don't think about that; don't imagine what that beast was enjoying.

He had to let her make her own choices, no matter how much he knew they'd cost her.

His bowie went higher on the next toss.

He'd promised her he'd wait for her all night, in case she changed her mind. He kept watch here, where he could see both her window and the rear door. Plus, he'd bribed the doormen to tell him if anything happened at the front.

The sun blazed across the steel, as deadly to his hopes for the future as any desert sunrise. Bright as the flames rising above that Kentucky sky fourteen years ago and leaving the ground below just as barren of life.

Hope twisted through his gut like a hangman's knot and vanished.

Gareth threw his blade into the hotel's doorframe, where it hung like a shattered bird.

The cop jumped up, startled into lucidity. "Now, now, young fellow," he began.

Gareth strode past him without a glance and retrieved

Portia's gift, which he'd need at his next job for Donovan & Sons.

William hadn't been able to find anybody who'd work in Southeast Asia. But halfway around the world should take Gareth far enough from his memories of Portia.

God willing.

Chapter Nine

Hanoi, August 1882

Gareth jolted awake, nightmare pillars of smoke pursuing him like jackals back to consciousness. His heart beat against his ribs hard enough to break them open, the same way he'd fought to get one more shot off in his dream.

Dead men's ghosts still sank into his flesh as if their souls sought to take root in his own. Their eyes were picket fences he couldn't escape, while crimson rivers of blood streamed faster and faster from their death wounds.

Sweat broke out across Gareth's skin, bitterly cold despite the humidity hunting every crevice like magma. Rain pounded on the roof and dived through the gutters into the sewers, almost loud enough to drown his gasps for air.

He was an adult now. He hadn't wept since he'd dug his mother's grave and The Nightmare hadn't roared through his dreams for months, until tonight.

So why the hell could he remember those satisfied pigs, snorting around his family's corpses? His stomach jolted into another knot.

Maybe it was the omnipresent scent of charcoal from all the local cooking fires that reminded him of racing toward the smoke rising through the Kentucky woods. Running until he puked, but never reaching his destination.

Where the hell was the damn light?

He flung his arm out and sent papers flying onto the floor. China shattered with a loud crash when his knife smashed into it. He barely managed to grab the hurricane lantern an instant before it toppled onto its side.

Cursing like the mule packer he'd once been, he sat up on the edge of the delicately carved bed. His pulse still drummed stupidly fast. It was an insane beat since he'd finished delivering all those critical railroad supplies, despite the every hazard corrupt politicians, foul roads, and filthy weather could hurl at him. Donovan & Sons would be very well rewarded.

His hands shook, as if he'd drunk himself to sleep. Not that he'd chosen that escape, of course. He'd realized within a month of Portia's wedding that whiskey wouldn't ease this pain.

He ground his teeth and looked for matches.

Chau peeked around the corner, her enormous brown eyes alight with concern above her thin silk robe. Despite the few months they'd been acquainted, she was confident around a disturbed male as only a previously well-pleasured woman could be.

At least he could do some things well.

Even so, words only trembled on her lips and never escaped into the air to disturb him further.

He finally managed to light the lantern and saw the newspapers scattered across the floral silk carpet. Ice ran down his spine, chilling him faster than his nightmare.

A single photo stared up at him. Portia and her husband— rather, the Earl and Countess of St. Arles—stood aboard their yacht at Cowes Week. Every inch was emblematic of Britain's finest society, from their haughty pose to the layers of furbelows which hid any reminders of the soft womanhood which had enticed him from underneath her wedding dress. Even her high collar seemed to bristle with superiority, like a woman's version of an imperial uniform.

Gareth closed his eyes and tried not to look at how carefully he'd folded the newsprint so it would highlight that single photo. He didn't need a reminder of his old playmate, some-how transformed into a magnet for his wayward eyes. If he had a nickel for every time his heart twisted at a thought of her, he'd be a millionaire.

"Would you like some tea?" Chau's cousin Quyen crept in-side the room, her robe concealing few of her well-sampled charms. A professional courtesan, she could make tumbling out of bed seem an erotic invitation. She was an enticing morsel like her cousin but, like all his play partners since leaving the States, she was dark haired and dark eyed. Her hair would never gleam in the firelight like Portia's.

He shook his head violently. Then he remembered how well they could read him after a few months of sharing his bed. He opened his eyes and tried a more charming tack. "Not at this hour, thank you."

"Perhaps you heard the cable arrive at the office next door." Chau offered him the folded bit of yellow paper.

Discern anything in this storm? Gareth added a smooth smile to his noncommittal murmur and read the message quickly.

He dropped it onto the newspaper, covering Portia's face. "My boss wants me to take over the company's freight routes in the Mediterranean."

"Paris?" Convent-inspired dreams flashed through Quyen's eyes.

"Algeria," Gareth regretfully corrected her. Another barren, blood soaked hellhole where Donovan & Sons could turn a profit as one of the few companies willing to do business.

"There's fighting there! War and rebellion. You could be killed," Quyen objected and bit her lip, tears swimming into her eyes.

Gareth gritted his teeth against easy agreement and the need to comfort her—or distract himself. Algeria was unfortunately far too close by ship and train to Paris, where Portia could surely be found primping herself for St. Arles' hellish appetites.

He would not, could not dally on that Mediterranean shore, no matter how often rebels stormed across its plains.

"And Turkey," he added. "Constantinople, and maybe some of the smaller ports." He did his best to look certain. Surely Donovan would agree to opening up a new business route into the Ottoman capital.

"The Turkish sultan is a bloodthirsty monster, who'll kill anyone." Chau caught his arm, surprising him yet again with her mastery of gossip. "He destroys missionaries and his own people, plus honest men who simply carry odd packages. You could die any minute."

But he'd be too damn busy looking over his shoulder and dodging government spies to worry about Portia or dream about his lost family.

"The Sultan attacks only fools who give him the chance," he demurred. "No, I must obey my master's bidding and leave this fair"—and wet—"land."

He lifted first Chau's, then Quyen's hand and kissed their delicate fingers. "While you, dear ladies, will stay here to prosper and be adored."

They hesitated for a moment like herons poised over a fishing pond. Then they relaxed and giggled happily at his emphasis on the word prosper. After all, somebody needed to truly enjoy all of their life and his bon voyage gift would ensure they'd have the opportunity to do so. As ever, the money he made from gambling when he wasn't at work went back to William to be invested.

He, on the other hand, would have a very difficult job to keep his hands busy and his mind from worrying about Portia.

Chapter Ten

St. Arles House, London, October 1885

Portia stirred the jewelry strewn across her table one last time. Her sitting room's soft gaslight picked out the exquisite details uncannily well and identified them as extremely high quality, even if most were old-fashioned. She'd picked her American jewels up from the vault that morning: she would not leave her mother's possessions near any banker who might feel more loyalty to St. Arles than to her.

It was the last step before leaving this house.

Nobody had touched her mother's sapphires and pearls in more than a decade, since all of Juliet Townsend's jewelry and possessions went to her daughter. Even so, Portia's fingers lingered longest on the tiny cloisonné watch where the phoenix crouched, ready to spring into flight. She'd hoped so much more would follow when Gareth gave it to her.

So many memories were bound up on this table, as they were in the servants facing her from across it.

"Are you very sure you won't do this?" she asked again. "I'd understand perfectly if you agreed to testify."

"It would be a lie, your ladyship." Mrs. Russell, the housekeeper and designated spokeswoman, sniffed ferociously.

"People tell untruths frequently, especially for the family they've worked for throughout their careers," Portia pointed out and ran her thumb across the watch's delicate gold threads. Gareth never seemed more alive than when she held his gift, even though she didn't know where he was.

"Besides"—Portia hesitated, unwilling to speak more frankly and make the situation worse.

"Servants generally provide complete details of lives in the households where they serve." Years of dictating other people's behavior rang through the housekeeper's severe tones. "It is our duty, your ladyship, to answer all questions put to us. It is not our duty to make up statements from whole cloth."

"Your absence from the proceedings will be noted," Portia pointed out gently and started to wind the watch. "It will probably cause considerable gossip in his lordship's circles and may darken his lordship's mood, something I don't want you to suffer."

"We all know you've taken the brunt of that upon yourself whenever possible, your ladyship!" little Maisie burst out, startling the entire group by a housemaid's temerity in interrupting such an august gathering.

"If you'll pardon me for speaking so frankly," she added, dipping her head. Jenkins, the under-groom, gently nudged her and she grabbed his elbow like a lifebelt. "But you've always been kind to all of us, learned our names, made our schedules easy as pie whenever possible." Maisie's eyes shone with tears and sincerity under her pleated cap. "It wouldn't be right to make you bear the full burden now."

"His lordship has already made it clear he expects his staff to testify according to whatever script he writes, including the details of the adultery committed by any staff member with your ladyship." Winfield's voice dripped poison for all its quiet, astonishing in a butler with thirty years service under the same family.

"There will be a divorce and St. Arles must have witnesses to my so-called adultery." Portia forced her voice around the knot in her throat. Duty, honor—all virtue demanded a price. Hadn't Gareth taught her that? "If you do not speak, his lordship will be forced to hire a correspondent, paid to swear he'd committed adultery with me—"

"No true man—" Jenkins muttered under his breath but Maisie kicked him hard in the shins.

"Plus witnesses to this adultery," Portia finished. "Spending money for what he must certainly consider disloyalty will anger him greatly. Are you and the other servants certain you wish to do this?"

"My lady, you have always been a most true and faithful mistress. We will keep faith with you by becoming very slow-witted when asked about you. And forgetful," Mrs. Russell proclaimed firmly. "Certainly we would never speak a lie."

"Even if that means being turned off and being sent to live with the lowest of the low in Spitalfields," Winfield added.

"All of us who know you, both here in town and at St. Arles Castle, have sworn to it," completed Maisie and Jenkins.

The four of them stood shoulder to shoulder facing her, like knights of old ready to ride into battle. Their plan might just work.

"Oh my dear friends, how much you've lifted my heart." How few friends she had left, except for her family. Gareth was lost to her since her wedding, since nobody spoke to her of him.

She fastened the exquisite bit of jewelry around her neck.

"While I'm sure it would never come to Spitalfields for you, I'll always be willing to do anything I can for all of you." It was the very least she could do for them.

Chapter Eleven

London, November 1885

Light sliced across Portia's eyes, sharp and fast as an executioner's axe after the holding room's darkness. She flinched and her gloved hand lost its deathly tight grip on the banister. Her foot slipped on the narrow tread. An agonizingly long moment later, her heel finally thudded onto another stair's ragged wooden edge.

A splinter cracked and broke off underneath. A chill breeze teased her skirts and petticoats then tried to slither up her wobbling ankles to terrorize her legs and her heart. Twenty feet below, a pair of gaslights buzzed before the door to one of London's most notorious prisons.

But she wasn't a criminal and her freedom lay ahead, no matter how high the price. Besides, she was damned—what an appropriate word—if she'd let Saint Arles win everything.

Portia tightened her grasp on the far-too-large handrail and hauled herself into London's finest courtroom before her guard noticed anything had gone awry. An instant later, she was firmly penned in a large wooden box, forced to view the world over a stockade of varnished oak planks.

"Ice Princess! Countess St. Arles!" The crowd's clamor swelled around her, more raucous than anything she'd endured to ar-

rive at this hellish place. How many hours had her lawyer—
no, barrister—said she'd have to survive the torment?

Portia firmed her stance and wrapped herself in an attitude
of arctic politeness, based on the one her mother-in-law had
always shown her. If nothing else, it should fend off the rabble
rousers and let her assess her true tribunal.

Winter's cold brilliance spilled into the great courtroom from
the skylight and windows, remorselessly exposing every tiny
detail to the judge's pitiless scrutiny. It drowned out the wall
sconces' feeble yellow glow as easily as the crowd outside ignored
the police's attempts to keep the surrounding streets clear. It
honed its blades upon the great mirror then dived upon its prey.

Portia tilted her head slightly, using her hat's lace trim to de-
flect the worst glare. She hadn't been permitted to wear a veil,
a decent woman's standard protection from prying eyes. Even
so, she didn't have to display every thought that passed through
her mind, even if she was the accused.

The bailiff's deep voice rang through the big room, like a
horn summoning hunters to follow their master. Heavy oak
paneling marched around the walls behind him, locking in
potential malefactors as completely as a stockade. "Edward
Henry Vanneck, Earl of St. Arles, Viscount Erddig, hereinafter
known as the Petitioner . . ."

Portia's husband smoothly shook out his cuffs, as calculat-
edly dispassionate as if he were negotiating an arms treaty.
The movement had the additional advantage of distracting onlookers from his narrow shoulders and viper-thin face. His
black frockcoat and white linen were perfectly tailored and
quite pristine, making them permissible to be worn by the fruit
of centuries of England's finest breeding. Dark eyebrows curved
over his heavy-lidded eyes, framing a high-born predator's watch-
ful gaze.

He focused all his attention on the bailiff and the judge, of
course—never the crowd, with their sharp, ill-bred whispers
and stares.

All around him, clerks and barristers took their places in a final blur of black robes, rustling papers, and heavy seats slamming down like a fort's gate ramming shut.

Portia instinctively, unwillingly flinched. The bitter taste of failure—of being forced back into St. Arles life again—surged into her throat.

She swallowed hard and reached for logic, whose cool shelter had protected her so well for so long. For five years, she'd tolerated St. Arles in her bed. But not anymore, thank God. Besides, if she acted with all the speed her ancestors had shown against the Barbary pirates, she might yet salvage something for herself.

She might be damaged but she was not yet utterly defeated. She was, after all, a golden Lindsay, at least on her mother's side.

"For divorce . . ."

Pencils stormed across pads while newspaper artists feverishly recorded the day's events. All those years of doing her best for the people on St. Arles' estate—building schools, starting new businesses, repairing roofs and replacing others for tenants, and other deeds, all of which St. Arles had derided or fought as a waste of her money, which should have been spent on his brilliant ambitions . . . All that work was now eclipsed by blocks of black ink screaming her name across every newspaper in Britain.

The words' stain seemed to have sunk through her clothing and into her skin, no matter how conservatively she dressed or how often she washed. Her carriage had been blocked this morning by newsboys shoving copies of the latest lies into a thousand grasping hands outside the courthouse.

"From Portia Anne Townsend Vanneck, hereinafter known as the Respondent . . ." The bailiff's head reared back and he glared at her, determined as any buffalo hunter unleashing a loaded Winchester rifle.

Her mother's family was here to fill the near gallery's first row, dangerous as a pack of wolves guarding their littermate.

Uncle Hal Lindsay, big and bold with Aunt Rosalind by his side, assessed the lawyers down below like hyenas to be carved up as quickly and neatly as possible. Grandfather Richard Lindsay sat still and erect like the naval officer he'd been, intensely aware of the judge's least flicker. Her Lindsay cousins occupied the seats beyond him, more menacing in their silent watchfulness than the courtroom's guards' twitching wariness beside the doors.

As for Uncle William and Aunt Viola, they sat at the edge of the gallery closest to her, ostensibly the best behaved of all her family. Yet the guards gave the big Irishman with his California accent and London-made clothes the widest berth of any Lindsay family member. And Aunt Viola—dear, dear Aunt Viola—was pale and slow-moving, due to her third bout of pneumonia in the two years since the twins had been born. Yet she still stared at the bailiff as if she wanted to dowse him in the foulest animal matter possible.

Portia longed to yell at her to rest, almost more than she wanted to make the bailiff fall silent. Yet she was caged, able to see but not touch or call out to her family. They might as well have been on another continent.

Gluttonous stares swept over her from the other onlookers, like locusts hunting for tidbits. United in black and white clothing, they swayed to and fro under the legalistic chant's hypnotic sway. Their jaws were poised to clack rapidly, their elbows ready to jostle their neighbors' ribs at the first hint of any weakness on her part.

Idiots. Flesh-eating beetles would have been more discreet, since they'd at least run back into dark corners if she stomped her feet.

Amabel Mayhew, St. Arles' mistress, leaned forward from her seat in the far gallery, her close-set eyes avidly scrutinizing Portia. Was she staring at Portia's attire, rather than her expression like everyone else? *Didn't the fool realize whose money paid for everything—and it wasn't the earl's?*

The legal chain of words reached out for Portia again.

"On the grounds of having held criminal conversation . . ."

A cold draft stirred her hem and dragged it back toward the drop through the stairwell down to the prison.

Portia immediately twitched it away from the verge and settled the ruffled, whispering mass safely away from danger. Gareth had always said her liking for feminine frills would get her into trouble—but, please God, not here and now.

Why couldn't the court's servants be honest enough to simply say adultery? Surely criminal conversation could be interpreted as something else, just as infidelity required more than words.

"Five times . . ." the bailiff intoned with notable satisfaction.

Five times? The same number as his mistress had borne children to her late husband, thereby proving her worthiness to become the next Countess of St. Arles. Unlike Portia's complete and utter failure as a breeder.

Only the past years' bitter lessons in how to become an acceptable British countess kept Portia from shrieking a denial.

St. Arles had only discussed one count with her, not five. Why the devil should she heap even more opprobrium on her head by accepting—no, standing here in court and agreeing to—so many more occurrences of infidelity?

The infernal bastard who still styled himself as her husband leaned back in his chair and studied his fingernails.

Portia measured the distance to the nearest inkwell. Too far below her on that lawyer's desk to grab, dammit, but perhaps she could hurl one of those appalling wigs instead?

No matter what words Shakespeare had placed in her namesake's mouth, she could not pray for mercy for St. Arles, only justice. If not from this court, then another.

The bailiff's phrases continued to roll inexorably onward like a sorcerer's incantation.

"With one Robert Brundage . . ."

A down-at-the-heels actor whose hair was so oily that it seemed to beg for the latest carbolic soap.

"How plead ye?" the bailiff thundered, cracking the question at her like a lion tamer's whip.

She caught the statue of Justice's unblinking gaze. Her mouth tightened and she quickly looked away.

But true justice would not be found between these four walls, only prearranged lies and half-truths. Gareth's watch ticked steadily against her throat under her collar, in a silent reminder that like time and tides, some things were beyond the power of man to change.

Today was her battle to fight—and win.

She stared back at the bailiff impassively, her hands firmly folded in a lady's formal public barricade. Now was the only time she controlled this public flogging. She'd do exactly what she wanted to with it, not what the men decided.

If she denied committing adultery, the divorce would take longer but it would still go through. St. Arles had made that very clear and she believed him.

If she agreed, matters would move far faster and she'd still keep one priceless asset, an item that would infuriate him.

Her continued silence had drawn everyone's nervous attention, even St. Arles. Very good.

"How plead ye, my lady?" The judge reiterated the bailiff's question, sharpening the whip's edge in an implicit threat to hurl her back down into the pit if she didn't obey him quickly.

How much choice did she truly have, if she wanted to start afresh?

"Aye." Her admission rang out through the room like a battlefield bugle call compelling attention and belief. After all, she would have done everything she was accused of, and more, with Gareth Lowell.

If she'd only had the chance.

Chapter Twelve

Newport, Rhode Island, February 1887

Viola Donovan fought to bring the spyglass back into focus. She refused to curse either the high winds that kept her inside, far away from the fast moving boats, or her own weakness which left her unable to hold the heavy bits of steel and glass for more than a few minutes.

William and Hal were outside, standing in the sun and probably chatting about the Navy's recent annexation of Pearl Harbor in Hawaii. William knew more about it than any of the East Coast-based Lindsays, thanks to his San Francisco home. Hal's Great Lakes empire was immense but he always had a keen eye for his Lindsay cousins' potential advantage.

She'd always worried how he'd treat his own son but she never fussed over his handling of the various male relations who sought their fortune under his auspices.

Marlowe and Spenser, her five-year-old twins, raced across the finely manicured lawn, their black hair blowing in the wind just like their Irish father's did. Fourteen-year-old Neil watched them warily, ever careful to keep himself between them and the sea, despite the stout brick wall hidden by the steep cliff edge.

Thirteen-year-old Brian, on the other hand, willingly chased his little brothers in yet another game of tag. He even pretended to stumble and fall over a non-existent bump, no doubt hidden under the sere grass by last night's bitter frost. Little Spenser laughed and jumped into the air to clap, while Marlowe raced to victory atop the garden wall.

Brian sat up quickly—and her heart eased. She should have known nothing physical would injure her fairy-blessed second son. Not for him was Neil's horrified frown when Spenser's coat came unbuttoned, bringing the attendant horror of possible bronchitis. No, Brian chuckled and teased and fastened his little brother up again, while Viola shuddered and prayed that her youngest might be spared to live another day.

She'd paid too high a price to have him. She'd even sworn to her frantic husband that they'd never have another child, lest they not be able to dismiss death from both her door and the babe's.

But she didn't have to think about that today. This afternoon was for sharing family joys. She was with her father again, able to talk about the Lindsay clan's passion for boats. She was warm and comfortable behind her cousin's observatory's thick glass panes, no matter what else they might think about. Like the upcoming finalization of Portia's divorce.

"There, d'you see the triple-masted yacht? That's Gould's latest." The old commodore, still unbowed by his many decades, pointed out to the foaming seas where a sleek black funnel sprang into life above the white caps.

"Very pretty," Viola approved, remembering old lessons from her hometown's shipyards. More of the boat revealed itself coyly, glimpses snatched between waves reaching for the sky. "She's very big—and very seaworthy."

"Aye, Gould builds them well."

"Them?" She set the spyglass down and tucked her shawl around her more closely. She'd somehow grown less tolerant of drafts since the twins' birth. If William caught her without a coat, he'd blister her ears—or worse, look terrified. But she hadn't had pneumonia yet this winter so there was nothing for him to worry about.

Heaven knows they both spent enough time fretting about Portia's refusal to come directly back to America, with its baying jackals called newspaper reporters. The trial's coverage had been hell for her, with its mixture of a few facts and much fiction. Every British and American newspaper had discussed her for months, painting her in terms which made Jezebel appear virtuous.

Her family had tried to silence them, or at least reduce the baying jackals to printing only what appeared in court. Nothing worked. They'd bought newspapers in America, blackmailed, bribed, called in favors from politicians and anyone else who might help. Viola suspected their most successful tactic was Hal's unacknowledged use of bricks thrown by gangs of young thugs.

Even so, the only apparent difference was a slight slowing in the torrent of purple vitriol.

"Gould and his sons collect yachts, as well as railroad cars." The former steamboat captain bit off the mention of railroads, despite his daughter in law's family attachment to his landbased rivals.

Viola tucked her hand into his and steered the conversation into less troubled waters. "Do they need so many?"

"I doubt it." He hugged her, putting himself between her and the cold air. "This one is a new design that Gould's testing for ocean cruising. Rumor says his wife doesn't approve of how the cabins are decorated."

"Does she plan to have them redone?"

"No, she wants an entirely new yacht—so she can have new paneling." The old millionaire's tone was very dry.

"A new boat? Even for the Goulds, isn't that rather extravagant?" Viola couldn't imagine how much it would cost to satisfy the whim. "Has he given in?"

"No."

"He's very thrifty," she mused, remembering tales of how the railroad tycoon had raised his children to understand and manage their own money. "Perhaps we can help them both."

"What do you have in mind?" Her father cocked an eyebrow at her.

"Portia has decided to see the world, once the divorce is final, rather than return directly to the States." Where she'd face so many reporters, the poor darling.

"Harrumph."

"What if she had a trustworthy ship and crew to match?"

The old naval officer stilled, as if he'd just heard drums beating the call to battle once again. Then he whipped his spyglass up and stared at Gould's yacht for a long time.

"Well?" Viola inquired, trying not to beg. This was the first time she'd ever asked her father's help in something more than planning a birthday party. "Do you think it would work? She wants to head east, through the Suez Canal, then on to Singapore, Hawaii, and California. I'm worried," she finished in a hoarse whisper.

"That's a very good idea which will help our Portia." Her father gripped her fingers reassuringly. "Once I buy that little lady, Hal and I will find crew for her. Don't worry, we'll keep our sweet Portia safe no matter where she goes."

Viola leaned her head against her father's shoulder and let his certainty fill her as it never had before, not even when she'd been Marlowe and Spenser's age. She had to believe—and she had to pray, too—that Portia would come home safely.

Chapter Thirteen

Cairo, March 1887

Horses' hooves and carriage wheels pummeled clouds of dust out of the street, like offerings to the ancient sun god floating overhead. Tall trees marched beside the curbs, providing color while great men's transient striped awnings supplied shade. White helmeted men rode strutting horses or hastened across the street.

Noontime had passed and the midday heat was rising inexorably to its brazen climax before Shepheard's Hotel, the highest example of Cairo lodging. Broad marble stairs led down to the street below a latticed, wrought iron awning. Tables crowded the terrace on either side behind finely etched railings.

A storyteller hooted at passersby, hoping for one last kiss from a coin. Dates, oranges, and slices of watermelon spun past on plates, their small vendors cheerfully willing to exchange them for silver.

It could almost—almost—have been Tucson on fiesta day.

Gareth Lowell would have spent hours among sights like these, wandering between the ancient river, the amusing tricks the young vendors played, and the tourists' slow saunter.

Portia Townsend Vanneck, who'd once been called Portia Countess St. Arles, dismounted from the barouche and turned to watch a particularly small, chocolate brown urchin. He was following a policeman, every step and gesture mocking all of the fellow's very self-important movements. He far outshone the snake charmer and trained monkey performing on the hotel's main stairs.

Best of all, unlike most of his brethren, all of his limbs were sound and muscles gleamed through his filthy rags.

Once, she too had dared the authorities like that, when she'd snuck out of her uncle's house with Gareth to gape at a burlesque show or leap for joy under forbidden fireworks.

Unbidden, her feet shifted into an answering dance, echoing a half-forgotten, insidious beat for a few steps. Some of the child's pure joy in successfully triumphing over his elders, even in so little as silently mocking one, slipped silently into her bones. Another day of sightseeing suddenly became a highlight.

She dug into her purse, the eye-catching movement which every guide cautioned visitors against. More than one person turned to look.

"There!" Cynthia Oates' voice rang with triumph. She caught up with Portia, an enormous parasol shading her petite figure. "She *is* smiling."

Portia sniffed loudly at her dear friend's teasing, even while laughter still lurked in her toes. Few of her British or American friends—no, acquaintances—had continued to speak to her after the divorce. Cynthia's warmth and the ability to return it were an ongoing delight.

"Are you certain, my dear?" asked Sir Graham Oates, neatly unfurling his large frame from their small carriage. "Perhaps the bright sunshine has addled your brain and we should take you inside."

"This was the third time today." Cynthia tapped her husband on the chest in mock dudgeon.

Portia tossed a few coins at the little mimic. Somehow the tiny fortune vanished like wisps of smoke between his fingers.

She giggled, hiding her mouth behind her hand.

He bowed to her as if he were a mighty wizard, all flourishes and twinkling eyes, then scampered away one step ahead of his jealous brethren.

Portia applauded him readily. She could celebrate a day if it brought sight of a success like his, which few did. Her own life was filled with silent, echoing spaces, albeit blessedly free of newspapermen's howling questions.

"There you see! I was perfectly correct!" Cynthia chortled.

Portia shook her head and paused on the hotel stairs to wait for her friends. Ever since they'd left London, Cynthia had made it a private crusade to make Portia relax, preferably by smiling. How could one be angry at a friend like that?

"Of course you were, my dear: all we needed to do was take Lady St. Arles far enough from London and she'd remember how to laugh," Sir Graham agreed, smothering what sounded suspiciously like a guffaw.

Portia raised her eyebrow at him as if wielding a lorgnette. He countered by inclining his head before shooting her a wink. The three of them dissolved into soft laughter, the same gentle friendship that had kept them together on the long journey from London.

Sir Graham offered each lady an arm and they turned for Shepheard's Hotel, the ne plus ultra of Cairo lodging. Originally a harem, fifty years of catering to the very wealthy had adapted its stone bulk into a palace which promised comfort and privacy, rather than flaunting vulgar ostentation.

Cynthia leaned a little closer to her husband, their steps falling into harmony with the ease of long practice.

Bittersweet joy, too painful to be called envy, twisted Portia's mouth.

What would it be like to have someone who adored you so much it showed in something as simple as your walk?

But the past was better left behind, with the dreams' dust it contained.

The hotel's wide terrace spread before them, scattered with

tables and palm trees. Red-jacketed waiters, topped by crisp red fezes and anchored by billowing white trousers, flowed between patrons like silent magicians, capable of any gift.

A man rose out of the shadows like a spitting cobra emerging from a basket.

Portia stopped, her feet immovably fixed to the stone paving and her blood spinning into Arctic realms.

"Mrs. Vanneck." His pitch-black eyes ran over her and her friends, noting every wrinkle on a once immaculate sleeve, lock of hair sagging from the heat, and trickle of sweat slinking down a flushed face.

The so-called gentleman looked exactly the way he had the last time she'd seen him in that London courtroom, flaunting the gaudy cleanliness of a man who hired others to do his dirty work.

"St. Arles," Portia acknowledged. The dust of ancient pharaohs would have tasted better than those words on her tongue.

What the devil was he doing here? The *London Times* had announced his marriage to That Woman months ago, within days of the divorce becoming final. He should be in England, breeding the heir who'd block his cousin from ruling St. Arles Castle.

A cup smashed down into a saucer only a few feet away, followed by hisses of surprise and the screech of chair legs being pushed rapidly backward. Clearly their reunion had acquired an audience.

Portia ignored them, something she'd learned far too well how to do, and instead scrutinized the man whose bed she'd once shared. In Arizona, she could have listened to her instincts and gone armed, however subtly.

Like him, she offered no gesture of greeting, neither handshake nor nod. If he collapsed before the whispering crowd on this busy Cairo street edge, she'd be the first to send the notice to The *Times* then drink a glass of champagne in private.

Something flickered behind his eyes and his diplomat's mask

tightened over his knife-edged features. Could he be angry she
hadn't immediately sought to placate him?

Surely not, given she was no longer married to him and
therefore no longer owed him any duty.

Cynthia swept around her husband and linked arms with
Portia to protectively flank her. Even her hat's feathers seemed
to bristle like a bull terrier.

"Sir Graham, Lady Oates." St. Arles gave them the same
curt recognition he'd give street signs, as if they were necessary
but not interesting.

Hot words protesting discourtesy to her friends surged forward but Portia forced them back, into the familiar cavern of
useless remonstrances behind her gritted teeth. St. Arles loved
only his country and his land; everyone and everything else
was judged in terms of their usefulness.

"My lord." Sir Graham's voice was even less friendly than
the other man's, for all that he was an Army captain facing
down an earl well-connected enough to crush him. "We were
on our way inside when you caught us. Is there ought we can
do for you before we depart?"

"I'll have a word with Mrs. Vanneck." He'd have shown
more consideration if he'd been ordering lunch at his club, the
bastard. "She must postpone her trip to India."

"Quite unnecessary, St. Arles," Portia returned, determined
not to argue with him again. She was free and he had no claim
upon her whatsoever. "Our lawyers have already said everything necessary."

"She has already booked passage with us for India and on
to Australia," Cynthia added.

"After which, I'll return to San Francisco and my family.
Good day, sir." Portia started to walk past the earl.

"You might want to hear the latest news from Mrs. Russell,"
St. Arles suggested and polished a fingernail with his thumb.

The housekeeper at St. Arles Court? Why would he carry a
message from her? He never troubled himself with the servants
except to make their lives miserable.

"And Winfield? Or young Maisie and Jenkins, I believe he's called?" He shot a speculative glance at her then returned his attention to his always important manicure.

The butler, housemaid, and under-groom? A chill, which had nothing to do with the spring breeze, or the verandah's shade, crept into Portia's fingers.

She tried to kick her recalcitrant brain into action.

What would Gareth look for in this situation?

St. Arles had just named the ringleaders of her supporters during the divorce. How much did he know or suspect?

Now that she was gone, they lacked a protector—unless That Woman had changed her stripes and become someone capable of considering others more than herself.

Portia sniffed privately, remembering maids weeping after being slapped by the over-bred, ill-mannered breeding machine.

No, she had to hear out the two-legged male rat. Her duty to her friends demanded nothing less.

"Yes, of course, I would." She started to move away from Cynthia and Sir Graham.

"Surely you can't mean to take her very far," Cynthia exclaimed. "We're promised to have tea together in a few minutes."

Actually in a few hours. What was she thinking of?

"Why don't you join us and share all the latest gossip from home?" Cynthia burbled, in the style most men expected from a blond of her looks but her friends rarely encountered.

St. Arles frowned, his disgust almost tangible.

Portia's lips curled, despite the ice fighting for possession of her skin under the brazen desert sky. The Fifth Earl only talked to women if he hoped to bed them or tease a state secret from them.

"No, I'm afraid I cannot stay that long," he refused curtly. "A few minutes should see us done."

"In that case, you and I can walk in the Ezbekieh Gardens on the hotel's other side, ahead of Sir Graham and Lady Oates," Portia said sweetly. She'd be safer roped and tied by Apaches than alone again with him. But everything Gareth had taught her about duty in the face of danger insisted she needed to learn what the brute wanted.

St. Arles opened his mouth to object then measured the intensity of their growing audience, spilling in waves across the hotel terrace. His gaze swung back to his former wife's rigid determination and her friends' wariness.

His jaw clenched. "I'd be delighted to escort you," he gritted out.

"Thank you," Portia returned with less enthusiasm and took care not to touch him. Sir Graham and Cynthia followed at a distance, close enough to see but not to hear.

They passed through the great hotel's shadowed dimness without speaking and into the great garden's verdant square surrounded by massive palaces and hotels. Closely cropped hedges and green grass echoed Paris's famous parks, while an ornate bandstand offered a place for the well-to-do to congregate. Only the ancient palm trees and the sweet scent of flowers for Egypt's famous perfumes evoked Oriental mysteries.

Gareth would have looked far more commanding striding across the grass, than any of the bronze statues of kings and emperors lurking behind shrubbery. Or the well-bred varmint beside her.

"How are they?" Portia asked, without glancing at her companion.

"Well enough—for now."

Exactly as she'd suspected: another bout of the haggling which had wracked their marriage. She waited, determined to hear him out then walk away. This time, she had no reason to beg her father for money to advance St. Arles' ambitions.

"A steamer trunk is being delivered to your rooms at this moment. You will take it to Constantinople—"

"What?" That had to take the prize for greatest harebrained conversational topics.

"Where you will receive instructions on who and how to transfer it."

She came to a complete halt and stared at him, her tailor-made suit snapping against her boots.

He didn't even pause but continued to stroll forward, armored as ever in arrogance—and the certainty he'd made the proper decision.

He'd tracked her down in Egypt so she could take a piece of luggage to Constantinople?

Fear, which she'd thought she'd forgotten, or at least escaped, bloomed in a rising tide through the hairs on the nape of her neck.

She shook herself fiercely. A quick glare warned Cynthia and Sir Graham to stay back before she caught up with her damnably confident ex-husband.

St. Arles planned to strand her in a very foreign city with an enormous oak box, which would be impossible to hide, and demand she wait until somebody happened along to take it off her hands? She'd carried gold into Apache country but it had been a small amount, hidden in a money belt, and taken on a scheduled stagecoach route.

Still, if she'd survived the Apacheria, she could manage this. Somehow.

She ignored the little voice which reminded her of Gareth Lowell's aid.

"Why Constantinople? Surely somebody else could take it to the capitol of the Ottoman Empire." She deliberately kept her voice honey sweet and rational, suitable for a proper diplomat's wife. It was one of the few weapons which had been useful during her bitter marriage.

"It's a woman's piece of luggage, not a man's. The Turks won't pay any heed to it." He paused to watch two little boys playing hide and seek behind a large hibiscus bush. His stern expression softened into something approaching charm.

"Why me?"

"You're American, not British. Touchy as the Sultan is, he won't be looking for trouble from an upstart colonial."

She blinked. "What do you mean by that?"

"Two years ago, the Sultan barred the Dardanelles to our Navy. It's the only reason we didn't have a full-out war with Russia—Baltic, Crimea, Afghanistan, Pacific, everywhere—at a time when India itself was at stake."

"The Penjdeh Crisis."

"Finally your tiny brain starts working." The little boys ran off after their nanny. St. Arles sighed and turned his attention completely to her, his brief ascent into humanity completely vanished.

"The Sultan is a bloody-fingered autocrat who looks for plots everywhere. A trunk this large in a diplomat's luggage, especially British, would be watched constantly. That's why you're taking it in."

"Never."

"You'll do as I say or every one of your so-called friends will be dismissed without a reference."

They'd be destroyed. They'd never be able to find another job, at least not a decent one.

"You wouldn't dare," she countered. "Your wife would be left to fend for herself, with no one to cook or clean for her."

"Only until I could replace them. It would be worth it, if it meant the traitors were gone."

Traitors?

"Most of them have served generations of your family," she countered, striving for logic.

"They should have testified against you when I told them to."

"They'd have lied."

"What of it? I wouldn't have needed to pay that greedy actor, plus witnesses at the coaching hotel to do so. Every other man can rely on his staff at all times; why couldn't I?"

Because you're a brute and I tried to protect them.

"Now it's time for them to be of some use."

As bait?

"The trunk can't be worth enough for that kind of black-mail." She flogged her brain for a way out of this impasse, as if she were riding through an endless thicket of cactus with no water in sight.

Think, Portia, think. You must have learned something from Gareth.

Perhaps if she sent word to her solicitor in London, he could do something in time. But she'd wager her best pearl necklace St. Arles was having her every move watched, including every cable she sent.

"The Turks will think it's jollier than old Humpty Dumpty." He snickered. "Don't try to open it; you won't have the key, of course."

"You need an American woman," she said slowly. Was this clue a glimpse into an oasis or a mirage? "Is this for yourself or the Crown?"

He stilled, like an angry rattler ready to strike.

"A matter of state?"

His hand shot out for her throat. She automatically jerked away, trained by far too much practice, and Sir Graham growled.

St. Arles dropped his hand an inch short of her jugular. He glared at her, the promise of gory death lurking behind his slitted eyes.

Old terror tried to climb back into her veins but she shook it off. She was not his puppet any longer, required to spout the prattle he fed her whenever she walked among other diplomats' wives.

"Good God, St. Arles, what are you planning to do? Buy conspirators for some harebrained scheme?"

"It's none of your affair. Simply do as you're told and there'll be no trouble from me for your friends."

What was in that trunk to evoke such a sharp reaction?

"Why me? Surely you could have found somebody else, perhaps paid a man to take it there." If she understood better, surely she could convince him to change his mind. He usually did, given enough money.

He laughed harshly, the noise as jarring as a crow's cry heralding death among these scented gardens.

"Not at all, my beloved former wife. You see, this is how you will work off your debt to me."

"I don't owe you a penny, St. Arles. You know perfectly well my dowry wiped out your father and brother's gambling debts on our wedding day. After that, you spent the spare change on cleaning up your home."

"A million pounds."

Even her heart stopped beating at the far too familiar sum.

"Yes, I thought you might recognize the amount. Or should I call it *five million dollars*? You owe me that much for rushing our divorce through."

"I owe you nothing!" Portia violently swept petals off a planter's rim.

"Remember the trust from your mother that you inherited on your twenty-fifth birthday? Townsend should have told me about it."

"What of it? Mother inherited it from her mother and it would pass only to her daughters. Father had nothing to do with it, so of course he didn't think of it." Her heart was beating like one of those erratic drums in a bazaar.

Stay calm, Portia. Gareth always remained poised during battle. Oh, dear Lord, if only he could walk by right now . . .

"If you'd contested the divorce, if it had taken the usual amount of time, we would have been married on the day you came into it—and all of that wealth would be mine. I would have the gold and Amabel's fertility a few days later, rather than your useless barrenness."

"You're . . ." She wet her lips at the deadly poison in his eyes.

"Angry? Logical? Exactly so, my dear," he sneered. "Don't think to tell anyone, even your precious companions here in Cairo. You're holding a Crown secret once again, as you've already surmised. Whitehall deals very harshly with loose lips and the ears they pour foolishness into."

If she was sixteen again and this was only a prank, Gareth would appear to tell her how to deliver the ugly chest to the

Sultan. Instead, he'd walked out and she had to outmaneuver her poisonous rattler of an ex-husband by herself.

She had to agree. It was the only way to play for time.

"Very well."

Blast the man, he'd undoubtedly have her watched every second from now on. But maybe a carefully phrased cable to Uncle William and Aunt Viola would make it through.

And surely the Constantinople police would not be as ridiculously fearful as St. Arles implied. It was far more likely her fiendish ex-husband simply wanted to make her miserable yet again.

Chapter Fourteen

Saladin's Citadel, Cairo, two days later

The wind pummeled Gareth the instant he stepped outside the ancient stone fortress. Saladin, the mighty leader who'd thrown back Richard the Lionheart's armies from Jerusalem's walls, had first fortified this steep hill. Mamelukes, that legendary warrior caste, had fiercely defended this castle for centuries until the last ones sallied forth from this gate to meet their doom less than seventy years ago. Their corpses paved the road to the future, while their tortured prisoners' skeletons no doubt cheered their ambushers.

Sand hung in the sky like a deadly disease, filthy brown and eager to send the unwary to a graveyard. The Nile's blue ribbon was only a vague smear on the western horizon past the tattered tenements. Green growing things were a vague memory, their scent trapped on the wind's fringe to be pounded against the southern desert.

Gareth flung his burnous around his head and shoulders to protect himself from the worst of the upcoming storm, grateful he'd chosen to wear native dress, including the full, heavy cloak.

He could have worn European attire but that would have cost him infinitely more baksheesh, the golden grease which kept Egyptian commerce moving in more or less efficient channels. The Suez Canal was a far faster route to Europe from Asia but Egypt held the perfume industry's heart and soul, with its vast profits for tiny, fragile parcels. The art was paying the minimum in bribery, while still staying alive.

He smiled faintly, remembering all the dead assassins who'd tested themselves against his blade before his business costs had become measured only in coins. Oddly, the natives seemed to award him greater respect after he learned the local language.

Gareth shifted his shoulders, settled Portia's knife's neck sheath more comfortably into place, and headed for his hotel. A hot bath, a good drink, and at least one willing woman couldn't arrive too soon.

Ranks of alabaster columns faded behind him, hidden by their guardian stone bulwarks. Two great minarets lanced the dirty air, while the mosque's great golden dome impassively observed both the songbirds fleeing for safety and the scarlet-coated British sentries. Last night, its halls and the entire city had rung with *Lailat al Mi'raj*, the Festival of the Night Journey when Muslims remembered patience, perseverance, and prayer.

A few tourists fluttered like ragged pieces of paper inside their open carriages. He ignored them, memories of his hotel chef's chicken rasping his throat more powerfully than the sand.

"Mr. Lowell!" A man shouted at him from the British Army barracks.

His ears pricked at the aristocratic drawl but he didn't break stride. The hot bath was far more important than answering a stranger's call, especially since Donovan & Sons now had other agents in this country.

The British consul general and his staff—everyone who meant anything in actually operating Egypt's government—had their offices in Cairo's Citadel. The British army was headquartered here, including the large force charged with retaking Khartoum and retrieving the wildly popular General Gordon's body. That very upper-crust bloke could have mistaken him for anybody.

"Gareth Lowell!" A woman's voice this time.

Gareth slowed, his feet dragging to a stop. An American female, here in Egypt, who knew him?

"Mr. Lowell, I'm Cynthia Oates, Portia's best friend." A small blond whirlwind hurled herself at him and grabbed his shoulders.

"Yes, I remember hearing of you." Vaguely, from scrapes she and Portia got into years ago at boarding school.

"This is my husband, Graham."

"Sir." Gareth exchanged a bare nod with the other.

What was going on? The fellow wasn't offended by his wife hanging onto a stranger in a public street, even though her attitude was that of an anxious sister.

He tried to peel her hands off but her fingers only tightened.

"Where have you been? We've been looking for you, since we left her at the dock in Alexandria."

"Portia? I was on the other side of the Red Sea, at the Arabian Sea." *Buying and selling pearls, but not glimpsing any truly priceless ones like Portia.*

Oates' eyes widened. He reassessed Gareth's clothing with a fierce stare, betraying how much he knew of men who could live among the natives, including Arabia's brutal Empty Quarter.

"St. Arles will hurt her, I know." Mrs. Oates' fingernails sank into Gareth through the rough linen, sharper than his conscience all these long years.

A mighty shock punched into his gut, grabbed his breath and darkened his world. He shook his head and fought for enlightenment.

The muezzin sounded the first call to afternoon prayer from high atop the mosque's minaret, the ancient city's tallest point. Other criers answered, their voices echoing across the stones and into the desert.

"Portia?" Gareth wheezed. "She's divorced from the bastard." He was too surprised to apologize for his language.

"He's sent her on an errand to Constantinople for him," Oates said quietly, his voice the clipped tones of an officer keeping to the facts because any emotion meant loss of control. His lady rejoined his side but watched Gareth constantly, like a falcon hovering over its prey.

"What kind of errand?" Gareth demanded. *Good God, may it be something simple like taking a message to one of that son of a bitch's mistresses.*

The husband and wife locked eyes with each other in one of those long moments of communication only deep love can bring. Then the man's face twisted, as if he'd accepted a necessity too bitter to be spoken of.

"She never mentioned it," Mrs. Oates said slowly. She glanced around for observers and found none. Even their carriage was parked in a half-ruined building's lee a few feet away. "But she took an extra trunk with her. A big, heavy one at that."

Gareth pounded his fists together, since St. Arles was nowhere close at hand. Smuggling anything into Constantinople could cost lives. How much did it matter to that brute? How far had he gone to force her into his game?

"Did St. Arles force her to do it? Was he pleased she agreed?"

"Very much so," the little lady sighed, a sound redolent with remembered horror.

What was that verse from the Koran his traveling companion on the journey across Arabia had quoted? *Be sure we shall test you with something of fear and hunger, some loss in goods, lives, and the fruits of your toil.*

Gareth shot a glance at Oates.

"If I wasn't a serving officer and he a diplomat, I'd have killed him myself for how he treated her." Rage ran through the very proper English tones like the finest steel carving a carcass. "Even so, I had a damned hard time containing myself when I found out afterward."

"Can you stop Portia before she's arrested?" the little blonde asked, every tiny inch blazing with outrage.

"It's too late." Gareth shook his head. "If she's been on a steamer for two days, the next customs official she sees will quickly report to the Sultan's secret police."

"There's no such thing as secret police!" objected Mrs. Graham Oates. "God won't let her be harmed."

But there was and their foulness wouldn't respect foreign ladies. Gareth shuddered, his appetite gone faster than the daylight.

He had to help her. His friend's voice came back. *Oh you who believe! Persevere in patience and constancy. Vie in such perseverance, strengthen each other, and be pious, that you may prosper.*

"I'll go to Constantinople. If she chose a steamer based on comfort . . ."

Gareth raised a desperate eyebrow and Oates nodded quickly. "Her courier chose such a boat. She hired a gentleman from a well-known Turkish family to escort her. He's a scholar who wanted to visit relatives in Constantinople."

"Plus, a good paying job would give him a better reason for the paperwork to enter Constantinople," Gareth said cynically, his brain flashing through the shippers he knew. How could he sail north across the Mediterranean first?

"Better than having family there?" Oates' wife stared at them both, her eyes darkening at the mercenary atmosphere her friend would be entering.

"In that case, I should be able to charter a faster one." His mouth twitched briefly at how much of a true smuggler's craft she'd be. He'd leave a message at the American consulate for any Donovan & Sons employees who might look for him.

"I promise you I won't let her be caught by the secret police." He could do that much at least. Then he'd take her home to San Francisco, where she could finally settle down with a good man.

Somebody totally unlike himself.

"Thank you." Cynthia Oates leaned up and kissed him on the cheek. "I knew you'd look after her."

Gareth's smile was as crooked as his past.

Chapter Fifteen

Constantinople, May 1887

The Customs Office was small, the lines long, and the over-heated air pressed down on every person waiting to be seen with far more energy than their official greeters did. Certainly the Ottoman bureaucrats sitting behind the high desks had spent more effort perfecting their wardrobes than they had honoring any concern for their fellow citizens.

"Relax, gracious lady," 'Abd al-Hamid, Portia's half-Turkish, half-Parisian courier murmured in French. "Soon they will realize you are a true European lady and not someone to be left swimming among these filthy mackerel. They will lift you up and you will shine like a star on the boulevards below Hagia Sophia and the Blue Mosque. You have my word on it."

"Hmm," she murmured, having been reduced to mono-syllabic responses by the dozen times he'd provided the same reassurance.

She brushed a non-existent piece of lint from her brocade lapel and promised herself never again to be nervous about facing down journalists. Anything on the other side of the Atlantic had to be a pleasure compared to this.

The Orient Express had only been running its high-speed train from Paris to Constantinople for four years. But it had already succeeded in monopolizing all the respectable, or at least moneyed, European travelers. Apparently, no Ottoman official believed that a titled British lady would stoop to arriving on a small Egyptian steamer from Alexandria, rather than aboard the gold-embossed blue cars with their startling abundance of polished teak, crystal, and liveried attendants.

Instead, they'd left her standing amid the hordes of ordinary supplicants for entry into a fading empire's capital, papers clutched in sweaty hands and bribes hidden in sleeves below eyes darting to find the most likely recipient.

In this dusty room, where honesty was even rarer than shafts of light, everyone sitting behind a desk was willing to accept money, whether or not they wielded any apparent authority. A single narrow door beyond them offered the sole entry into Constantinople's fabled urbanity.

Even the ushers welcomed coins faster than any Egyptian street urchin.

But nobody ever changed their behavior, except perhaps to utter a few extra platitudes.

At least she hadn't seen any gold find its way into the cold-eyed policemen's hands. But she didn't want to move close enough to know for sure. There were far, far too many of them whose police baton formed an appallingly efficient metronome to their lounging.

Sweat slithered down the nape of her neck and under her dress, like Cleopatra's asp. She yanked herself rigidly upright, back into her best impersonation of Aunt Viola's Southern belle manners.

Heaven forbid somebody think she was too nervous—or follow her twitching eyes toward St. Arles' appalling gift. First-rate maker, solid oak, and bound in painted black iron, it weighed more than any other piece of luggage she owned.

She couldn't possibly look scared now. Not possible—or were the police watching them?

Surely not. They had to have an open mind; otherwise, she couldn't tell them about the trunk and whatever plot St. Arles had concocted.

"Ah, *sacré bleu, madame,* the heat," her maid Sidonie sighed and fanned herself even harder, like a homing pigeon longing to break free. "If we were in Paris . . ."

"I promise you that once my family arrives, all will be well. Plus, I was named for our illustrious Sultan—God be pleased with him!—so the luck will soon be with us."

Portia shot her courier a dubious look at that piece of pious optimism. Bitter necessity had forced her to hire a courier for the mechanics of escorting her through Moslem countries on Moslem ships to Constantinople—buying boat tickets, conveying her luggage between ships at various ports, and so on. The half-Turkish, half-French 'Abd al-Hamid had seemed ideal in Cairo, where he'd spoken longingly of seeing his father's family in Constantinople once again and be welcomed under his nickname of Abdul.

But any idealism rasped her nerves all the way north, especially when she was near a reminder of St. Arles.

"'Abd al-Hamid?" the clerk called. He consulted the piece of paper in his hand again. "'Abd al-Hamid of Cairo, plus two foreign ladies?"

"That is us! What did I tell you? Soon we will be out of here." A smile burst across her courier's face and he quickly chivvied their neighbors into bringing her mountains of luggage forward.

Portia hoped her expression was as confident as his. She planted her parasol firmly on the mercifully clean floor and crossed her hands on its handle in a European lady's most self-possessed stance, ready to command the respect due to a woman of means and station. God willing she'd soon be facing somebody who could help her with that awful trunk.

Sidonie lined up beside her. She probably hoped her silent support would release them more quickly.

Moments after they reached the customs officer, the door to freedom opened and a pair of Turks entered. Their suits were the equal of anything in Paris and their fezzes—the tall, conical, flat-topped felt hats worn by Turks—were of equally high quality.

A flood of joyful Turkish burst out between them and her courier, who leaned around the massive desk to gesticulate better.

Portia tweaked the folds of her overskirt so it draped more evenly. Surely she'd been too skittish in looking for a threat where there was none. Even so, it wouldn't hurt to make sure she looked her best.

The customs officer tapped his pen on his inkwell to demand proper respect.

"Ah yes." Her courier swung back and instantly dropped into French with an apologetic glance at Portia.

"Pray forgive me but it is a very long time since I have seen my father's family. I did not know if they would receive my message and meet me here. I am 'Abd al-Hamid and these are my charges, Portia Countess St. Arles"—he did so enjoy rolling her title around on his tongue—"and Mademoiselle Sidonie Armand, her maid."

Clearly unimpressed, the bureaucrat's fingers silently demanded their paperwork. "Where are you staying?"

The documents slid forward, accompanied by a truly ridiculous number of pound notes.

"The Countess and her maid are staying at the Pera Palace, while I have reservations at the Yildiz."

The official's hard countenance abruptly lost its resemblance to marble. Instead his eyes looked like twilight gleaming on a revolver, the last light of day before eternal night.

"Yildiz?" the official repeated, making the name sound like a place he'd never allow his son to utter, much less enter. He tapped his left shoulder with 'Abd al-Hamid's identity papers.

"Yes, it's a hotel near Al-Sarkaji. I'll be moving, of course, now that my family's here." 'Abd al-Hamid waggled his fingers at the older newcomer, a burly, well-dressed fellow whose dark eyes moved with the same bird-like quickness as Abdul's.

But her courier's looks must have come from his French mother, given how slender his waist was when compared to his relatives. The other two grinned back at him and mimed dancing, their hands rising toward their shoulders as if ready to clasp him.

The bureaucrat assessed all of them like mackerel lined up on marble, ready for the fishmonger.

Portia wanted to grab a mantle to ward off her sudden chill.

"A man named for our beloved Sultan plans to lodge at a hotel matching the Sultan's palace?" the bureaucrat barked.

His voice carried through the entire room, like Satan entering a circle of hell. A ripple of silence spread outward. Truncheons slid into policemen's fists.

Portia's skin lifted, desperate to flee. Sidonie's cold fingers slid into hers and she gripped them, offering a reassurance her heart didn't quite believe.

"I will cancel my reservation immediately," 'Abd al-Hamid asserted, far more desperately than she'd ever thought he could speak. He started to back away from the big desk. "I'd never dream of setting myself up as a figurehead for any movement against our beloved Sultan—"

"Guards! Take him!"

Policemen sprang upon 'Abd al-Hamid and knocked him down to the floor in a flurry of blows, never pausing to see whether he fought or not.

Sidonie screamed and hid her face against Portia.

"Now see here," Portia shouted, trying to defend her employee. "He did nothing wrong. He only came here to serve me."

Something crunched, achingly close, and 'Abd al-Hamid screamed.

Horror rose in Portia's belly, more urgent than nausea. None of her youthful escapades had brought her this close to violence. Vile as the burn victims at the ranch had been, they'd been almost a mile away, not literally next to her elbow.

A truncheon swung past her ear and she took a quick step back to protect the sobbing Sidonie.

A flood of Turkish entreaties and curses poured out of 'Abd al-Hamid's relatives.

Jostling arms shoved Portia out of the way. She staggered a few steps farther before she caught her balance and wrapped her arms around Sidonie.

"You can't take him," she shouted again before realizing she was speaking in English. She tried again in French but nobody was listening.

More men charged forward and helped drag the heaving, bloody lump that had been 'Abd al-Hamid out of the room. His family chased them, arguing vehemently at every step until an iron-barred door thudded behind all of them.

Portia turned on the customs officer, her arms still wrapped around Sidonie.

"Why did you arrest him?" she accused, angrier than she could ever recall being, even at St. Arles. "He did nothing wrong, except being born. I demand that you have him released at once."

A few heads turned to listen, even the other officials who'd not yet started to reexamine the desperate applicants at their desks.

The superstitious fool's face flushed and his eyes narrowed. He brusquely flipped through the paperwork on his desk, the fat bribe nowhere in sight.

"You, countess, have been consorting with a known traitor to the Sultan." Even his moustache seemed to sneer at her passport.

"Traitor?" Indignation grabbed every word from her tongue.

"In fact, I believe the situation warrants a detailed examination of all parties, starting with your reasons for traveling here, your luggage . . ."

Luggage? Oh, dear Lord, if he opened St. Arles's damnable wooden box, they'd all go to prison. She barely managed to hold herself upright, despite the harpies carving out the inside of her skull with razor-edged blades.

"Is there a problem, officer?"

An American drawl had never sounded so divine to Portia before, even when it was speaking French.

Did she know that voice?

She pivoted, Sidonie a half step behind her.

"Gareth," she whispered. What on earth was Gareth Lowell doing in Constantinople? She'd seen him for the first time when she was twelve, at a taffy pulling party. He'd walked into the San Francisco mansion's kitchen from a winter storm, windblown and alert, rough around the edges from his time in the mining camps.

Now he touched his hat to her, silver eyes clear as spring water in the Sierra Nevada mountains. He still had broad shoulders, strong hands marked with old calluses and scars, the easy grace of a man who could explode into action between one breath and the next. Or, worse for her heartbeat, the level brows over deep-set eyes above a rock-solid jaw, all framing the firm mouth every woman understood could bring either heaven or hell.

Hope sent a little warmth into her fingers, at least for her friends.

"Mr. Lowell." The obnoxious customs official dropped her passport onto the floor and rose from his chair, as if lifted by a superior force.

"Sir." A single syllable but every bureaucrat flinched. Most went speedily back to work, while the one dealing with Portia launched into an incoherent explanation.

Gareth studied him pitilessly without responding. Power swirled around the Westerner now like a fine perfume, the casual ability to give orders to strong men and have them immediately obeyed. A first-rate London tailor had made his clothes but she wouldn't have been surprised to see him produce his beloved Colt or even a bowie knife.

His eyebrows drew together when he saw hers and Sidonie's tumbled passports. He said nothing, only shot the greedy official a single, barbed glance.

The fool flinched. "But, sir, madame is a—"

"My friend," Gareth said implacably. "As is her maid."

"But they were with—" the superstitious idiot tried again.

"How high in the Almabayn do you wish to continue this discussion?" Gareth asked, friendly as the soft whoosh of a revolver clearing its holster.

Almabayn? What was that? All important business was supposed to go through the Grand Vizier's office. Was Gareth running an enormous bluff?

But she had to support Gareth or they were all done for. She jabbed Sidonie sharply in the ribs to make her stand erect.

The customs officer blanched under his better's stern gaze and quickly stooped to fumble together the fallen documents.

Gareth was actually pulling it off. The harpies started to flee Portia's skull.

"Please forgive me, sir, for having disturbed you and your friends," the bureaucrat stuttered. "I can assure you I would never have done so if I had known who they were. If you will but give me the chance, I am sure I can explain everything."

He emphasized his point with his customs stamp but missed Sidonie's passport entirely.

"Really," said Gareth dryly. "However, I'd prefer to have my friends enjoy a quick arrival upon Constantinople's streets."

"Oh yes, of course, what was I thinking?" The customs officer flashed a narrow smile. He almost became an octopus in his flurry of eagerly flailing arms and shuffling hands, desperately working to process their documents.

Gareth accepted the third properly approved passport.

"Where is my lady's manservant?" he inquired calmly.

"In the jail—" The hapless customs official abruptly realized what he'd admitted and slammed shut his ledger book. His eyes darted like a rat trapped between two gigantic cats, between Gareth's implacable countenance and the damnable paperwork, which officially admitted 'Abd al-Hamid into Constantinople.

A desperate sweep of the room proved that none of his fellows would so much as glance at him. Even his superior had turned away, ostensibly to straighten some record books.

Why were all of these bureaucrats so terrified of Gareth?

Even so, the customs officer still tried to recover some of his lost dignity.

"The fellow is a dangerous brute," he announced and shuffled his gear together as if done with the subject.

"Would you care to defend that description within the Almabayn's walls?" Gareth cocked an eyebrow, as brazenly as he'd draw and aim his Colt.

"Oh no, sir, not at all." The official choked and ran a finger under his collar, his eyes very wide. "That will not be necessary, since he's vouched for by someone of your sterling qualities."

"Indeed." Gareth's tone was so brusque that Portia was hardly surprised to see the supervisor stop eavesdropping and head over toward them, wearing a very anxious expression.

"He shall be delivered into your custody immediately, sir," the former obstructionist declared, deliberately not looking at his boss.

"Into the bosom of his family," Gareth corrected him.

"Ah yes, yes, of course. May Allah bless all of us with such loved ones!"

"Exactly." The harsh lines deepened beside Gareth's mouth but Portia had little attention to pay them. She was too busy joining in the general praise to the Almighty and hoping her party could leave quickly, before anybody changed their mind and made all of them stay.

Moments later, Constantinople's salt-laden air teased Portia's nostrils with its reminder of the sea's freedom and the tears she'd shed so many times in England, regretting what she'd angrily, foolishly discarded.

She stood beside Gareth to see 'Abd al-Hamid being gently

lifted into his family's cozy equipage. Sidonie had recovered herself to supervise their luggage being loaded into Gareth's vehicle, although her orders lacked their usual crispness. Gareth's men were local, neatly dressed, and more than brusque enough to discourage passersby from stopping to watch.

How could so much harm have occurred to Abdul in so few minutes? He could only hope to see out of one eye, given his poor battered face, and days would probably pass before he could eat anything but soup. His left arm hung useless at his side, while he curled his right hand protectively against his chest. His legs were little better than his arms.

"Ah, gracious lady, thank you," he slurred.

"For what?" Portia blinked back tears and tried to keep her voice level. "I brought you here."

"I would have come home to Constantinople, no matter what the risks. You and the gentleman rescued me quickly"— he paused to swallow with great difficulty—"from my folly of the ill-omened hotel, while I waited to be reunited with my family."

"We are in your debt," his uncle added. "You need only ask. He says you know how to find us." He tweaked the blankets tucked around the invalid one last time before fully facing Portia.

"Well yes, but—there is no obligation between us."

He grunted, relegating her statement to the realm of polite fiction, before looking at Gareth.

"This is no place for a lady," he observed, ancient eyes studying the larger man without fear.

"She has a suite booked at the best European hotel—and I will continue to keep her safe."

"Most excellent." He bowed. "Peace be upon you."

"And upon you be peace," Gareth returned in equally excellent Arabic.

Portia could read nothing in Gareth's face after they'd left, unlike her wedding day, the last time they'd met. She sighed, wishing for so many things.

"Hmm?" Gareth asked noncommittally, just as he would have when she was an adolescent. Back then, he'd been surprised at her presence on his expeditions out of Uncle William's house. But he'd never refused to take her along and he'd always answered her questions, even if he didn't start any conversations. At least in the beginning, he hadn't.

"He looks so helpless, unlike the charming—"

"Charming?" Gareth's tone sharpened fractionally. He turned toward the large, comfortable barouche that Sidonie had just climbed aboard.

"Parrot? Or maybe a mynah bird?" Portia spread her hands a little helplessly, before following his lead. A seagull soared overhead, effortlessly free unlike herself. "Abdul Hamid always reminded me of a tropical creature, with his vivid waistcoats and eternal, colorful chatter. Seeing him crumpled up like this makes him look like a broken bird."

"I doubt there's any serious damage." Warmth softened Gareth's eyes for the first time until they gleamed blue as the water behind him. He offered her his hand and she took the first step up into the carriage.

"Are you sure?" Standing on the metal step, she was almost at eye level with him.

"They didn't have enough time to tie him up and truly start working him over. The police here have a pattern they like to follow." His expression hardened for a moment then he kissed the tips of her fingers. "But that didn't happen. Once he sees a good doctor, is bandaged up, and has a long rest, he should be fine."

"Are you truly certain?" She searched his face. They had never, ever lied to each other.

"As much as I can be."

"Very well then." She tightened her fingers around his, feeling his strength flood into hers once again. "Thank you for rescuing us."

"It was my pleasure, Portia." He kissed her hand again, brushing his lips across her knuckles. It was still no contact at all, nothing like all the men who'd tried to seduce her into an affair while she was married, saying she needed to distract herself from St. Arles. She'd always refused them, telling herself and them it was because St. Arles would never tolerate a cuckoo in the nest. He'd have known in a minute if another man had sired his heir and heaven knows, the son of a bitch kept hauling himself back to her bed to breed one.

She hadn't realized until now it was because no other man made her bones shiver, even when her skin hadn't been touched.

"We need to talk," she said more than a little desperately.

"Of course. But not here—and not in the carriage."

Oh dear Lord, she'd have to be truly private with him.

Jumping off the pier would have been easier than boarding the carriage but she did it nonetheless.

Chapter Sixteen

The carriage lurched and jolted forward again up the steep
hill overlooking the great city.

Portia swayed beside Gareth and gracefully adjusted to its
ungainly gait yet again. Her maid sat in the opposite seat with
her eyes shut, her fingers busy with her rosary.

Unfortunately for him, Portia was even lovelier now than
the day she'd married that English prig or in any of the newsprint photos since. Wisps of golden hair teased her face from
under her high-brimmed hat with its mass of blue feathers,
until she seemed a lightly ensnared bird.

She deserved a better introduction to Constantinople than
she'd received. With any luck, she'd be on tomorrow's train for
Paris—and away from the idiotic lump in his throat when he
looked at her.

Her hand crept across the carriage seat toward him.
Tentatively, as if the slightest rebuff would send her running,
she linked her fingers with his, the same way they had during
their escapades.

His chest tightened.

He held hands with her and told himself it was only to comfort her for the nastiness she'd endured. He didn't need any
such warmth.

*   *   *

Gareth's eyes swept the hotel lobby once again, suspicious as if he stood in a crowded saloon full of cowboys using their Colts for wagers.

Yet nothing could have been more civilized than his surroundings: the tall black marble columns which divided the great space, the gold-paneled walls bordered in black fretwork and which offered pastel hymns to Constantinople's glories, the high ceilings etched in more gold to reflect the enormous French chandeliers, and the white and gray marble floors floating like a winter sea from the front door up the stairs to main lobby and hence to the rippling main staircase, which led to the suites.

Liveried attendants lined the walls or glided across the floor, eager to fulfill a guest's slightest wish—whether a speedy check-in, directions, or a cup of English tea. Anything and everything was available here for its very well-heeled European patrons. Discreetly, of course, especially the heavy security.

So why the hell were his fingers twitching for the gun he never carried in Constantinople?

Maybe it was because this was the first place men openly looked at Portia.

Yes, that had to be it. They'd journeyed through the Old City, primarily among Moslem men who'd never let their glances linger on a woman, especially if she was accompanied by a man. But here the fellows were European and they felt free to show their appreciation of her beauty.

No matter how politely they did so—however glinting the smile, quirky the lift of an eyebrow, or jaunty the tip of the hat—their reaction was unmistakable.

Just like Gareth's automatic response to them: tuck her hand more closely into the crook of his arm and glare. He might look a fool but she didn't need to be bothered with them, not when she'd just gone through that bitter divorce.

And so what if any whiff of her scent made his breath catch in his throat? He wasn't accustomed to smelling a polite European lady's perfume. And if that made his chest tighten and his loins ache—well, some reactions were simply instinct that a fellow had no control over, especially when he hadn't had a woman for a few weeks.

He'd have to take care of that tonight, though, or put Portia on the first train out of town. Otherwise, he might look a fool in front of her if he spent a full day with her tomorrow.

"You'll take me to evening prayers at the Hagia Sophia then?" Portia asked. She turned to face him on the main staircase, placing the gilded wrought iron between them like a harem's screen.

A driving need inside Gareth roared an objection to any distance from her, startling him by the presence of something whose birth he hadn't quite noticed. It had to be because he wasn't close enough to guarantee her protection.

"Yes, of course." He patted her hand—and checked out the distance to the closest guard.

Damn, nobody on the stairs, which left only the men in the lobby. But there were many at the doors, plus others moving through the crowd.

He stretched his shoulders and told himself not to be a fool. Maybe he should find a woman immediately. Or maybe not; he didn't want to reek of cheap perfume when he saw Portia again.

Two men headed past them up the stairs, dressed in cheaply made French suits which didn't fit well. Both were probably Turkish, given their heavy mustaches and clean-shaven jaws, and neither was young.

They were polite enough not to display any reaction to Portia's presence, except to veer well past her skirts. Yet when they reached the landing, the elder one looked back at Gareth, not her, with a fighter's measuring stare.

Gareth countered it with a matching glance and waited, equally calm. Were they making sure he could defend the most attractive woman here?

The younger man tugged at the other's sleeve. He nodded to the American and moved on, having never broken stride.

Gareth slid his knife back into its wrist sheath, faintly surprised instinct had readied it for no overt threat to him.

"You have time to rest and change first," he reminded Portia and his drumming pulse. "We'll dine together afterward."

"If you won't mention tomorrow's Orient Express to Paris," she said demurely.

"Portia!" he protested, barely managing to keep his voice down.

"I came to see all the sights." She shrugged, as charmingly obstinate as she'd ever been. "Besides, Sidonie has friends here she'd like to visit."

"We'll talk more at a later time." Gareth flicked an eyebrow at her, warning her that she'd won the argument but only for the moment.

She winked at him but there was a shadow hidden in the depths.

"You've already had a very long day." He kissed her fingertips, careful not to allow himself any closer proximity. "Now go upstairs and pamper yourself."

"Yes, Gareth." She thinned her lips into a schoolgirl's placidity then suddenly blew him a kiss.

"Portia!" He jolted backward, his heart pounding against his ribs as if a horse had kicked him.

"Not here," he got out, hoping he sounded more like a heavy-handed chaperone than a skittish colt.

She laughed, the sound as musical as when they'd first scandalized San Francisco. She waggled her fingers at him and trotted up the stairs, whistling softly.

Gareth grumbled under his breath, furious that he undoubtedly sounded like her father after one of her more memorable escapades.

He raised an eyebrow at a hotel guest, silently daring the fellow to say anything or even cast a look askance.

The glossily clad man promptly reduced himself to a state of milk toast, assuming an expression of vacuous amiability created by no apparent thought.

Gareth nodded curtly and moved on, cutting through knots of men and past servants better-dressed than the patrons.

He paused to consider the doormen.

Everyone here wore wealth and power like a uniform. Even the flunkeys donned it as their passkey for admittance.

Where the hell had those two men come from, in their cheap, ill-fitting French suits?

Frenchmen would never allow the glory of France to be besmirched in such appalling fashion. He'd learned in Algeria that fabric might lack quality but the fit would be precise, or at least tolerable.

If they were Turks, what were they doing at Constantinople's most expensive hotel for Europeans?

Gareth slowly turned around and damned himself for acting like a lion with a thorn in its paw.

A woman's scream ripped through the lobby's pretentious bustle.

Gareth had leaped over the balustrade and was running up the stairs before a porter could pick up the first shattered teacup.

Portia tried to ignore the forearm gripping her like an iron bar across her throat. Her wrists had been bound tightly behind her with a sash cord and her skirts' fashionable folds muffled her kicks. Thanks to St. Arles' bedroom manners, she had far too much experience with this sort of behavior.

But in case somebody hadn't heard her first scream, uttered when she'd unlocked the door and beheld poor Sidonie's hooded form heaving against a chair, she had to keep on fighting.

Her pulse was ricocheting inside her skull hotter and faster than from anything St. Arles had ever done to her, black was bleeding into her vision, and bells clanged an alarm somewhere.

The thug's foul hand was clamped over her mouth while his forearm squeezed her throat into her spine. His mate searched her luggage, scattering clothing, shoes, and parasols like cheap bric-a-brac. Even her jewelry garnered no more than a cursory glance.

She caught the ruffian's callused thumb's edge and bit down hard, giving it all the anger she'd ever longed to deal St. Arles.

The brute jerked and cursed in Turkish, not French.

Emboldened, she clamped down again twice as forcefully, despite the foul taste and the dizziness scattering her brains, and bit into his entire finger.

Guttural curses spilled over her head and he yanked his hand free.

She screamed again, more hoarsely this time. She gulped for breath, thankful her high collar had blunted the brute's attack, and tried once more.

The suite's main door slammed open and Gareth roared wordlessly.

The searcher slammed shut the lid to her evening gowns' trunk and raced for the bathroom. Her captor freed her so suddenly she staggered, before he too dashed for the more distant room.

A window screeched in its frame, accompanied by guttural expletives.

Gareth stormed into the bedroom, knife in his hand. A single glance, brilliant as sunlight on a drawn sword, reassured him that she was alive. He jigged, his steps heading in two directions at once, like the anger and concern warring in his eyes.

The window complained vehemently again. Sidonie wailed from underneath the enormous black hood like an abandoned kitten.

Portia waved him toward their foes, her heart burning a hole in her chest for him. Was she sending him into an ambush?

He snarled soundlessly but nodded curtly and ran past her, silent as an eagle on the hunt.

Her lungs didn't remember how to breathe until he emerged again, moments later. Unscathed, thank God.

"They escaped out the window and over the roof, the slimy

thieves." He tossed his knife into the air and cut it, as if ready-ing it for throwing.

"Not thieves," Portia husked and sank down sideways onto a chair. Logic said her pulse wouldn't tumble through her feet onto the carpet, no matter what sensation and instinct insisted.

"*Not* thieves?" Gareth echoed and glanced at the room's wild disorder.

"Mrs. Vanneck?" the hotel manager called from the door. "Are you well? May I enter?"

Portia sighed and tilted her head back. She could answer for herself but what about Sidonie, who'd never wanted to leave Europe's friendly havens behind? "Certainly, monsieur."

"Definitely not burglars," Gareth confirmed her estimate very softly and stooped down beside her. "Hold still, honey."

Honey? He'd never called her that before, although he'd used it with others like Uncle Hal and Aunt Rosalind's daugh-ters.

Even so, she held very still indeed.

His knife sliced quickly and surely through the cord impris-oning her. Her arms separated and she was free again, just as he'd always helped her to be.

The hotel manager filled the room with a covey of his min-ions and a storm of apologies before she could catch a glimpse of Gareth's face.

Had he realized he called her honey or had the endearment slipped out?

Gritting her teeth against a thousand questions which could only lead to more heartache, she untied Sidonie.

Chapter Seventeen

"I will not remain in Constantinople!"

An hour later, Sidonie's declaration still resonated in Portia's ears. She rotated slowly in the middle of her hotel suite and wondered what on earth she'd do now. One hand held her arm while she rested her mouth against her knuckles.

"Where do you want to spend the night?" Gareth asked quietly. Only an old friend could have found the anger underlying the genuine concern in his voice. "You're free to change suites, since Sidonie did an excellent job of repacking before she fled to her cousin."

"Yes, she was very glad to receive the first-class ticket home on the Orient Express," Portia remarked. She trailed a finger over her evening gowns' trunk, so much alike yet so different from St. Arles's damnable trunk. All of her luggage had been made by Louis Vuitton and was monogrammed, even that abomination. The only obvious differences were the size and weight. She could tell it apart in an instant but who else?

St. Arles undoubtedly could.

"You should be on the same train," Gareth said.

"No." She barely uncoiled herself from her fist to speak clearly.

"Portia, somebody broke into your room to search your luggage, not steal your jewelry. I don't know why you're in danger but you're not safe here."

What did safety for her mean if Mrs. Russell's, Maisie's, Winfield's, and Jenkins's lives were destroyed, together with all the other servants who'd fought for her in their own way?

The chill deep within her bones strengthened.

"I can't leave yet."

"I'll hogtie you and put you on the damn train. You have my word on it, unless you tell me why I shouldn't."

Her eyes flashed up to meet his. Determination waited within those silver eyes, harsh as the Arizona landscape.

"You could be killed," she whispered, her voice softer than the wind whistling outside.

"I've risked my life before and will do so again." He impatiently waved off any such concern. His eyes narrowed, turning colder. "But anyone who'd burden a woman like you with a secret worth killing for, warrants a hanging himself."

She shook her head, an unwilling chuckle breaking loose somewhere deep in her belly. "Ah, Gareth, you do say the sweetest things when you know nothing at all about what's going on."

He scowled and she patted him on the shoulder consolingly. Her hand lingered for a moment, startled by the sweep and strength of his muscles under the fine wool, the solidity of his bone, the straightness of his carriage. All offered to her service without asking for any recompense.

He put his hand over hers and kept it there for a moment, light as a warm woolen blanket against winter's last cold winds.

She stepped back reluctantly and hid her reaction to Gareth by a kick to St. Arles's abominable luggage. It thudded dully, like a monstrous barricade against her future.

"Nobody wants to hurt me. They only want the trunk St. Arles saddled me with."

"Trunk?" Gareth frowned and squatted to examine it. Iron bands, lock—even the oak planks—received a freight master's exacting scrutiny. He ran his hands over it, examined scratches through a jeweler's loupe, confirmed the handles' strength by tugging it, and tested the wheels' smooth movement.

"A gentleman's small trunk, probably a courier," he pronounced finally. "Approximately three and a half feet long, two feet wide, a foot and a half tall. Metalwork's been very freshly painted so any attempt to force or pick the lock can be easily seen. Damn—excuse me, very heavy for its size, although she's built to carry larger loads."

"It could carry more?" Portia almost squeaked.

"Indeed. A fully loaded gun case would be the same size but weigh more, for example." Gareth rose to his feet. "What did that brute tell you?"

"'The Turks will think it's jollier than old Humpty Dumpty,'" she quoted.

"A bomb perhaps? But for who?"

"I think it's gold to trigger a revolution."

"That would explain the *jolly* and *Humpty Dumpty* aspects of his explanation. But my gut doesn't agree." He walked around the trunk again. "You take the Paris train tomorrow and I'll dispose of this."

"You can't do that!"

"Why not? I've worked for Donovan & Sons for eighteen years and high-risk freight to high-risk places is our business. If I can't make something like this disappear, I deserve to be fired."

"St. Arles—"

"By the time anybody figures out what happened, this piece of hogwash will be long gone."

"He promised he'd fire all the servants who helped me throughout the divorce," Portia said desperately, forcing the words past the tightness in her throat. "They'll be put out on the street without references. They won't be able to find a job."

"Hell and damnation! That miserable piece of Satan's spawn isn't worth sharpening a scalping knife for. Why, he should be . . ."

Portia wrapped her arms around him and hid her face against his chest.

He stilled, his heart thudding like a startled deer.

After a moment's hesitation, he clumsily put his arms around her and patted her back. "There, there now, honey, don't you worry. I'll make sure St. Arles can't harm any of your friends."

"We could cable Uncle William's contacts in London and ask them to help." She sniffled and tried to speak more clearly. "But that will take time."

"Not too long." Gareth thumped her again. "They'll be fine."

"But he can dismiss them faster than we can help them. Plus, I'm surely being watched." She craned her head back to look at Gareth. "Look at how easily those men found me."

"Oh, hell." The eager glow of securely offered sympathy vanished from his face, to be replaced by gnawing worry.

She tore herself out of his arms' distracting shelter.

"Isn't there someplace safe I can stay here in Constantinople until it's time for me to hand over the trunk to St. Arles?"

"Honey, you'd have to be watched over constantly. This is the best hotel in town yet you weren't safe here."

"What about where you lodge?"

He shook his head promptly. "I don't have rooms at a hotel. I board with a family instead and I can't bring you home with me."

"Why not? Would the trunk be stolen there?"

"Hardly." He snorted, dark laughter curling across his face. "Even the most reckless thief wouldn't take on a senior member of the Almabayn."

The dread organization whose mere mention had cowed the Customs Office? She frowned and tried to find another option.

"A British steamer leaves tomorrow morning for Athens." Enthusiasm brightened Gareth's voice. "You'd be safer onboard her than a train since she can't be hijacked once at sea. I'll take the trunk and—"

"No, you will not!"

His clenched jaw warned her that her explanation needed to be very good.

"It's my responsibility and I won't yield it to you or anyone else."

He propped his fist on his hip and glared at her. "Do you have another choice?"

"What if you told your friends I was your cousin?" She tried to think of a convincing lie.

"They're a very conservative Moslem family who generously let me stay among the unmarried men, in the *selamlik*. You'd have to reside in the harem where your luggage could be searched in an instant."

"Surely they wouldn't . . ."

"Maybe not. But this town lives on spies and corruption. Bribe a servant with a few pounds and they'd find that trunk fast enough."

"Oh." She beat on the high mantelpiece with her palms, ignoring the elegant plasterwork and etched mirror above it.

"Honey, the only place you'll be safe is on the fastest train out of town."

"No. St. Arles ruined my honor and I can't let him destroy my friends' honor, too, by saying they're worthless."

Gareth went very quiet behind her, a murderous look in his eyes.

"Isn't there some way for a European man and woman to share quarters in a Moslem household?" She turned to face him, tired of fencing through a mirror. "That is, if you'd be willing to."

"Share a suite to protect you? Yes, of course."

Her heart thrilled at his emphatic willingness to look after her—until he went on.

"But it's impossible here, especially at Kerem Ali Pasha's house. Moslem sensibilities would never tolerate two unmarried people living together."

Marriage, the focus of a thousand shattered dreams. She cast the images aside yet again with all their remembered pain.

"We could pretend—" she began.

"Impossible." He grimaced. "He already knows I'm not wed, since it came up while I was carousing with his son. Plus, the spies would probably mention the lack of a local wedding."

Marriage. What did she have to lose? She'd already been pilloried for her failures.

She might gain some memories of Gareth, to banish the nightmares of St. Arles with.

"Then why pretend?"

"What do you mean?" He shoved his hands onto his hips, forcing his jacket back from his broad shoulders, and glared at her.

"Will you marry me? Whether in a church or the embassy, I don't care, so long as it's legal and keeps me here in Constantinople." Her mouth was drier than the Arizona desert and her heart was flinging itself into her throat like a frenzied jackrabbit.

"Are you insane?" His face went dark and he stormed away from her. "We'd have to share the same bed. Ottoman families prefer very small houses so they can see more of each other; we'd never pull off a platonic relationship."

Her heartbeat kicked up its heels and cartwheeled through midair.

"Whatever you believe is necessary and are comfortable with," she gasped. "Or will you offend your friend by showing up with a wife?"

"I doubt it, since he's always asking me when I'll find one. But I can send him a note, asking him to hold your luggage while we get married. If I know him, he'll invite us to stay with him rather than rent a house."

"Good." Perhaps his manners were the only reason he'd been so disturbed. If so, why wasn't her pulse settling down?

"I'm not St. Arles," he stated clearly.

"Thank God."

He looked at her then and his lips curved in what was almost a smile.

"I've never hurt a woman in my life, Portia. But I am only a man. You have to understand that if we're alone frequently together, sometimes I may think and act solely for our immediate pleasure."

"Oh." She carefully considered the warning in light of what Aunt Viola had taught her about men, rather than her stepmother's sayings. "Are you telling me that you'll frequently take advantage of me?"

"You're a beautiful woman and a charming one. Better men than I have been driven insane by lesser temptations." He continued to keep his distance from her, his expression unreadable. "You should return to Paris."

"No!" She could be intimate with Gareth, possibly often. It was everything she'd once dreamed of, no matter how much St. Arles had made her shudder away from a man's advances. "But I might disgust you."

"What do you mean?" His brow furrowed.

She blushed and hung her head. She'd never considered discussing this with a man. Truly, she'd planned to never marry again.

"I don't enjoy being intimate with men," she whispered, every word hard-won against the past seven years' habits.

Silence grew until the carriages rattling over the street outside seemed only inches away.

"Men?" Gareth inquired very gently. "Or St. Arles in particular?"

"Oh." She stared at him, her heart thudding against her ribs. He hadn't moved, yet his eyes were blue-gray like sunlight breaking through fog.

"Oh," she said again and reconsidered.

"St. Arles," she pronounced and the nightmare seemed to fade slightly, thanks to being dragged into daylight.

Gareth growled something under his breath that made her eyes widen.

"Gareth?" she questioned.

"You have nothing to fear from me," he announced firmly. "We are both free to seek pleasure together, whenever you want."

Pleasure? She eyed him dubiously. She'd found that alone, with her hand. But to do so with a man? When *she* wanted?

His lips quirked, reminding her how often she'd once dreamed of kissing him.

"Very well, let's get married," she said, forcibly ignoring the silly blush heating her cheeks, and held out her hand to him.

"We have a bargain then." He briskly shook hands with her. "I'll pay the bribes to get us a marriage license and we can be married tonight in Christ Church."

"Tonight? Thank God."

He gave her an encouraging nod, obviously reading her enthusiasm as a reaction to danger.

"Our bargain lasts for as long as you're in danger here on the edge of Asia. After that, I'll give you a quiet divorce or annulment, whatever will cause you the least scandal."

Portia's jaw sagged toward the floor, closely followed by her wits.

A *short* marriage to Gareth? But that could be worse than her first marriage's hell.

"No children, of course," Gareth added.

She nodded dumbly, unable to protest the loss of something she'd had next to no chance of gaining anyway.

She'd just lassoed the wind. Now all she had to do was survive the ride.

Chapter Eighteen

Nothing he'd ever done before had prepared Gareth Lowell for this moment. The shadows creeping across the church's gray stones from the memorials to dead soldiers didn't help steady him. Even the sun's last rays seemed to only highlight the altar's cross and white cloth.

As if he needed a reminder that ghosts watched him.

The white-frocked minister offered Gareth another encouraging glance. His little brown sparrow of a wife stood by with her hymnal, ready to witness the religious ceremony necessary under Turkish law. He'd already paid a Turkish clerk a year's pay to overlook the rules and give them the necessary license.

Shaking like a drunk at his first gunfight, Gareth tried again to swear the dreaded oath.

"I, Gareth, take thee, Portia, to be my wedded wife . . ."

He didn't deserve her. Didn't deserve any woman, but especially not her.

Ma, if you're anywhere near this earth, please help me now.

"To have and to hold from this day forward, for better for worse . . ."

Worse would come when Portia found out she'd tied herself to a fellow with dozens of dead men's blood dripping from his hands.

His fingers tightened convulsively around hers and she gave him an encouraging smile. She was more beautiful now, in her simple white traveling suit and white boater than she'd been in that fancy New York wedding.

"For richer for poorer, in sickness and in health, to love and to cherish, till death us do part . . ."

He didn't know anything about love but he'd give his life for her; was that enough?

"According to God's holy ordinance . . ."

He was vowing this in a church, to make it all right, tight, and legal with his conscience. That should do.

As long as they were married, he'd treat her right, go to church with her whenever she wanted, do all the polite things Pa had done for Ma.

But he'd set her free as soon as possible, so she could have a good man to end her days with. Somebody who didn't want to run and hide every time he caught sight of an altar.

"And thereto I plight thee my troth," Gareth finished hoarsely.

The preacher's wife and curate heaved audible sighs of relief that he'd finally completed it on his third try.

Portia launched into her oath, her beautiful voice making music of the ancient words.

The preacher held out his hand and his assistant gently placed the slender circle of gold on his palm. For a moment, Ma's ring gleamed like an angel's halo before he handed it over.

It came smoothly into Gareth's hand and glided easily onto Portia's finger.

Maybe Ma was here today, to guide this wedding.

"With this ring . . ." His voice was very hoarse.

Ma had died with her left hand tucked under her. Gareth had never understood why he hadn't buried the ring with her nor sold it later for food.

At least not until now.

"I thee wed, and with all my worldly goods I thee endow."

The simple gold band looked just right on Portia's finger, especially when she smiled up at him with tears dancing on her eyelashes.

He took her gently by the waist afterward, intending only to hug her. That would be the proper thing to do in a fine stone house of God like this one, with arches flying overhead and fancy windows making music out of light. Just something to reassure her that he cared for her first of all and wouldn't embarrass her, the way St. Arles had.

Portia stepped confidently up to him, the way she always had as a teenager in California.

Like a fool, his blood warmed and swept faster through his veins, until all he knew was how infinitely perfect it felt to stand here, in this holy place, in this circle of light, with Portia smiling up at him like her blue eyes opened every door to homecoming.

And when she fanned her hands over his sleeves like he was a rock to hold onto and tilted her head back for his kiss until her golden curls rippled and flowed over his mother's ring— well, his heart thumped like a circus band was beating time.

Portia Lowell. His wife, at least for the moment.

He kissed her lightly, warmly. Her lips hesitated, then opened cautiously under his like a young girl's who'd never been tasted before.

What the hell? Didn't she know this much at least of men, and joy?

He lingered on her mouth, taking his time to tease her into relaxing. Stroking her lips with his tongue, shaping his mouth to match hers, gently sharing his breath—anything to catch her interest.

Portia moaned softly, deep within her throat.

The preacher's wife coughed louder than any doorbell.

Gareth lifted his head with considerable reluctance but was delighted to leave a dazed look on Portia's face. For once in their relationship, he had the advantage of the better social mask.

There was no point in considering how much his hands were still shaking—or how hard his cock was. He'd survive his wedding night somehow, no matter what happened.

* * *

The caique, a fancy cousin to the gondola, plowed its way across the Bosporus toward the distant Asian shore, its small steam engine humming briskly amidships. Daylight's balmy skies had given way to a crisp evening breeze and the waves constantly jostled the hull. Sparkling lights to the rear outlined Constantinople's ancient bulk, while fizzing sparks trailed like fireflies from the boat's smokestack.

The shore ahead was filled with rolling hills, marked by only a few lights against the moonlit sky. Except for the engine chugging below decks, this could have been an ancient Greek boat sailing these seas for the first time.

Portia linked her fingers more tightly with Gareth's and leaned her head against his shoulder, grateful for the loan of his jacket. Sitting on a bench in the stern might be the place of honor but it also attracted every chilly wind.

"Only a few minutes more, honey. We're almost there." He gave her hand a quick, comforting squeeze.

Hope for something more than their old friendship stirred inside her heart, dispelling second thoughts.

"Are you certain Kerem Ali Pasha will welcome me?" She couldn't bring herself to ask how long Gareth would accept their marriage.

Her trunks seemed to weigh down the boat like a guilty conscience from below decks. Like any good Donovan & Sons freighter, Gareth had produced a handful of sturdy men to transfer her luggage from the hotel and stand guard over it during their wedding.

"His note said so, didn't it?" Gareth kissed her fingers then rubbed her hand lightly to bring warmth back into it.

Her free hand lifted instinctively toward him but he spoke again, dispelling the magic.

"See those lights dead ahead? Where the dock cuts into the water?"

Her arm dropped back to her side and she answered him as practically as possible. What did it matter if she was clumsy at showing affection? He'd always liked conversing with her.

"But those are long windows with the rooms fully lit inside." She leaned forward. "The house looks like a lantern swinging over the water."

"It's Kerem Ali Pasha's *yali*, a seaside mansion with a boathouse built into it underneath."

"So many windows must allow inhabitants to enjoy the view—or catch the sea breeze."

"Exactly. It's been so hot he brought his family out here very early in the season." Gareth lowered his voice. "It's isolated enough you'll be safe."

The hair lifted on her neck and she nodded quickly.

"It's almost a fairy castle," she said wistfully, disliking the need to sully its delicate beauty with St. Arles's abomination.

"It is also pink," Gareth commented.

She gaped at him, searching that stalwart profile for any sign of mockery.

"And ornately carved," he added.

"You're joking," she pronounced with complete conviction.

"Not at all."

She made a burbling sound of disbelief but couldn't bring herself to express it more explicitly.

"Kerem Ali Pasha also has a scarlet silk tent, which he erects in his garden for parties."

Now that statement rang with the same simplicity which he'd use to discuss how to pack a mule for high-country freighting, or her stepmother Albinia would describe the menu at a successful dinner party.

Hope began to sift into her bones. "Does he decorate it with lanterns?" she asked.

"And flowers. The entire family is famous for their gardens—and love of literature."

She sighed happily.

"One door opens to the sea, the other to the gardens. One side of the house opens to the harem, the other to the selamlik."

"Rooms for the single young men?" Portia remembered what she'd heard of other Moslem customs.

"Yes."

Were there people standing out on the dock?

"Your trunks will probably be stored in the other half of the boathouse, under the house. If we're given the guest suite in the harem, we may be able to put them in the dressing room." His voice was low and rather rough.

She glanced up at him then nodded tightly. This wasn't the time or the place to argue, no matter how much she wanted to jump to her feet and look for herself.

Or did she want to stand up so she could hurl herself at the ever-polite Gareth?

She bit her lip, her heart's answer making her even more intensely nervous.

The helmsman cut the engine and the boat glided smoothly against the dock. Torches blazed at the ends, allowing glimpses of a fine garden with a massive tent erected inside.

Even the desperate tightening of her stomach couldn't stop Portia from craning her neck to see more.

Two liveried servants quickly secured the tidy craft.

"Lowell, my friend!" A slender man, clad in a long, elegant black coat and red fez, almost quivered atop the wharf like a gray wolf eager to greet his family. Two younger men flanked him, clearly his sons judging by their joint likeness to finely honed swords.

"You should have told me sooner what you planned. We would have made you the most splendid abduction of a bride ever seen in Constantinople!" He reached out a startlingly tanned hand and lifted Gareth onto the dock in a single easy leap. Clearly, these two had long since discarded civilized tricks such as steps. The Turk embraced the much taller American enthusiastically and kissed him on both cheeks, a salute that Gareth returned with a smile.

Portia pressed her hand to her mouth, unable to truly relax despite the welcome. Would they freely offer sanctuary if they knew the threat she brought?

"If you had the chance to seize the perfect woman, Kerem Ali Pasha, would you hesitate?" Gareth inquired.

"No, never! I too would have carried off such a pearl, especially after she was threatened by barbarians. She is the one who was tied up and whose luggage was searched, yes?"

"Very much so."

"Appalling." The patriarch's two sons muttered something unprintable in Turkish which earned a stern glare from their sire.

Gareth's grin grew wider and he gallantly brought Portia out of the caïque to join him on the dock. He brought her hand formally onto his arm so that they stood facing his friend.

"May I introduce my lady wife to you? Kerem Ali Pasha, this is Portia Townsend Lowell, my patron's niece and adopted daughter."

The great man studied her as if uncertain how to greet her.

She started to don a polite diplomatic smile then shook it off. No, she needed to be warm. This wasn't St. Arles's circle where knives were only inches from the surface, whether forged in steel or carved in poisonous tongues. These were Gareth's friends and she wanted him to stay close to them.

She smiled a little shyly, uncertain what expression to wear, and moved closer to Gareth.

The patriarch's expression softened and approval flashed through his eyes under the torchlight.

"Ah, you did not mention her lineage before, my friend. Indeed, you are fortunate among men to ally yourself with such a noble family." He bowed to Portia with a distinctly Gallic flourish. "Peace be upon you, dear lady. I beg that you will forgive my city for the attack you suffered and not allow those ruffians to poison your opinion of us. Pray consider my home to be yours. I swear you will be safe here."

"Thank you, sir." She gave him a curtsy, his exuberant welcome smoothing some of her worries.

"Lowell, I know your family is far from here." Their host

returned his attention to Gareth, with an air of polite finality as if she needed time to recover from the journey. "Will you allow me to give you at least a little of the celebration your father would, on this happy occasion?"

Gareth frowned.

"It might also distract your lady from this afternoon's alarms. A simple affair, rather than the forty days we gave my son or the three days even the simplest villager enjoys."

"Three days?" Portia queried. That would be a very long party, far more than anything her stepmother had ever dominated.

"Yes, indeed, there are many traditions to ensure both bride and groom are welcomed into each other's family. But since you are Americans and therefore probably already know each other's clans, my mother believes you will be content with the banquet traditionally held on the third day."

Portia slipped her arm through Gareth's, too curious to remain still. Perhaps someday she'd learn about Gareth's family, of course. But she wouldn't ask here and now. She would have to be satisfied by discovering more about these unusual traditions.

Gareth glanced down at her. "Would you mind?" he asked in English.

"Will it be embarrassing?" Heaven forbid it include anything humiliating.

"No, certainly not, especially from Kerem Ali Pasha's family. But it won't resemble your previous wedding."

"Then—yes, please," she said emphatically. Anything to erase the memory of that awful banquet would be a blessing—the endless toasts while her face stiffened into a smile born of dread and Uncle William looked more and more as if he couldn't decide whether to murder her husband or her father first. And the horrific night afterward with St. Arles . . .

"You honor us by your gift," Gareth told Kerem Ali Pasha and bowed slightly, an acceptance which Portia matched.

"Splendid!" The older man clapped his hands twice.

More servants promptly appeared, led by three carrying drums.

"Oh, Lord," Gareth muttered.

Drums?

She flicked Gareth an inquiring glance but before he could answer, she had to be polite once again.

"My sons Adem and Kahil," Kerem Ali Pasha said proudly. "All of us will help escort you to the wedding celebration. That is, if you don't mind?" he added a clearly perfunctory question.

Portia nodded agreement, unable to even form a question as to why only men would escort her. Their drums would surely cause an incredible ruckus, too.

She started to grin.

"What is it?" Gareth whispered.

"I must do this; my stepmother would be appalled."

He whooped—and the drummers promptly echoed his joy with a brilliant cascade of sound.

"This is my family's *bindalli* cloak, which we have wrapped around our brides for generations." Kerem Ali Pasha held up a crimson velvet cape, whose sweeping folds were magnificently embroidered in dozens of golden branches sparkling with crystals. A princess would have counted herself lucky to wear it only once.

"Lowell?" He coughed significantly and his eldest son nudged the American forward.

Gareth accepted the priceless mantle and wrapped it reverently around Portia. Their eyes met and for a moment, it seemed as if being enfolded by his protection in this ancient tradition, was just as much of a wedding as any fancy ceremony in a stone church.

"For better or for worse," he whispered.

"I thee wed," she answered, equally soft and completely heartfelt.

The drummers launched into an ecstatic din of celebration. Adem, the eldest son, tied a crimson sash around Gareth's waist which matched her cape.

Portia accepted her husband's arm and turned her back on the bobbing boat, with the skulking trunk. Head high and heart barely daring to hope for more than survival, she strolled toward her wedding dinner, surrounded by singing and shouting friends.

Chapter Nineteen

Portia was utterly comfortable, snuggled in a nest soft enough to make eider ducks envious. Darkness ruled there, full of coziness too complete to seek change. Even her ribs, normally encased in a corset tightened just beyond necessity into fashion's tortuous realm, rose and fell freely.

Her bed was firm enough to offer support yet soft enough to caress her skin, which had been slightly chapped during her voyage to Constantinople.

Yet she was uncommonly warm for someone covered only by a fine linen sheet and silky soft blankets, given the morning chill crisping her cheeks. In fact, she could have hurled the covers away and burrowed back into her blissful dreams.

She rolled over and groped for the cloth's edge.

Instead her fingers glided over the warm satin of a man's bare shoulder.

"Eek!" Shock ripped every nerve apart and hurled her to the other side of the bed.

"Good morning, wife." Her very naked husband nodded respectfully to her from where he now stood beside the bed.

She'd never seen him without clothes before.

Dawn's first light filtered dimly into the bedroom through the slatted windows. Seagulls called to each other like magicians, while the waves renewed their acquaintance with the shore. Two men quietly chatted in the distance, using the desultory phrases of a conversation's end.

The bedroom glowed like an exotic jewel in the dim light. Everything was scarlet and pale gold, from the delicate silk rug underfoot to the embossed ceiling overhead. The bed was so intricately carved it looked like lace, yet it sent four gilded poles soaring toward the ceiling. Delicate frescoes of local landscapes and seascapes graced creamy walls between shuttered windows. A single low divan provided the only seating.

All of that was an insignificant background to Gareth's stalwart body. His face and chest had been tanned by the sun to a burnished gold, which faded to a soft cream over his hips and below. His raven black hair moved like a living shadow around his head and blue veins laced his skin to his heavy muscles and straight limbs.

Evidently satisfied she was well—despite her speechlessness—he turned to scan the room, a heavy, broad-bladed knife at the ready. His eyes searched every shutter and nook, on the alert to protect her without thought to his own safety. Scars slashed and pried at his muscles in shades ranging from deep crimson to shadowed mauve, as if old battle wounds' poison still haunted him.

Her fingers curved to touch and hold, comfort and heal.

"Good morning, Gareth." Blood heated her cheeks brighter than the curtains and she tugged the sheet higher up on her shoulders. Oddly enough, she was only wearing a day chemise with its deep neckline and short sleeves, rather than her more enveloping nightgown. "I'm sorry I woke you."

"That's quite alright. I usually rise at this hour." He glanced at her from beside the shutters. "I'm sorry if I disturbed you. I only slept with you to be sure you were warm."

"I understand. We need to sleep together since we're married, after all." Her eyes slipped sideways toward his naked hip but she dragged them back. "It would look very odd if you slept on the floor."

But he too had been fast asleep until her fright woke him

up. Portia's heart sunk a little further and she curled herself further into the covers.

How could he be willing to fight for her, even when roused from a sound sleep? Tears touched her eyes at the sight of the highly distinctive bowie knife she'd given him almost fifteen years earlier.

She'd bought it when she was fourteen at San Francisco's annual mechanics' fair from Michael Price himself, where she'd had to beg the great man to part with one of his finest knives. Unlike his more recent work which was made for surgeons and indolent Easterners, this one had a modern blade's fine steel but the inconspicuous hilt of Gold Rush Era pieces. It hummed with quiet readiness to be carried into dangerous places by equally deadly men, instead of worn strictly for show.

Had it saved Gareth's life as many times as she'd hoped?

Moving very, very slowly and keeping his hand behind his back at all times, Gareth carefully hid his bowie knife under a book on the nightstand. He stood so close she could only see him from the waist up.

Her heart twisted. Now he treated her like a hothouse flower, unable to withstand even the slightest reminder of danger, such as the sight of armed protection.

"Would you like me to send for a cup of tea or coffee?" He lowered his voice to the same deep croon he'd offer a skittish horse.

"Oh no, certainly not." And let strange servants know what had transpired between her and her husband on their wedding night? Never!

"You must be chilled," she ventured, softened enough by his concern to offer an equal token. "Would you like a blanket? Or come back to bed?" What a dangerous thought that was.

He shook his head, a faint smile teasing his lips.

"Thank you." He caught up an embroidered quilt and settled onto the divan like an Indian wrapped in a blanket.

Surely she was satisfied at seeing only his face, hands, and feet, rather than the male beauty of a few minutes earlier.

Still, would he be comfortable there? His battered body deserved better.

"Can you sleep there? You should definitely get your rest." She tried to tuck her toes a little farther under her knees to give him more space on the other side. A cool breeze teased her arms.

"I've been colder. I'll stay here and let you breathe easy."

"Me?"

"Aren't you doing better now than when you first woke up this morning?" he countered.

Neither St. Arles nor her father had ever put her comfort first. Portia's chest loosened and warmed. Her fingers stretched, longing to reach out to him.

"But you're my friend and you're uncomfortable. How can I relax when you're uneasy?"

His eyes searched hers with the same intensity he'd given the room's hidden nooks.

"Please?" she added and bit her lip. He needed to believe she wanted him beside her for more than marital appearances. He needed comfort, the same way his scars should be healed. "Please come back to bed, Gareth."

"If you're sure, Portia."

"Yes, I am."

He came swiftly, probably so she'd have no opportunity to view him. He was on the other side of the bed, to her surprising disappointment, before he spoke again. "When is St. Arles expected in town, Portia?"

"Today perhaps, if he pretended to be an indolent tourist and came by train." She shivered, chilled by more than the air. "Or he could already be here, if he commandeered a fast warship."

"Do you want to lie down again, too, honey? Do you need another coverlet?"

"I, ah . . ." Did she want to flee? Or did she want to dive into the comfort of his arms and try to forget St. Arles' looming presence?

Gareth truly hadn't taken advantage of her the night before. She was certain of that, since she wasn't chafed and raw between her legs the way St. Arles had always left her.

"We've only been in bed a couple of hours," Gareth coaxed. "You must be exhausted. You still have time to sleep before we say goodbye to your maid."

"True." The Orient Express didn't leave until early afternoon, even though it arrived in the morning of the same day.

She stroked the inviting hollow she'd made in the pillow just above the perfect niche in the mattress. Both of them seemed to beg for her to return, to forget the coming day's cares.

Her hair swung forward onto her breast, tickling her cold shoulders. It had been only loosely tied with a hair ribbon, rather than sternly repressed in braids.

"How late were we up?" she asked, without looking at Gareth. Her fingers ached, half from the morning chill but far too much from the surprising need to touch him.

"Past three. Don't you remember?"

"Mostly as music and dancing, not hours and minutes."

"It was a fine wedding party, all laughter and friendship." He flipped the embroidered quilt invitingly out toward her. "Come closer, honey, and let me warm you up."

Another brisk breeze down the nape of her neck decided her. This was Gareth, her most reliable friend who'd always told her the truth without regard to his own betterment. He'd slept with her without taking advantage of her. Surely she could trust him—and him alone.

She dived back under the covers, straight for the most reliable heat source in the room.

"Argh!" Gareth grunted then clasped her close to his chest. She wrapped her arms around him, careful to keep her cold hands on his waist, and buried her nose against his chest.

"My poor darling," he crooned and smoothed a blanket up around her ears. "It can be a mite chilly around here in spring."

She sniffled and held onto him.

He was safe and solid—and hairy, too, above all that muscle clothed in silky skin. His body was a miracle of curves and planes, sculpted in three dimensions like one of Michelangelo's mighty masterworks ready to dare great powers. Not an animated watercolor maintained to be a living, breathing showcase for fine clothing, like so many men she'd met.

Clothing. Where was her dress?

"Since Sidonie isn't here, who put me to bed?" she queried. Warmth was slipping back into her bones, together with the most delicious lassitude.

"I did, best as I could," he admitted. For the first time, a little caution snuck into his voice.

"*You* did?"

"You were so sleepy, you started stumbling on the way in from the garden. You told me not to summon any of the maids."

"You must have thought I'd had too much to drink." She untangled her hands from under his ribs but remained tucked up against him, where her feet could get warm. Her nipples had somehow become aching little spikes, pressed deep into her breasts by his chest. But she couldn't pull away.

"Two glasses of wine?" His snicker quickly put her conscience to rest. "But your eyes were shut before I had finished undoing all those buttons."

"I'm sorry."

Her ankle slipped between his, as if holding onto him.

"You were charming." He kissed the top of her head. "You wore my watch."

She flushed at the realization he knew she still thought of him and sidestepped that issue without considering the alternative's risks.

"How could I be charming, if you didn't have your wedding night?"

"Who says I didn't like the outcome?" he retorted, triumph rippling through his voice, as subtle and final as a Colt entering its holster.

Their gazes locked.

"But you haven't . . ." She stopped. Her tongue darted out

to lick her lips, a move which he regarded with considerable interest.

"Yes, honey?" he drawled.

"You haven't *had* me," she whispered and blushed, wishing she could disappear under the bed.

"I've slept with you, haven't I? Maybe not in the Biblical sense but that doesn't matter, not when you spent hours wrapped in my arms."

"I wish I remembered it." She nibbled on her fingernail and wondered how he could be so calm, when she wanted to either run or grab him. But his body was hardly relaxed, given that his heart was drumming under her palm.

"You don't need to. Your body's happy, right? So why worry?"

"But I'd like to remember enjoying *you*, so I wouldn't have all the horrid thoughts of St. Arles when I think about sleeping with a man."

"Of course we can make another memory for you."

"What do you mean?"

"Anything you want." His eyes were very blue under their heavy lids. "All you have to do is ask."

"Kiss?"

"Of course."

"Or,"—she hesitated, impulses she'd never dared voice to anyone tumbling through her mind—"touch?"

"Anything." The syllables rasped his throat like the most heart-felt promise. He delicately stroked her hair back from her face. "And everything."

She smiled, relaxing in the surety of his promise, and traced the long muscle of his cheek, under his beard stubble. It was uncompromising, just like him, yet it seemed to have potential for more.

Surely she could safely handle Gareth. All the things she'd never wanted, never dared with St. Arles.

He turned his head and caught her fingertips in his mouth. She squeaked and shivered at the slow, steady caress. The gentle pull of his lips on her softer flesh seemed to ricochet straight through her arm and circle her breasts, tightening them as it went until she could barely breathe.

He did it again and her eyelids drooped, closing out the world so she could better savor the magic of this simple gesture. And when he kissed her other hand, and the palms of her hands, her heart lurched into a deeper, stronger beat that consumed her lungs.

She moaned softly, as much a plea for more as expressing bewilderment at her own reaction. She'd enjoyed playing with herself before but that had nothing to do with finding pleasure with a man. Didn't it?

"Ah, sweet Portia, you're so tempting with your lips parted. Will you mind if I steal a single kiss?" Gareth crooned against her cheek.

She shook her head, blindly seeking the source of the warm breath which ruffled her hair.

"That's my Portia." Gareth's mouth met hers.

She opened willingly but a little shyly, fascinated by the contrast between his lips' supple curve and his beard's roughness. Gentleness and strength, both aspects of protection all in one.

He kissed her a little more and she snuggled closer. Somehow her hand slipped up his shoulder and into his hair, entrapped in the heavy strands like a sorcerer's web.

Time mattered little, compared to the delights of tasting and touching him so intimately, tongue to tongue, lip to lip. Even their teeth gave texture and meaning, adding emphasis and depth—while her breath sighed in and out, sending his warmth down her throat and into her veins. It pulsed through her blood and tightened her breasts, stealing her wits.

He kissed her eyes and cheeks, then nuzzled her throat.

"Gareth, please," she whispered, although she couldn't have clearly defined what she wanted.

"Of course, Portia darling." His mouth came back to hers and she caught his head in her hands. He chuckled and she kissed him fiercely, certain now she could do this much at least.

He swept his hand down her back and pulled her close. Their legs tangled and her day chemise, far shorter than a nightgown, slipped up to her hip. But who cared when his magical mouth sent the stars spinning so fast that only he existed?

When he moved away, she could only gasp for air, dazed yet ecstatic. The hot tide of lust riding her veins was throbbing between her legs.

When he ran his finger along her jaw, his eyes were the blue of truth. He caressed her throat and her collarbone as delicately as a kiss—and she arched to meet him. "Ah, Gareth."

She ran her hands down his back and impatiently gripped the fine muscles of his ass to pull him closer.

"Portia, honey, you're a delight." A jolt of laughter and answering hunger ran through him.

He slipped his hand inside her chemise and cupped her breast. His big hand was shockingly hot, yet her hard little nipple craved his palm, stabbed at it, and shot surges of lust down to her toes.

Yet he stayed perfectly still—and Portia moaned, frustration adding a startlingly harsh edge to her wordless plea. A fine sheen of sweat helped her wriggle under him.

But nothing brought her needy, dripping core the final stimulation it craved. Just a touch from her hand or his, soft or harsh, fast or slow, she didn't care, not with this madness firing her blood. But she was blocked, condemned to climb higher and higher toward a pinnacle of pure need she'd never known before where nothing existed except the blurring of body and desire.

The only reality was the man in her arms, the one she'd craved for so very long. Gareth's shoulders filled her hands and his thigh was between her legs.

She rocked against him, unconsciously circling her hips. There was no place here for fear.

He slid her chemise aside and sucked her nipple deep into his mouth.

Portia cried out. Hot, wet—and teeth?

"Didn't expect that, did you, darling?" he muttered and set about driving her mad with tongue and teeth and fingers.

Vision faded first. Sound existed only for his voice urging her on and her own broken cries, begging for more, and her body writhing against his echoed by fine linen's susurration. The rich aroma of sex mixed with the salt water's tang to perfume the air, driving lust deeper into her veins.

And hunger, desperate and achingly sharp for the man above her. Hot and heavy as the slap of the waves on the pilings below the house, sharp as the bite of lust every time he suckled her. Deep and strong as the pulse building in her loins for the man beside her, his shaft blazingly hard against her knee.

"Gareth, please." She tossed her head from side to side and groped for him again, desperate, uncertain how to spur him on.

"Take it, Portia, take it for me—and for yourself," he purred like a tiger, that creature of shadows, offering to play in the sunlight.

His hand slipped between her thighs and found her most intimate flesh. He stroked her pearl—and Portia bucked, hard, and tumbled into orgasm. Fireworks exploded through her body, stealing breath and melting every bit of flesh and bone like magma.

She cried out, a long wordless, joyful sound like an unknown bird.

An instant later, Gareth grunted and jerked. Hot liquor splattered onto her thigh and her chemise's hem, just above her knee.

For a moment, his heartbeat drummed between his palm and her thigh, vital and demanding as the Arizona noontime sun. Then he shifted his arm and his pulse faded into the distance, leaving her to face emotions she'd never thought to manage.

Chapter Twenty

Moving as clumsily as if she'd run across the Arizona desert, Portia laid her head against her husband's shoulder.

He rumbled approval, lifted his arm, and gathered her against him. At least he didn't seem to be angry with her.

A single hot tear gathered on her cheek.

"What's the matter, honey?" He cleaned her delicately with the sheet's edge then smoothed her chemise down.

"N-nothing."

He tucked the covers up around her. She sniffled and burrowed closer, insensibly comforted by his heart's steady beat under her cheek and his arm's solid strength around her.

"Did I hurt you?" He spun the question out with the same idle intent he used to lure trout to his fishing line.

Like them, she couldn't resist responding, even though sweet lassitude was melting her body into his hold.

"I enjoyed myself but,"—she sought for the most tactful phrase then settled on the truth—"you didn't."

"Of course I did." He stroked her head, unerringly finding the spot where her headaches gathered. "Couldn't you tell? I had an orgasm, too."

If she could have sunk through the house, from their top floor bedroom, through the main floor to the boat house and the ocean, she would have done so. No matter how bluntly

Aunt Viola had spoken of intimate matters, Portia had never expected to do so with a man.

She closed her eyes and tried to be brave. Curiosity came to her aid. "But didn't you need to do something, anything to amuse yourself?"

He chuckled deep and soft, like a well-fed cat. His belly was so close to her elbow that she could tell his shaft was relaxed and quiescent between his thighs.

"I enjoyed myself very well, sweet Portia." He petted the small of her back under the covers.

"How? You never touched yourself," she blurted and blushed again at probing further into his most intimate needs.

He huffed in surprise and leaned back slightly to look at her face. She managed to meet his gaze, startled to find his gray eyes crystalline now with no veils raised against her probe.

"Why should I? You gave me more than I expected when you fell asleep in my arms. I didn't know you still trusted me after so many years."

"I didn't plan that," she protested.

"Exactly; every part of your body was utterly relaxed, which your brain could not have commanded. Thank you."

She shrugged, wondering a little uneasily why she was so comfortable in his arms now. Could it have been how well he made love to her? Or was that truly making love?

"And when you woke up all amazed at being in bed with a man, I knew you'd never slept the night through with St. Arles." Gareth's lips curved into a fiercely predatory line.

Portia gaped at him, caught by a barely leashed triumph she'd only glimpsed in the most high stakes power struggles among diplomats. "Is that so important?" she whispered.

"Oh yes, sweetheart. It was far more exciting than a dozen caresses." His eyelids swept down for an instant, granting him privacy for remembrance.

"But, even so," she stammered, returning to her original argument, "when I climaxed, you didn't even touch yourself. How could that satisfy you?"

"Well now, honey," Gareth's gray eyes flashed open to embrace her, "I reckon that every time I hear you take your pleasure, it's something St. Arles never heard. That makes me the winner."

"You're crazy!" She sat up to stare at him, heedless of her chemise falling off her shoulder.

"Are you telling me that you ever had an orgasm with that man?"

"No," she admitted warily. Were there any etiquette manuals which addressed discussing first husbands with the second one, especially regarding life's more intimate aspects?

"Then every time I hear you sing in pleasure, I win—and he loses." Her old playmate grinned at her, full of lazy, confident anticipation. "There's nothing I won't do to make you holler like that again."

Her jaw dropped. Her breath seemed suspended, together with her thoughts, somewhere she couldn't reach.

"Now relax and come back to bed, honey." Gareth stroked her wrist and forearm. "We have plenty of time and no need to rush. You must still be exhausted after last night."

"Exhausted?" Did he refer to the attack at the hotel or—

"Or relaxed, maybe—and sated from this morning?"

"Gareth!"

He swept her arms out from under her and tugged her down on top of him in a wrestler's move. He held her like that, close and warm, and petted her very gently.

Every inch of her met its match in his intimate flesh. Warm skin, smooth curve, crisp hair. She couldn't breathe, couldn't think, could only feel—and know herself utterly content.

"So tell me—why the dickens did you stand up in court and lie about having committed adultery?" His soft drawl made the question all the more lethally placed, like a well thrown knife.

Portia's jaw dropped like the shell cracking around her heart. Nobody, not even Uncle William or Aunt Viola, had ever disbelieved she'd been unfaithful to St. Arles. They'd all tactfully refused to discuss the matter, thus confirming that they thought her guilty or at least wouldn't care if she had cuckolded her obnoxious husband.

Gareth, on the other hand, had just restored her lost honor.

But how could he understand so well what she'd done in public, when they hadn't seen each other in years?

"How do you know I wasn't telling the truth? After all, you're the one who said he was an unsatisfactory lover."

Gareth harrumphed, as arrogantly sure of himself as any March gale clearing the way for spring.

"Remember who you're talking to, Portia. I'm the fellow who had the gall to take the boss's niece through the dens of iniquity along the Barbary Coast."

"To see jugglers!" Nothing more scandalous, despite her adolescent hopes. But they'd had a splendid outing anyway, worth every bit of the penalties afterward.

He nodded, his silver eyes linking them in a net of shared memories.

"I can imagine you in a courtroom for murder, but not perjury, Portia. What happened?"

He'd always been able to read her like a marked deck of cards. She could either tell the truth or lie yet again.

"Publicly, the marriage was more or less a success." Years of public deceit fell away all too easily.

"By those asinine British standards." She raised an eyebrow at his aggravated tone and he clarified, "I saw photos."

"Journalists." She sniffed unhappily and Gareth tucked her comfortingly against his shoulder once again.

"St. Arles was a successful diplomat and I was an acceptable hostess—"

"A damn good one!" Gareth rapped out, as if he'd prefer to plunge the words into the hearts of those who'd denigrated her.

"Too young to claim that title, but thank you. We both enjoyed yachting and . . ." She paused, trying to think of something else she'd done with St. Arles.

Gareth's silver gaze swept over her like a lantern, illuminating far too much.

"Hmm," he said, dismissing those bygone facades from both their memories. "What else?"

"No matter what we tried, I remained barren," she whispered, her face crimson with remembered humiliation. The long nights, the shouting, the pointed fingers from society . . .

"Son of a bitch!" Rage surged behind his eyes yet no fear leaped through her bones in response. Perhaps it was because his arms offered only protection for her and warmth. Perhaps she was hiding within a dream. Perhaps.

"Did he try to blame that on you, when he'd been married before and that wife had never had a baby?" Gareth asked more quietly but just as angrily.

Portia nodded, stunned he knew about St. Arles's brief first marriage.

"Goddamn bastard should be carved up like the skunk he is," Gareth muttered. "Doesn't he realize the stallion must flourish before the mare can?"

"Truly?" Portia blinked at him, never having heard that explanation from a man before. The husband had to be fertile, too?

"Of course. What happened then?" he asked brusquely.

"He demanded a divorce so he could marry his mistress. He was certain she could breed"—Portia gulped over the painful word but went on—"because she'd borne so many children to her late husband."

"And you agreed." Gareth's tone offered no hints to his thoughts.

"I wanted an end to the marriage." Lord, how she'd hungered to have it over and done with.

"Why couldn't he plead guilty? He was the adulterous rat dripping evidence through the backstreets."

"They'd have to admit she was the other party—and she'd never be accepted again in society."

"Mealy-mouthed bunch of hypocrites, the lot of them." Gareth crumpled the sheet between his fingers, as if crushing an insect under his boot heel. "Could you have held out a little longer, just to see him squirm?"

She'd wanted to do exactly that.

"I'd been married to St. Arles for five years. I was certain that, sooner or later, he'd find some way to force me into swearing I was the one who'd committed adultery—the only workable grounds for divorce."

Gareth grumbled something about stupid British laws.

She grabbed his strong wrist.

"If the divorce went through very quickly, I would be free by my twenty-fifth birthday—when I would inherit my mother's trust fund."

"A fortune?" Gareth's gaze sharpened.

"Five million dollars, all of it from my grandmother."

"Coming from that side of the family, your father wouldn't think about it. He wouldn't have informed that high-and-mighty Englishman."

"No." She released him, hoping, praying he'd understand.

"You turned the knife in St. Arles that day in court."

"Yes." *By swearing to my fantasies when everybody thought I meant the greasy swine my husband had brought forward.*

"And St. Arles didn't realize it." Gareth's hand circled her back.

She shrugged, old ice crystals falling away from her bones.

"Very clever of you, my good girl." He stretched underneath her, as if he offered his own body for her bed. "We should take some rest before we explore the city."

How deliciously simple he made it sound, as if she was sixteen again.

"You're very unusual, to calmly sleep with a perjurer." She whispered the words against his heart. She should have known he'd hear.

"Sometimes a person does what he must, honey, even if it's outside the law's limits."

The bitter knowledge in his voice stopped her throat.

She shuttered her eyes and let the dawn's glow drift around them.

Chapter Twenty-one

Early morning fog retreated like a cowardly foe across the Bosporus until the great harbor sparkled like a victory parade. The world's greatest nations' ships lay at anchor under clear blue skies, while tiny rowboats flitted through every available gap. A salt breeze stirred the air, touched by a promise of fresh fish from the local market.

Asia's hills rose in the east, shrouded in shadows against the dawn. A few lights glittered along the waterline, emblematic of the wealthy who slept there in seaside mansions.

For now. Florence Nightingale's hospital had marked those shores thirty years ago. Those lavish little mansions would make excellent officers' clubs for the British Empire's finest.

St. Arles made a mental note to add them to his inventory of property to be *requested* from Turkey's next sultan and allowed himself another swallow of tea.

"More tea, my lord?" the captain's steward asked, his white uniform crisp as the white canvas awning stretched overhead to shield the warship's teak deck from the sun. White paint gleamed beside brilliantly polished brass, and ropes were coiled like sleeping dragons on the pristine deck. Two boilers rumbled deep within, a reminder of how fast the warship could leap into action.

St. Arles held out his mug without a word, unsurprised the stolid Welshman read him so well. After all, he'd chosen tea over wine at every opportunity since he'd come onboard. What the devil else would they expect of a former British naval lieutenant?

Nobody made tea like the British Navy. It had been far too long since he'd last savored its milk-laced beauty.

"Very fine harbor, St. Arles," Southers remarked and closed his spyglass with a snap. "No wonder Jason and the Argonauts established camp here." Two years younger than his guest, his blond hair gleamed with youthful enthusiasm against his tanned cheeks. "She'll make a very tidy eastern outpost indeed for our fleet, almost equal to Dover, I do believe."

St. Arles gritted his teeth against another surge of frustrated rage and silently cursed his indolent older brother Philip yet again.

Dammit, he should have been the one comparing this anchorage to the British Navy's fortified home port in the English Channel.

Ten years ago, he'd thought himself the luckiest man in Britain. He'd dodged his father's boring, barracks-bound Army into a glittering naval career, full of good mates and constant travel. No need there to worry about awkward questions from discarded females, who might be a bit worse for weather, not when tomorrow always provided a new port or a new ship. He'd been so bloody happy until Philip had ruined everything once again.

The fat, drunken ass fell asleep in a brothel, while smoking a filthy cigarette—not even a manly cigar! He thereby transformed himself into a torch and the entire establishment into his funeral pyre.

Even the Navy's worst ship offered fewer rats than St. Arles House ten years ago. Water only ran down the bulkheads during a gale, rather than seeping out of the walls in moldy patches.

"Beautiful harbor indeed," St. Arles agreed. "An excellent jumping off point against the Russians."

A pack of young officers prowled across the foredeck, ostensibly checking the great guns' brass work. One by one, each deadly muzzle rose toward its assigned target in the Constantinople skyline—and took St. Arles' spirits with it.

"Did you notice the shipyard on the other side of Hagia Sofia?"

"Quite so, old chap. Once we put our men into her to add some western efficiency, she'll make a very nice addition to the Navy family, don't you think? There's a jolly good promenade nearby on those old Roman walls for the wife and children, too."

"Yes, indeed." Old frustration rasped St. Arles again. He should be the first one to fire a shot, instead of plodding through back corridors.

The Foreign Office was the only place where a peer of the realm could serve his country. Cotton-headed dunderheads wandered the diplomatic corps' hallways.

Or so he'd thought until he'd been offered this jaunt by a backroom chap. A simple ploy, similar to some of his old cutting out expeditions in the Navy. No questions asked about methods because the highest possible stakes were involved for Queen and Country.

"Constantine became an emperor after he founded this city. Crusaders and a sultan conquered it." Southers unleashed his spyglass on the great mosque's glittering golden dome, which dominated the hill overlooking the city.

A deep, barked command and a drum roll announced a rumbling surge of Royal Marines onto the deck in perfect order, scarlet uniforms blazing like promised sunshine.

Turkey had been called The Sick Old Man of Europe for decades. But only the greatest of history's generals had ever attempted to conquer its capital, while still fewer had succeeded. The entire strait was a natural fortress, enhanced by man until only the most foolhardy would want to attack it.

There'd be a splendid reward for snatching it before the Queen's Golden Jubilee in June, possibly even a marquisate to add to the family collection of titles.

Even better, this stunt provided revenge against the slut who'd stolen his money.

At least he had Amabel for wife now, more eager than he to add danger to sex play. She hadn't bred yet, damn the luck. He'd rather have an heir than a marquisate.

Hunger ran through him, fierce and bright for Amabel's blood dripping along a knife edge and laughter in her eyes above it, for the fierce joy of lighting a bonfire on St. Arles Castle's front lawn for his son.

Another round of barked orders—and the Marines shouldered their rifles. Sunlight poured over their bayonets like blood—or victory.

How could the Ottomans possibly match these men?

Suddenly who commanded the *Phidaleia's* power and speed mattered very little indeed.

How soon could he remove the filthy Sultan from his throne and get back home?

"High time for the old city to welcome some true civilization, don't you think, Southers?"

He'd host next year's Trafalgar Day banquet at one of those big seaside mansions. And, by God, when he and the other British naval officers raised their glasses of the finest port in the Immortal Memory toast, to honor Nelson and his fallen officers, a proper silence would fall in the banquet hall and throughout this city—because the conscienceless heathens here would finally have learned who were their betters.

St. Arles lifted his mug to the sea dog. "To Queen and Country!"

"Queen and Country!" Southers echoed immediately.

Afternoon sunlight blazed on the customs official's polished badge when Gareth held the train station's gate open for Sidonie, Portia's maid.

"We hope you will return soon to our beautiful city, madame. We would like to show you more of its glories on a longer stay."

"Thank you very much, sir." On the hillside behind her, Hagia Sophia's great domes and spires reached for the sky like a chorus of prayers. Men and women rushed between ancient buildings to visit their friends or sell goods. All was hustle bustle and the hot, spicy scents of a living town, washed by the salt sea. Dogs barked, children laughed, and men sang their success in the market.

Portia was very proud of how composed Sidonie was, given yesterday's terrors. Of course, she had spent last night and today with her cousin, who served the French ambassador's wife.

Portia would wager those two ladies had taken turns pampering Sidonie: Her graying hair was now braided into a much more becoming style and she'd advanced to a blended fragrance, rather than simple lavender water. Plus, her new hat was a miracle of restrained Parisian elegance.

She, on the other hand, had slept so late in Gareth's arms that she'd barely had time to dress before boarding Kerem Ali Pasha's personal sailing craft to reach here.

Sidonie escaped into the depot without any audible sigh of relief and paused, her eyes narrowing at the crowds bustling past.

"This way, ladies." Gareth tipped his hat, somehow as immaculate as a tiger sauntering through a jungle.

The little Frenchwoman bestowed upon him a beaming smile, which reawakened her countenance into youthful freshness amid flashes of beauty. She accepted his arm like a great lady and strutted down the platform, with Portia on his other side.

"I'm sorry we couldn't have spent more time together," Gareth said politely.

"Let me know if you don't like the spa at Aix-les-Bains," Portia added. "You need a good rest after the last few months and I'd be happy to send you anywhere you like. Dax, Deauville—"

"Deauville! Hmmph! Aix-les-Bains will suit me and my mother very well, not anything that grand. Thank *you*, madame, for your consideration. I wish I could stay longer." She shook her head, her color fading faster than the ancient stones outside. "But Constantinople is civilized and, at the same time, not civilized at all."

Portia's mouth tightened. For an instant, all she could see were black clad arms rising and falling above a man's prostrate body, while crimson drops complimented their aim.

"Perhaps you caught only some oddities of the current situation, rather than the entire pattern," Gareth murmured soothingly. "But France is beautiful in spring, while we could still catch a late winter gale here by the ocean. You can rest there, while my wife helps me finish my business here."

"Of course, she must stay here," Sidonie agreed and patted Gareth's arm. "Madame deserves a gentleman like you."

Portia almost tripped on her hem.

But—but the marriage was only for a short time until she and Gareth somehow dealt with St. Arles' blackmail and that loathsome trunk.

After that?

Gareth had proven years ago when he rapped her over the head with his gun, he didn't see her as a wife. Only years of loyalty to Uncle William had made him step forward yesterday to rescue her and, perhaps, some residual friendship with her.

"Madame will have whatever she wants," Gareth returned lightly.

He must be referring to that quiet divorce he'd promised her.

Oh, she could stop Sidonie's mouth easily enough. Heaven knew nobody was more discreet or loyal.

But did she want to be freed from her marriage? How could she keep him if he wanted to go?

Gareth handed Sidonie up the stairs to her first-class compartment.

"Goodbye, ma'am." He bowed, doffing his hat.

Sidonie beamed down upon him, framed by embroidered linen and fine teak. "Promise me you will cherish madame," she admonished him.

"With my life."

The three simple words stabbed Portia in the heart—yet he hadn't mentioned love.

He replaced his hat and stepped back beside her, his expression only that of a polite farewell.

The engineer blew the whistle, long and piercing like a portent of times to come. Machinery groaned softly and wheels began to churn. Steam hissed and blurred the tracks, hiding the future from the present.

"Au revoir, madame!" Sidonie called.

"Au revoir, Sidonie!" Portia cried back. At least she believed she'd see her maid again. She could not have said the same if she'd had to say goodbye to Gareth at this moment.

Chapter Twenty-two

Portia fanned herself again with the painted Japanese fan and glared at the barren table in her bedroom. She'd thought the unseasonable heat would be the worst of the day's trials. But, no, St. Arles hadn't yet condescended to send word where to deliver his vile trunk.

She couldn't do anything about the weather. But she had donned her favorite silk tea gown the minute she was alone. It was a silk confection, made from a blue and cream Japanese kimono that had been embroidered in chrysanthemums. Even better than all its claims to fashion was the fact she didn't need to wear a corset with it, allowing her to savor the heady freedom of silk floating over nothing more than a silk chemise and drawers.

A light tap caught her attention. "Yes?"

"Dinner," Gareth announced simply and closed the door behind him, balancing a large covered tray.

"You should have told me you needed help," Portia scolded and rushed to assist him.

"Weddings here are lengthy affairs, which frequently last up to a week. Since you seem to be getting on so well with me, Kerem Ali Pasha's family doesn't want to disturb you."

Portia balanced the tray and tried to decipher his meaning. "Do you mean that marriages here are frequently arranged, leading to wives who don't want to see their husbands?"

"Let's just say others frequently employ tact to ease newly-weds' relationship." Gareth stepped outside for an instant and returned with several flagons, which he placed near the long divan.

"But we"—He shot her a reproving glance, swift as an eraser over a blackboard—"*I* am behaving differently from those stranger brides. Therefore, Kerem Ali Pasha's family is happy to encourage us by granting us privacy."

"Exactly." He removed the tray from her hand and set it down on the low table near the flagons. "Come eat."

"European food?" She approached the delicious smells eagerly.

"No, these are some dishes from their own meal. What you would call hors d'oeuvres, or finger food."

She sat down on the divan and sniffed happily.

He nodded, his thick lashes veiling his thoughts. Like her, he'd changed into lighter weight clothing, notably a linen suit instead of tropical weight wool, and had even taken off his jacket. He had to be wearing a sleeveless undershirt since she could see the muscles in his arms through his shirt every time he moved.

She tore her gaze away and tried to forget what he'd felt like that morning under her hands—desperate, iron hard, straining against her, and the hard thrust when he found his own climax without ever hurting her.

He needed to cough to catch her attention before he could serve the first item.

She blushed scarlet and stared down at the plate, rather than his face. "What is this? It doesn't look like anything I've seen before."

"It's called dolma—or stuffed food. These are stuffed grape leaves." He sat down beside her on the floor, as comfortably cross-legged as if he was still in Arizona.

"Grape leaves?" She considered the small cylinder even more dubiously.

"The Turks include raisins in theirs." He took a bite, with the same insouciant air he'd once used to dare her onto three-storey high roofs.

She shoved the morsel into her mouth, chewed—and her taste buds applauded. "It's delicious."

He chuckled and poured her a glass of red wine from one of the flagons.

"Italian?" she asked.

"No, local. The Greeks have been making wine here since before Jason and the Argonauts sailed past."

She sipped cautiously, eyeing him over the rim. The Gareth Lowell she'd first met at age twelve couldn't have discussed wine. Even the man who'd so arrogantly cleaned up problems for Uncle William in Arizona didn't talk about fine wine, although he knew how to handle the morass of silver knives and forks on a fancy dinner table, plus the crystal goblets to match.

But his mature version raised an eyebrow at her and her heart skipped a beat, no doubt because of the very smooth wine flowing down her throat.

"I like it," she approved. Of the beverage, of course—and held out her plate for more food. Heaven help her if her senses started swimming, because of either alcohol or her husband.

"St. Arles didn't leave a message, while we were gone," she commented a little later.

"No, it's probably too soon. He only arrived in town this morning." Gareth tore off a piece of bread and dipped it into sauce, rather as if he wanted to shred St. Arles.

"How do you know that?" Portia firmly commanded her fingers to snatch another fresh fig, not throttle her husband for keeping secrets.

"I hired men to keep watch on all arriving tourists, especially those on the Orient Express."

"*All* arrivals? Wasn't that difficult to do?"

"No. If the train didn't bring him, I was betting he'd stay at the same hotel you did."

"Why?"

"Honey, that bastard requires his creature comforts and they'll only be coughed up for him there."

Portia blinked, as much in surprise at his profanity, as in agreement with its cause.

"Even if he decided to rough it, I've put in a solid bribe at the Almabayn where all the spy reports come in. That nest of snakes will know within a day when he shows up and exactly where he lays his head."

"And they'd tell you?"

"For enough money, they'll send me a copy after the Sultan and all his folks know." Gareth ripped up several more inoffensive bits of bread. "If I was trying to avoid attention, I'd play the game exactly the way St. Arles has: Arrive looking exactly like the world's biggest tourist and check into the hotel offering the poshest digs."

"The same one I'd been at." Portia wiped her hands. If only she could rid herself of memories as easily.

"Yup. By tomorrow, or maybe the day after, if he behaves himself, only routine spy reports should be filed on him."

"If not?"

Hope must have been too loud in her voice because Gareth slanted a quick glance at her.

"If the authorities get suspicious, they'll have a covey of spies following him. He'd never be rid of them and he'd be a fool to try, since they'd only add more or boot him out of the country as a nuisance. No, St. Arles' best bet is to lie low until he's sure he's not being watched—and then start causing trouble."

"Drat." Portia gazed into her wineglass's depths then poured the liquid down her throat, its only sure use.

"Honey." Gareth gently wrapped his fingers around her wrist. "He's just giving us time to figure out how to stop him."

"I wish he'd do something more helpful, like leave town or drop dead," she muttered and held out her glass for more wine.

"A pleasant thought but unlikely. Let's try talking about

something more common." He filled the fragile crystal to the halfway mark, rather than higher. "The weather perhaps?"

"Now you sound like a diplomat, always sticking to the safe topic." She traced the rim with her fingertip. "But since it's so hot, why don't you get a little more comfortable? Maybe take off your vest and necktie?"

She tasted the wine's residue on her fingertip and glanced at him. His pupils were very dark and completely fixed on her mouth.

Instinctively, her tongue flicked over her lower lip.

His adam's apple bobbed in his throat before he could speak. "Yes, of course."

He set his plate down awkwardly, as if it no longer belonged to him, and his fingers clumsily worked at his necktie.

"Where did you learn French?" Portia inquired, trying to adopt enough savoir faire to carry off a casual conversation while a man undressed before her.

"I never heard anything about what you did, except that you were well," she added.

"No, I asked William and Viola not to speak of me to you unless you asked. After that disastrous confrontation at the wedding, I didn't think you'd want any reminders of me."

His voice held the bitter calm of long acceptance. How could she tell him she'd both hoped and feared for news?

She shrugged away either agreement or denial and waved at him to continue.

"I've always found it easy to pick up languages—"

"And any skill you needed," Portia inserted, still far too fiercely proud of him for her own good. Leaving him would be painful.

He glanced up at her, from where he'd just laid his folded vest and necktie, his expression startled. An instant later, his countenance smoothed into a more pleasant mask. She could have cried over the lost intimacy.

"Most skills," he temporized. "In any event, you know how I always grow tired of seeing the same places."

She frowned and drew herself back into a corner of the divan, closer to where the seabirds sang through the slatted windows. "Go on."

"I asked William to send me abroad so I could enjoy some new sights," he said lightly.

"Europe?" she guessed, hoping against hope, judging by the hard grooves settling into his cheeks.

"China first, in 1880."

"You must have left immediately after my wedding," she guessed, "to have arrived there before year's end."

He shot her a glare which would have flattened a symphony's brass section. "You know Donovan & Sons' motto."

"High risk freight to high risk places," she said impatiently. "But you didn't learn to speak French in China."

"No. I visited Shanghai, Hong Kong, and finally landed in Indochina, to bring in spare railroad parts. A monsoon season there left me with a working knowledge of French."

"And malaria, too?" Good Lord, was he condemned to burn at unpredictable dates for the rest of his life, thanks to a hellish fever?

"No malaria, honey." For the first time, his familiar crooked smile flashed at her. "I'll admit I was damn lucky but I visited Viola's quinine powder more religiously than any preacher's altar call."

"Thank God." She'd attended church as seldom as possible after her wedding to St. Arles. But Gareth's safety might deserve some special prayers. "Is that all?"

"No, I headed for drier climates after that." He lounged back on his elbows, like a big, lazy cat ready to either purr or show its claws. "I've crossed Arabia's Empty Quarter to the pearling fisheries in the Persian Sea. I worked with the French archaeologists in Egypt, who wanted to sell their finds to American millionaires."

"You have more scars than that." The whisper came from Portia's heart, not her throat. Even so, Gareth heard.

"Egypt doesn't offer everyone perfumed luxury, honey. There are flies and dust, gunshots and knives in the dark."

"There are knives at diplomatic banquets, too. But only the verbal ones cut your throat or are left in your back," she retorted.

"Sorry, honey." He caught her hand and kissed it, his silver eyes glinting like winter rain. "I forgot not every scar can be seen."

She twisted her fingers to clasp his, silently sharing her own nightmares of times when she too had been the target.

"Algeria, mostly, and here in Constantinople," he added after both their grips relaxed. "French notions of how to colonize are brutal. But I can stomach the work to be done in hauling goods between these parts, France, and back to the States."

Portia frowned, teasing out the violence and savagery which underlay French stories of conquering their new territories in North Africa from the original Muslim holders. How much had Gareth seen of that? He'd always treated Indians more than fairly and had even had very close Indian friends. He could not have enjoyed watching the local tribesmen being torn apart to make room for Frenchmen, no matter what rights and wrongs dwelt on either side.

Why had he stayed away from home, from Arizona, from Uncle William and Aunt Viola for so long?

He seemed to have avoided civilization as if it was almost literally a plague.

She kissed his hand, offering what comfort she could. Tears touched her eyes but she blinked them back, refusing to show weakness lest she remind him of too much.

Chapter Twenty-three

"What about Constantinople?" Portia asked when she thought she could form words. As unhappy with the results as with his memories, she tried again. "What brought you here?"

"The Turks are hungry for learning and to build whatever they can afford. Mostly they buy from the British and the Germans but occasionally they trade with Americans."

He selected a green plum from the tempting array on the table, clearly willing to change the subject.

"Is that how you met Kerem Ali Pasha?" She studied him, glad to discuss a happier topic.

He shook his head and mopped his mouth with a napkin, unabashedly enjoying the succulent fruit.

"Adem and I were both guests of the Paris gendarmes after a—" He paused.

"Brawl?" She proposed the most succinct explanation.

"Thank you for describing me so well." His eyes twinkled at her. "After I got us out without needing to call upon his embassy's influence, he introduced me to his father."

"Who was very grateful." She rewarded herself with a delicious strawberry for stating the obvious.

"Extremely. He's helped Donovan & Sons bring mining supplies into the country, including dynamite. The Sultan considers simply possessing the stuff indication of an attack on him so it's extremely hard to get."

"You're joking." Several pieces of fruit dangled unnoticed from her fingers.

"Not when there's so much money to be had, simply for providing the basics." A baffled, angry look crossed his face. "Kerem Ali Pasha also helped us escort American professors here, when they come to take up teaching posts."

"As private tutors? It's obvious why well-behaved folk would want assistance coming here." She'd have given half her inheritance to watch Gareth's icy protection of Abdul Hammid, if he'd been there from the beginning at the customs post. "But wouldn't that be paying rather much for a child's education?"

He shook his head vigorously and finished his last plum.

"Universities?" she asked.

"The Turks give them a fancy name, taken from their religion. But, yes, they're building universities. And they're starting to educate their girls, too."

"Heavens." She slid out of the divan and onto the floor facing him. "Here, in a Moslem country?"

"Yup." He grinned at her, looking a little more like the young man she'd so adored. "The Ottoman Empire has its problems. What country doesn't? Plus, the weather here is better than Saigon."

"What wouldn't be?" she asked tartly, tears drying on her cheeks.

"Sea breezes here are more pleasant than the Algerian desert winds," he added, full of spurious innocence.

She grabbed a pillow from the divan and swung it at his head.

"Sweetheart, you'll knock over the yoghurt," he protested and snatched at the tufted silk.

"You'd deserve it for such a saccharine platitude," she shot back and launched herself at him. "Working in a place solely because of its weather is asinine!"

She dug an elbow into his chest and he let out a startled yelp. Well pleased, she fought even more strongly for the cushion.

Gareth wrestled Portia down to the floor, until she lay on top of him, their arms trapped between them, linked by the silken upholstery.

She lifted her head and glared at him triumphantly.

"I won," she announced and tossed her hair back over her shoulders. Her loose upsweep had somehow come loose, sending masses of curls tumbling down her back. "I've got the pillow."

"So do I," he pointed out, "and I'm holding onto the button."

"But I have the bigger button." She tried to smirk. She was suddenly acutely aware of her legs straddling his hips—and the very large, hot bar rubbing against her.

"Portia," he warned, "my fingers are longer than yours."

She flushed, remembering just how well he'd used those digits that morning.

"Portia?" His voice deepened to a darker, more intimate note.

If she released the pillow, she might be able to feel his chest again. But they were both dressed, no matter how lightly.

Would he want to?

Nothing ventured, nothing gained.

She took a single hand away from the cushion. But where should she put it? Behind her back or on his arm, his thigh, his—?

He slipped his fingers through hers and guided them to his shoulder.

Her lips rounded in surprise.

He pulled the pillow out from between them, threw it across the room, and slid his hand up behind her neck.

Of course, he'd know exactly what to do.

She leaned forward into his kiss, letting all of herself rest on

him. Her breasts flattened against his chest and his ribs lifted
air into her lungs, as fast as his lips claimed hers.

She moaned happily, eager to taste more of what he'd given
her earlier.

He kissed her thoroughly, sweetly. His hands roamed her
back freely, sweeping from her shoulders to her waist, over her
hips and curving to fondle her derriere. She wiggled closer, enjoying the warm pulse rocking between his mouth and her
breast every time he kissed her, the lazy sparks of lust drifting
through her veins.

She sank her fingers into his shoulders but his shirt's crisp
starch rejected her. She made a disconsolate little sound and
pressed closer, seeking more contact with the warm male flesh
under her mouth.

"Portia?" He nuzzled her cheek, barely moving his head
away from her. "What do you want, honey?"

She needed a moment to recover her dazed wits. "I'd like to
touch *you*, not your clothes."

"Are you certain? Matters may—probably will—go further
than they did this morning." He considered her, sprawled across
the silk rug in the late afternoon sunlight like a sultan.

"I think I want them to." She nibbled on her fingertip and
watched him hopefully. Her breasts ached so much for his
touch and his shaft was so very large inside his trousers.

Yet she could never be sure he wouldn't do exactly what he
pleased, which might not suit her at all. All she knew was that
he'd never hurt her.

"Please, Gareth?" she added.

"Very well." He looked as if he was leashing himself, although not a muscle moved. "Do you know what steps you'd
like to take next?"

His voice deepened and slowed until it wrapped around her
bones, luring her forward.

She dragged her teeth across her lips, a move he watched
with fascination.

"You're wearing too many clothes," she whispered.

"Take them off," he countered.

Every bit of her skin suddenly flushed with warmth and the desperate need to do exactly what he said.

"I, uh, I—you mean it." She stammered to a stop, heat crackling into sparks between them under his heavy-lidded eyes.

"Of course. We've always told each other the truth."

She closed her gaping mouth, acutely aware of how taut her breasts suddenly were. He stroked her waist but didn't move his hands any higher.

She'd have to prove her willingness to him before he'd know she was ready to step out of St. Arles' shadow.

Surely the rewards would be worthwhile for doing this.

She climbed off him unsteadily and knelt on the floor. Her skirts fanned out around her in a billowing pool of embroidered flowers, like a promise.

The first button seemed to be made of butter, judging by how it slid away from her jerky fingers and refused to move from one side of his vest to the other. By the time she finally saw a wider vee of shirt, she'd tasted blood from where she'd bitten through her lip.

"More," Gareth commanded harshly.

Her eyes flashed to his, unbearably drawn by his tone.

"Undo my vest, sweet Portia," he said a little more gently, his breathing as bitterly controlled as a tiger pacing out his territory's limits.

"I can't," she stuttered, fascinated beyond thought by how crystal bright his eyes had become behind his thick lashes. And how untamed his hair was when it fell over his forehead.

"If you unbutton my vest," he coaxed, his chest rising and falling underneath it, "I'll undo my cufflinks for you."

She ran the back of her finger down one wrist. So very big and strong—but the hands they guarded? Heavens, the delights they'd wrought upon her that morning.

His breath creaked to a sudden halt.

"I can manage them," she bargained, suddenly more confident. "But you have more fastenings than I do."

A black eyebrow slashed upward like an artist's brush stroke. "What do you mean by that?"

"If I unfasten those few, how will you help speed up our undressing?" she asked, startled at her own frankness. She knew she hungered for him but why was she speaking so boldly about it?

"By taking my shirt and boots off," he answered promptly. "Or your gown."

She closed her eyes against the reckless instinct to simply hurl herself at him.

Her fingers were vibrating faster than her heartbeat when she bent over him again. Only the knowledge that her hair shielded her face kept her close to him.

But she sighed when he stroked her shoulder and down her arm.

"Beautiful silk," he murmured, "but not half as lovely as my lady."

The last button undone, she stayed where she was, head bent and panting far too much for breath.

"So many flowers." Gareth undid her gown's top button very slowly. She could feel his eyes on her like a caress, warming her from the inside out. She turned toward him further, fireflies taking flight from her skin.

He brushed his fingertips against the base of her neck, like the gentlest of kisses. She arched her head back and let herself float into a sea of lust, sparkling like sunshine over waves through her body.

"Delicate and strong to survive winter's harsh winds, yet bring beauty in the spring." He undid the second button, then another and another.

She swayed toward him, like the flower he called her, and met his mouth. Joy floated between them, pure and bright as the ocean waves reflecting off the ceiling.

He rolled her onto her side and she caught his head in her hands. His shirt rasped her aching nipples through her fine lawn chemise and she twisted against him.

"What is it?" Gareth murmured against her throat.

"You promised," she murmured disconsolately—and gasped when he nibbled the pulse at the base of her throat.

"Promised? Ah, my shirt." He trapped her gaze, his mouth a passionate invitation to carnal folly.

"Yes," she gasped. "And your boots."

His eyes narrowed at her demand for everything he'd promised, rather than a more ladylike minimum.

He came to his feet with a panther's speed and removed his shirt, tossing it carelessly toward the door. His boots and socks received the same cavalier dismissal, thudding to the floor as emblems of masculine dishabille.

Portia's core became a furnace, melting itself into a slick river of hungry cream for him. Nothing mattered except looking at him. Even fear, once so deeply embedded in her bones, seemed unimportant compared to his glories.

"Your eyes are very dark, Portia honey." Gareth's voice lured her, rich and slow as fine brandy—or the Kentucky bourbon she'd stolen once as an adolescent.

"Still too many clothes," she complained. But whether to herself or to him, she couldn't have said.

She drew up her legs and began to tear off her beribboned slippers, cursing the fashionable idiots who'd insisted on so many bows.

"Whatever you wish, my dear." He sounded satisfied—or anticipatory. But she didn't care, not when hunger ran hot and fast through every iota of her flesh and she could smell his need over the salt sea. For the first time, that scent drew her, made her want to luxuriate in it.

Cloth whooshed through the air, thudded against the wall, and slithered onto the floor.

Gareth swept a sheet onto the floor and lay down upon it, on his side.

Portia's breath stopped. His stalwart frame was magnificent and deadly, he was graceful and quick as a great cat—yet he bore so many scars. Somehow those imperfections drew her even more than seeing one of Michelangelo's statues come to life would have. She wanted this man, hardened and experienced as any medieval warrior engraved at a chapel. She needed to touch him, to rub herself over him, to reassure her every fiber that he was real and not cold stone—and to keep hot life vibrant in the steel gray eyes watching her.

She shrugged off her tea gown and threw it over his trousers.

His eyes flamed, blue leaping in them like the hottest flames' core.

She licked her lips rapidly, then undid her drawers and tossed them aside. Her chemise dropped down to her knees, concealing her.

"Ah, sweet Portia." Hoarseness rippled through his voice like fuel being added to a fire.

"Gareth." She knelt beside him, eager to finally lose herself in him. *Darling*, she added privately.

He pulled her into his arms and above him.

She tugged her chemise over her head, heedless of any scattered buttons.

He roared his approval and suckled her fiercely, making love to her breasts as if that morning had been the lightest sample.

She sobbed her pleasure, lust lancing between his mouth and her core. Heat pulsed in her blood, hotter and faster.

His muscles steadied her, while his crisp body hair pricked her into a world of wilder sensation. Her senses swam, engorged with his scent, drowning in a myriad of new sensations where everything was Gareth—sight, sound, scent, touch.

His hands were everywhere, fondling, probing, adding just the right touch to drive her wild. His deep voice was like the magic smoke from a genie's lamp, seducing both her ears and her bones.

She burned for him, her muscles ached to hold him. She

stropped herself over him, her lust's bright edge growing sharper with every new inch of his body she discovered.

"Dammit, Gareth, please." She wrapped her hand around his shaft and squeezed gently, transfixed by the contrast between strength and velvet.

"You've a lovely way of expressing yourself." Gareth groaned and lifted her up but she never released him.

When she came down, his shaft entered her precisely where she craved him. She bowed into an arc and her entire body became an instrument to envelop him.

Both of them worked to find pleasure during that wild ride, hands, legs, thighs, hips—who cared whose muscles brought it, so long as passion flourished? Body drumming against body, hot musk perfuming the air, and insatiable lust burning hotter and brighter in Portia's loins.

She was a being of pure sensation, existing only for the delight of this moment with Gareth.

Then he rubbed her pearl hard, the hidden nubbin only she—and he—had ever pleasured before.

She sang out his name and leaped for the stars, tumbling into orgasm as if she'd never felt its delights before. Every bone melted and dissolved in a ribbon of lights.

She pillowed her head on his chest, too content to be irked at his usage of a condom with a barren woman. She might have liked a small bit of hope for his child, no matter how unlikely.

Or should she simply concentrate on praying that St. Arles would behave like a gentleman and leave town?

Chapter Twenty-four

Gareth handed Portia into Kerem Ali Pasha's personal carriage, as carefully as if she were the Ottoman princess whose dowry had provided the luxurious vehicle.

Damn, but she was beautiful enough for royalty, even if she did keep falling asleep immediately after she'd had an orgasm. And with the most adorably bewildered expression, too, as if she'd never before been safe enough to totally yield to pleasure and the relaxation it brought.

She took her time settling into the fine carriage, fluffing out her skirts to make sure the acres of black, furbelowed silk remained crisp. For a nickel, he'd take her back to their bedroom and explore those enticing ruffles, both silk and feminine flesh, under her striped underskirts. She'd dressed as properly for an audience with the Pope on the outside. But what lay underneath was infinitely distracting to him.

But he hadn't yet earned that privilege. More important than anything else was seeing her laugh and maybe, one day, watching her throw herself at life the way she had before that hellish marriage.

Before he'd betrayed her and let her be swept into that damnable union.

"Ready, Gareth?" Her voice sliced through his heart. He'd have tolerated constant accusations better.

"Of course." He stepped inside the open barouche and reached for the door.

"Cable for you, Lowell." A yellow envelope was thrust into his hand. He barely had time to nod at one of his best men before Selim was gone, blending into the dockside crowd like the pickpocket he'd been.

Gareth slid the latch home and rapped his cane on the floor. The carriage swung into motion, its pair of beautiful horses catching the eye and causing onlookers to step back.

"Congratulations," Portia murmured. "You look and behave quite the man about town."

"Their shirts are too well starched and their neckties too tight." Gareth snorted. "But sometimes it helps to blend in with the scenery."

"Especially when we're about to see the Sultan?"

"Especially then," he agreed.

He measured his finger against the envelope's flap then sighed and settled for a pen knife. His fancy gloves were too damn thick to fit inside much, let alone something this tightly sealed. A few seconds later, he passed the contents over to Portia without a word.

He couldn't think of anything fit for a gentlewoman's ears, anyway.

She stared at him. "Why, that filthy, double-dealing, lying, conniving . . ." She crumpled up the paper and hurled it onto the carriage floor.

"Skunk?" Gareth suggested.

"Bastard!"

The unusual profanity made Gareth's eyes widen.

"He must have known when he spoke to me That Woman was already starting to dismiss the servants. People who'd been with his family for years." Color flew in her cheeks like battle flags.

"But not all of them, and not the four he named to you." Thank God the coachman only spoke Turkish, not English or French.

"Does it matter?" She tightened her lips and shook her little fists, as if begging for a target.

"It might, if you're holding to the letter of a bargain and not the spirit."

"Are you defending him?" She pulled her voice back from a shriek an instant before it echoed off the stone walls beyond the carriage.

"Hardly; I'd rather kill him." Very slowly, using some of the nastier Apache techniques.

Christ, what he wouldn't do to simply throw Portia over his shoulder and lock her up on the next London-bound ship to weigh anchor. But she'd simply jump ship or leap aboard the Orient Express, determined to come back here so she could protect her friends.

He ignored the cavity sucking out his stomach and forced reality back into her calculations as he'd done so many times before.

"Portia, you still have the chest which St. Arles needs."

"He will destroy my friends." Agony wrenched her voice out of its usual music.

"He will try." Gareth caught her hand. "We have other friends in London who can help."

She looked up at him, terror distorting her expression beneath her feathered hat. "Are you sure?"

"Always remember that you have something St. Arles needs." He urged courage into her with his grip.

"But if we meet him before we know my friends are safe— Maisie and Jenkins and . . ." She caught herself an instant before a hysterical sob. "What will I do if he demands the loathsome trunk then?"

"Choose what your heart demands," he answered slowly, "and I'll be at your back."

The reception hall at Yildiz Palace was large, extremely gilded, and very full of rustling Europeans and hard-eyed Turkish soldiers, all arrayed in their best.

Late afternoon sunlight streamed in through an enormous window, framed by cream curtains. Inlaid white and gold panels glowed like jewels above the crystal chandeliers. Mother of pearl panels adorned the walls, while garlands of painted flowers stretched up the columns before uniting with their embossed capitals. A single carpet rippled underneath like a cornfield, uniting the vast room and the crowd gathered within it.

Portia might have called it inviting except for her strong desire to be at home, nestling in her husband's arms where the world couldn't harm her.

"Please take your place wherever you wish, Mr. and Mrs. Lowell." The court flunkey bowed and stepped away without waiting for an answer.

He probably meant wherever they could find space at the window.

Portia considered the horde gathered in front of the gilded frame and shuddered. Between the adults pressing forward to reach the glass and the children squirming like accomplished spies to pass through, the entire mass resembled a snake pit far more than a civilized encounter.

The dozens of soldiers watching everyone present, as if anyone was worth a sudden shot or knifing, only added to the impression of barely contained primitives.

And for what?

The window displayed a beautiful little wedding cake of a mosque, almost breathtaking in its ivory purity. It was surrounded by dozens of ministers, Moslem priests of every sect, rank, and country, plus hundreds of soldiers, all of them dressed in their finest uniforms and glittering with decorations to outshine the sun. They were arrayed in concentric rays, like beams of a living sun, vibrant and warm with life.

"Can you see the courtyard?" Gareth asked quietly, wise enough not to jostle his way into the throng.

"Where all the soldiers are? Yes."

"The Sultan will ride into it, followed by Ottoman guards, all of them on some of the finest Arabian steeds you'll ever

find." A rare display of awe threaded his voice. "The most senior religious leaders will greet him and escort him inside,
where he will pray."

"There are a great many priests there, even to visit a sultan."

"He's also the caliph, the leader of the Moslem religion, and
this is Friday evening prayers, the holiest time of the week."

Good heavens, he sounded as if he considered their cere-
monies equal in symbolism to Christian ones.

"That's not a very big courtyard." She strained to catch a
little more of what impressed him. "How long will we see anything?"

"A few minutes."

"All this pomp and ceremony for that?" She shot him an incredulous look.

"All this *protection* to ensure the Sultan, heir to a centuries'
old line, stays safe at one of the few occasions evildoers can
surely find him," Gareth corrected.

"There must be a thousand men there," she protested.
"Who—or what—could get through that?"

"You've spent time around mining camps, Portia. Apply
your brain." Gareth all but hissed the last three, clearly enun-
ciated words.

She frowned at him then caught his sideways glance at the
circulating flunkeys.

Spies? She mouthed.

He nodded, his mouth very tight.

Here?

He didn't bother to dignify that question with a direct answer. "Isn't it glorious that so many men are willing to die for
their Sultan?" he asked, more loudly.

"Quite so," she murmured, borrowing a phrase from her
most despised former in-law.

"Do you suppose the Sultan feels guilty for taking so many
men away from their Friday prayers to guard him?" St. Arles'
studied, hateful drawl interrupted.

Portia's fingernails cut into her palms inside her sleeves.

Who could she denounce him to? Would anyone pay attention if she screamed?

"I'm sure the men in question consider their attendance an honor," Gareth parried and discreetly guided them to the far end of the room, well away from anyone else. "Who are we, to argue with another religion?"

"Blithering idiots, wasting men like that. Do you see how they've put so many men on the mosque's roof that it looks like ants trying to carry off a gingerbread house? They should simply shove him into a back corner and let him babble his nonsense there." St. Arles shook his head. "We know to do things more efficiently in England."

He called what all these people had gathered to celebrate, *babbling nonsense*?

Rage surged through her, icily crisp as a desert wind scrubbing sands with snow.

Portia regally turned to survey its loathed source, immeasurably stronger for the support of Gareth's arm under her hand. Any decision would be hers, but having him beside her limited St. Arles' potential for violence.

The source of a hundred nightmares shot her another one of his impatient glances which had always ripped through her defenses. "Come along; we can't talk in front of him."

"My *husband* stays with me."

"Husband?" For the first time, St. Arles truly measured the other man.

Gareth gave him an equally insolent stare, the vicious appraisal of two predators assessing each other's readiness for battle.

Portia licked suddenly dry lips, uncertain who had the advantage. St. Arles' nasty cunning had outwitted more than one opponent.

The court flunkey's voice rose slightly from beside the window, answering a question.

"The procession is about to start," Gareth translated. His

cool tone could be interpreted as anything from anticipation of a social event to sorrow that a prospective fight had been postponed.

St. Arles' faint snarl promised that the battle would occur.

"Bring the trunk here tomorrow." He shoved a small card toward Portia.

It somehow looked and smelled like a cobra, ready to spit poison at anyone who touched it.

"No." Her fingers dug slightly into Gareth. "I can't deliver it to the people here."

"What the devil do you mean?"

"Giving it to you would be like opening Pandora's box—and Constantinople's people have done nothing to deserve that."

Gareth's strong arm tightened under her hand, providing silent agreement with her decision.

"You crazy slut!" St. Arles took a step toward her and Gareth blocked him immediately.

"Do you realize what you're doing? By God, I will destroy those sniveling servants."

"You can try—and you will fail," Gareth snarled.

"We have the trunk—" Portia tried for a civilized conversation, given their audience.

"All I have to do is reach out my hand to take it back from you," St. Arles snapped, the muscles in his neck standing out like ropes ready to fling themselves at his enemies.

"Gentlemen, lady," the court flunkey reproved, sleek and dignified in his uniform. "May I ask you to join us at the window? Prayers are about to begin."

"Prayers? I'll show you what that nonsense is worth." St. Arles shoved past him and elbowed aside a high-ranking Moslem priest in his haste to depart.

The courtier's alarmed gasp made more than one head turn to see the cause. Only the British ambassador's quick gesture of apology stopped a guard from arresting St. Arles for insulting the priest.

For two cents, Portia would have stolen the guard's rifle and used it herself.

The door's violent slam marked a boor's exit and a rattle-snake's return to its lair, ready to build poison for another strike.

Chapter Twenty-five

St. Arles strode warily down the narrow alley, alert for the promised glimpse of a mosque. In this world of rolling roofs, arched lintels, and slender windows, stray cats were more confident than mere humans. Foul brown liquid dripped onto green vines from ancient bricks. Wooden buildings jostled each other like drunkards and crackled at every corner like hags good only for one last bit of gossip.

For some good rum, he'd have brought all of his old shipmates along with him to ward off the prying eyes watching every step.

The excuse for a road jogged right and then left again immediately, bringing the nearest hovel's eaves over the pavement.

A small gray tabby drowsed on a windowsill, the lone observer. He rolled and stretched a paw high in the air, as if to raise the all clear sign.

Amused, St. Arles returned the salute, grateful for the good luck token.

A single minaret rose directly ahead, like a candle on a banquet table.

At least something still behaved according to plan.

St. Arles took a quick step to the right, spun, and ducked through an open doorway into the meager excuse for a room behind it.

Here an ancient oil lamp spluttered and fought the shadows to reveal broken stools scattered amidst furniture makers' clamps. The attics at St. Arles Castle were cleaner and more welcoming. But he'd wager a year's rents that if he returned in an hour—or if the Sultan's spies appeared—only impoverished, ignorant upholsterers would be discovered.

Four men spanned the wall facing him, clearly blocking the best escape route from this rat hole. They were undoubtedly natives and possibly kinsmen, given their dark hair and stocky build. Everything about them, from their suspicious expressions to their hands only millimeters away from their weapons, suited this district. Except for their well-fed air.

"Greetings," he said shortly. The sooner he finished with them, the sooner he could have a decent meal at the ambassador's home.

"Sir," the eldest returned in a tone which implied the title was only a formality.

"When can you fetch me the chest?" St. Arles went straight to business. At least these foreigners had enough education to speak French.

"That's not part of the bargain," the appointed speaker retorted. "You were to bring us the trunk, then we would *secretly* deliver it to the palace."

"That problem is your fault. If you hadn't gone against my orders and tried to steal it from the hotel, the stupid female wouldn't be frightened enough to hide behind that American."

"At a state secretary's heavily guarded yali," his so-called ally added. "I thought she had brought it here at your command."

St. Arles sincerely wished a single glance would make them all choke on their own cleverness.

"How many men will you have to proclaim the revolution after we deliver the chest?" he asked and moved in, close enough to split them. "I'm sure you'll want to proclaim your reformist decrees in as many places as possible."

"Enough." His opponents didn't quite look at each other.

"Are you certain?" he prodded, pleased with their response. Poor bastards couldn't even attack him, since it would be months before the embassy would send out a replacement. He was their only hope for a speedy revolution.

"If we hold Constantinople, we hold the empire," answered the slender one in the rear. He brushed past the others to come forward into the light, bright as a freshly sharpened knife.

"We guarantee we'll control Rumeli Hisar, plus the other forts here and along the Dardanelles, sailor boy," their foremost speaker added far too quietly. A blade spun casually between his fingers. "You may want to sail your fleet through here to attack Russia—"

Damn their eyes, they knew all too well exactly how to block him, while he could only bargain with gold or a new Sultan. Bullets in their obstinate backs would be far more satisfying.

Was there nothing the Turks held dear, other than their damnable pastel palaces which they'd built by selling their revenues to foreigners?

By God, he'd demand nothing less than a marquisate for pulling this off.

He stretched his lapels and tried to pretend they were proper Europeans.

"Two years ago, Russia nearly swept into India through Afghanistan. When we tried to protect her by all means necessary, your Sultan stopped us."

"You mean he would not let you start *your* war from *our* territory," the other youth stepped forward into the light, betraying fashionable French attire. Entirely too much intelligence sharpened his gaze.

"Taking our fleet through the Dardanelles and past Constantinople to attack Russia's only warm water port," St. Arles spun to face each of them in turn, his fingertips only millimeters from his gun. "Your lives and land would never have been at issue."

"But our honor and national pride would have been. We

would have become a British satrapy," the younger man added bluntly and stepped back to assume his guard post again.

Damn the fellow for plain speaking on a matter of foreign affairs. St. Arles shook out his coat, wishing it was a naval uniform.

"Your ships will have safe passage, Mr. Englishman." The elder's broad shoulders almost blocked out the room's few rays of sunshine. "But it will be done by treaty after we have our revolution. We will have reforms, as in the days of the Tanzimat."

"You can't turn back the clock to fifty years ago." Damn, but it was enjoyable to turn the knife in their pride even a small bit. He eyed each one of their outfits in turn then curled his lip at their pitiful attempts at fashion.

Somebody stiffened and metal snicked against leather.

St. Arles allowed himself a small, contented smile and returned to the main door. Unfortunately, the superiority of British styles and customs was recognized for all too short a time.

"Will the revolution still occur next Friday?" The leader's voice boomed through the house, stately as a minister reading the Sunday lesson from the pulpit. "Even though you don't have the chest?"

Damn, damn, damn. St. Arles caught himself an instant before he would have killed the filthy heathen for implying an Englishman could fail.

He should have strangled the bitch instead of letting her off with a divorce. A more obstinate, uncooperative guarantee for trouble he'd never encountered.

He could not show weakness, especially not there and now. He needed time—to win this game, then kill the slut.

He made his turn into an excuse for lounging against the door. Would any of these idiots break ranks? No, they were all back in their mulish circle, eyeing him like the jailer come to lock them up again. *Dolts.*

"Yes, of course, the revolution will still go forward exactly as planned," he answered, his bonhomie smooth enough to please even Whitehall.

Because no matter how much he loathed dealing with these idealistic donkeys, they were still his only chance of blocking the Ottoman garrisons. Without them, there'd be no revolution—and no British warships in the Dardanelles or at Russia's throat.

Chapter Twenty-six

The evening sunlight drifted over the Bosporus, turning it into a fools' highway paved with gold. Dozens of steamers huddled at its crossroads, as if hoping for a prurient glimpse into the Topkapi Palace's harem. None of them were warships, only merchants.

The Moslem call to prayer echoed faintly from dozens of minarets, then silence. The perfect peace of prayer and meditation. Even thieves didn't tend to disturb sunset prayer.

Gareth enjoyed Moslem countries for that accomplishment. Only they could guarantee him at least one hour every day when no fighting made ghosts erupt out of his past.

Portia was triggering rustling noises from the dressing room. She'd been doing much of that for the past day, ever since they'd come back from seeing the Sultan visit the mosque—and talking to that filthy British earl.

As long as Gareth heard her like this, he knew she was well. She spooked a little too easily if he tried to help her dress or watched her too blatantly.

As soon as he got her out of here, he was going to grant himself the pleasure of hunting down her bastard of an ex-husband and destroying him like a cockroach. He'd already discarded at least five methods as being too gentle.

Lovely ladies like her should be cherished. Anybody who did differently should be destroyed.

She pushed open the door. The shutters' filtered light framed her brighter than any rainbow and just as unlikely to fulfill a man's dream.

"Plums?" she asked, holding up a bowl of the tart green fruit.

He had to clear his throat before he could speak.

"Not now, thank you. It's too close to dinner."

She sat down on the divan to watch the Bosporus with him, clad in yet another of those frilly tea gowns. His blood promptly remembered the pleasures that lay underneath the silken confection and the barriers which did not, such as a corset, and surged into motion.

He cursed under his breath, not in English or French, then settled a little more against the yali's bedroom window and stretched his shoulders. Adjusting his trousers would be better but there was no easy cure for their tight fit. Leaping upon his wife—God help him, what was he doing with one of those?—to satisfy his own lust would be a sure route to hell for both of them.

Perhaps he'd borrow some horses tomorrow and take Portia riding, with grooms in attendance, of course. Or maybe he'd try to take her a little farther north to one of the summer resorts; that should be safe enough for both of them.

Somewhere she could relax and become a hoyden again, as she'd been before that damned ride across Arizona. Somewhere she could laugh and yell her objections to idiocy and hurl herself into life.

She'd never been the same since she headed back East after that trip. She'd been a high-strung filly who warranted gentle handling, and his clumsiness, when he knocked her cold, had hurt her badly. Now it was his duty to heal her.

Nothing else mattered. Certainly nothing he wanted for himself did, even if he had any right to those desires.

POP! POP! The small explosions burst through the room, almost rolling over each other.

Gareth whirled toward the source, his knife automatically sliding into his hand.

Portia looked up, ready to throw another plum pit through the window into the water. Her blue eyes were as large and round as her mouth. They were also far guiltier than any time her stepmother had caught her throwing rocks as well as any boy.

Gareth rubbed his forehead then sheathed his big bowie knife. He'd never previously seen much need to carry a smaller blade.

At least she didn't look frightened of him.

"Sorry," she said in a very small voice.

He waved off the problem, wishing he could escape what she looked like as easily. The blond curls so loosely pinned up and meant to caress that slender white neck—or wrap around his hand while she pleasured his cock . . .

"It's not important," he assured her quickly. "I should have warned you I had one."

She leaned forward and ran her hands down the front of her thighs, stretching the fine silk over her waist and hips.

"It's just that I can't stop thinking about our meeting with St. Arles," she confessed.

"Are you worried that he'll hurt you?" Gareth dropped his knife and its scabbard onto the table beside the bed then knelt beside her. "Honey, he can't touch you."

"He was furious. What will he do to—"

"Your friends?"

"Or the people here in Constantinople? He's already gone back on his word to me and started destroying his own servants, the cur." Angry and desperate, her goddess's face would inspire men to take up arms. Then it crumpled into desperation.

"But what if he's so angry at my refusal to help him that he becomes nastier to Constantinople's inhabitants? He could shatter any deals he'd made with them. Perhaps start a revolution and turn this country into an empty husk, even kill his current allies lest they prattle about him."

"Portia." He grabbed her hands before they crushed a plum into oblivion.

"Gareth, it would be my fault," she whispered. A single tear swam onto her eyelash.

"For the love of God, Portia, do not blame yourself for another man's deeds. Any evil St. Arles does is because he himself chooses to."

"But I can't stop wondering—"

"If you don't stop thinking about it, you will go mad. God help me, I know that all too well."

Because I spent that entire monsoon season in Indochina, trying not to let the rain remind me of Kentucky mountains and make me escape into a bullet.

"Gareth, it would be my fault if—" she persisted.

He gave her the only escape he'd ever found which worked for any time.

He snatched her into his arms and kissed her with a man's hunger, heedless of any shyness she might still have. She stilled, her hands fluttering on his arms like butterflies, before she tentatively held on.

He kissed her again, stroking her with his mouth, sharing his need, drowning her in hunger and desperation, where nothing existed but passion. Thought had no place here, only the body's demands—and somehow an instinctive recognition of the other person with him.

She made an indistinct noise deep in her throat. Her lips opened under his and her tongue matched his. She softened to match his angle, surged to meet him.

His skin heated, blood rocking through as if it could leap across to her veins.

Her slender fingers lightly caressed his head, like angel's wings.

"Portia." By God, he wanted more. He pushed her back onto the divan and undid her tea gown, his fingers fumbling at the tiny buttons like a boy. Him, who'd undressed dozens of concubines and bored matrons.

Silk ripped, short and sharp and rough, like the sound of their breathing above the seagulls' sibilant cries.

His cock thrust against his pants like a wild beast, desperate to find sanctuary between her white limbs.

She wrapped her leg around him and lifted her hips, needy little sounds breaking from her throat. She smelled of sweet cream and salty musk, woman and spring and homecoming.

And absolutely not his future.

With his last remnant of sanity, he forced himself to find a condom and rolled it onto his now-free cock.

He pushed her skirts aside and tested her with his hand. Wet, more than wet enough, yet he lingered to pleasure her and tease her.

"Gareth, please!"

He rolled her onto her back and knelt between her legs. God help him, she threw one leg over his hip.

He lifted her hips and plunged into her, tormenting himself with possessing her utterly, as if he owned her, as if she'd always belong to himself alone, as if she was his past, his present, and his future. As if the sweet sheath clamping down on his cock was meant to welcome him.

And he rode her like a madman, seeking only wild pleasure for them both.

She gave it back to him, hurling herself up at him, sinking her fingers into his shoulders and rubbing her legs over him.

It was too much—and he came far too soon, shouting her name like a teenage boy. His seed bolted out of his loins as if the only safe haven was her body, wrenching him apart in a series of long paroxysms. He hung suspended, somewhere in midair, ecstatic—and appalled that Portia Townsend could tear his world apart.

He barely had wits enough to fondle her pearl and ensure she too would find rapture.

Holding onto her afterward felt like grasping the greatest risk of his life.

He panted, sweat congealing on his skin like glue to bind them together. He began to count the seconds until he could speak soberly again.

Her slender fingers slipped up his chest in a trail of fire to unbutton his shirt.

And his mindless cock promptly swelled against her thigh, as if it hadn't shattered every tenet he'd laid for conducting his life.

But why the hell not? They'd only be married for a week or two at the most.

He tilted her chin up and refused to consider the starved hunger which went into his kiss.

Chapter Twenty-seven

"Thank you, Gareth." Portia sat down in the carriage and tried to keep her words polite. Years of striving to achieve perfection as an always disciplined British countess was no help at all when faced with the man who'd made her body ache in so many wonderful ways. She'd never realized she could be stiff and want to become even more so.

Or look at the cause—and hunger to touch more of the man under the fine clothing. Such as his big hands, which had so easily lifted her for his thrusts last night and eased her onto the quay this morning.

Gareth sat down beside her and sent the high-strung vehicle rocking. She flung her hand out for balance and it landed on his leg—his big, muscular thigh which had so wonderfully propelled her into ecstasy only a few hours earlier.

She hastily snatched her hand back and silently cursed her fingers' lamentable tendency to linger. A quick tug on both of her short kid gloves hopefully discouraged any further tendencies toward impetuosity.

Fondling Gareth in any manner whatsoever would be dreadfully embarrassing, since Kerem Ali Pasha's son Adem now sat directly opposite them, ready to assume his duties as guide.

He'd leaped at the opportunity to escape his mother's fond clucking. He undoubtedly saw this simple bit of sightseeing as an opportunity to show his superior officers he was ready to return to duty. He could have served as an artist's model for a dangerous young commander, even if their destination was the royal palace.

The clear blue sky hung lazy and welcoming overhead, as if nobody could ever wish ill to this country or want to attack stealthily. The Bosporus flowed steadily south, its waves shifting quietly as desert sand dunes. The Old City glowed under the great mosques' minarets and domes, like a set of treasure boxes—or scorpion nests. Gareth had flatly refused to take her there, calling it too dangerous.

Their carriage stood on the eastern side, on the great road running north beside the ocean. Forests of Judas trees, vibrant with pink flowers, flowed up the hillsides behind them.

Portia leaned to see where Kerem Ali Pasha's yali lay to the west, on the Asian side. Her breast brushed against Gareth's arm like an arpeggio's completion.

Even through her severe, dark blue dress, a jolt ran through her, stronger and sweeter than a lightning strike.

She shivered and tried to pull away. But Gareth captured her hand, trapping her against him.

"Do you see the yali?" he asked, in that deep, infinitely seductive drawl.

"Yes, of course," she answered and tried to yank her fingers free. "It's the pink one, a little northeast of us."

"It was a gift to my grandfather from the old Sultan," Adem volunteered. "He was the Chief Secretary, in the days when Topkapi was still the Sultan's palace."

"If you look south, toward Hagia Sophia and the harbor, Topkapi Palace is on the promontory." Gareth was watching her face more than the sights.

Portia eagerly swiveled in her seat, trying to overlook the warm hand holding onto her.

"It's spectacular." She turned a little farther, her attention caught by the ships riding at anchor. Dozens of rowboats filled the waters like iridescent beetles, while their larger brethren, the caiques, paddled steadily onward like swans. Small merchant ships swarmed close to Hagia Sophia's hill, like grubby workmen resting from a hard day's work.

All of which made the great, white ship in their midst look like an eagle amid a gaggle of pigeons and sparrows.

"What on earth is the *Phidaleia* doing here?"

"Which ship?" Gareth swung around to follow her gaze.

"HMS *Phidaleia*. She's Britain's newest armored cruiser."

Speaking the blatant truth sent ice diving from her lips into her gut. Had the warship come to help St. Arles?

She sank back into her seat and tried to chase her skittering thoughts. If the Royal Navy thought highly enough of his plots to back him with one of their best ships . . .

"Armored cruiser?" Gareth queried, his tone far too soft.

"Ten six inch guns plus six torpedo tubes. She's fully armored but can make seventeen knots, with a crew of almost five hundred." She gripped his hand hard, desperate for comfort.

He turned his palm up and locked their grasps, silently uniting them.

The carriage was trotting past an enormous palace, built of glittering white marble. Surely even the most extravagant sultan would not have inlaid his walls with gold or carved them in fantastical shapes like a cross between Versailles and the Arabian Nights.

"You're very familiar with her and her type," Gareth observed. His voice was all Kentucky drawl now, which meshed oddly with French words. He must be thinking hard.

"St. Arles is a former naval officer. He only left Britain's senior service to take up the title when his brother died." How little he disguised his homesickness for those days, too. "We spent considerable time with his naval friends."

"On board their ships?"

"Yes, but not the *Phidaleia*," she answered Gareth's unspoken question. "She was only launched a few months ago and is the Admiralty's pride."

"She's here to pay Great Britain's respects to the Sultan,"

Adem announced cheerily, deliberately ignoring their tension. "Next Friday is the Night of Absolution, when Almighty Allah forgives all his creation. Except for a very few of the lowest scum, who we will not soil your ears with, gracious lady."

His manicured fingers dismissed those vermin like an executioner flinging aside decapitated skulls.

"Is it a festival?"

"It's one of the five nights, or *kandili*, when the mosques are lit with candles," Gareth said brusquely, his mind clearly elsewhere.

"We will pray and lament in the cemeteries for our departed friends and relations," Adem contributed. "Then we return home, where the elders receive the younger people. There are special foods served, especially desserts to celebrate the dead who walk among us that night."

"Ah yes, it reminds me of how my grandmother's relatives decorate the family graves outside Louisville." Her shoulders eased and she started to relax, pleased she understood at least a little of this unusual country.

"The Sultan always lights the first candle. It's one of the very few occasions on which he does not attend the mosque next to the palace." Gareth rapidly drummed his fingers on the carriage's rim.

Portia's heart slammed into her throat.

St. Arles had five chances every year to attack the Sultan—and one occurred next Friday? When a top British warship just happened to be in town to support him?

May God have mercy on the Turks, they didn't know what was about to happen. But how could she tell them? She had no proof; a trunk full of gold was not a sin.

The great marble palace gave way to verdant gardens bordered by the blue ribbon of the Bosporus. Another white palace rose on the opposite shore, as if transported from Renaissance Italy. Two fantastical tents rose beside the water, almost as if fairies had recreated a genie's pavilions into stone.

A ferry steamed past, promiscuously scattering cinders and

fragments of conversation. Two fishermen struggled with a heavy net and a small boat, pulled ever closer to shore by the strong current.

A new palace appeared ahead, standing tall and proud beside the water. White marble like the others, it was carved into narrow, vertical blocks. From a distance, they could have been filled with windows or giant steel bars, despite their fanciful carved frames. A great marble terrace surrounded it, edged by dozens of armed guards.

"What is that building?" Portia raised herself up to get a better view.

"Don't look at it!" Gareth wrapped his arms around her, heedless of Moslem prohibitions on displaying affection in public, and pulled her face against him. "For God's sake, Portia, they'll arrest you if you so much as glance at the windows."

"Gareth, don't be silly." She tried to pull away from him but manacles would have been more flexible. "You're crushing the feathers in my hat."

"Mrs. Lowell, the previous sultan, Murad V, is imprisoned in Chiragan Palace," hissed Adem from barely a foot away.

Portia's fingers dug into Gareth's arms, this time for stability in a spinning world.

"If Murad is still alive," she fumbled for phrases to express her horror.

"He must be," Gareth said with an experienced street fighter's brutal assurance, "else Abdul Hamid would never waste so much effort to guard him."

"And he still has a stronger claim to the throne than his successor." Years of curtsying and biting her tongue under diplomatic protocol had taught her how to read the nuances of court politics.

"Any revolutionary could use him as a puppet to bless their radical ideas—or sign treaties with a foreign government, if they held him," Adem added. Passionate entreaty to understand his country's pain wracked his voice. "He could even invite foreign warships to use his harbor to attack another country."

Dear God in heaven. Or rather, may Allah have mercy upon the Turkish people.

Portia's head fell back and she stared into Gareth's glacier gray eyes.

"Do you understand now?" His thumbs rubbed her shoulders lightly, offering a smidgen of comfort.

"Of course." She patted his lapels back into place, careful to look nowhere else. He released her and she returned to her previous seat. This time, she sat straight and proud, haughty as any dowager duchess who'd ever snubbed an American heiress.

"If we're not supposed to cast our eyes upon it," she remarked and flickered a single glance sideways, "what happens to anybody who sets foot on it?"

"Immediate arrest," Gareth said simply.

"That's not too dreadful, is it?"

"And interrogation." Adem seemed to be deeply involved in counting Judas trees far away from the palace. "There's a dungeon below stairs, so matters can begin immediately. The Superintendent is the best in the Empire."

"Dear God," Gareth whispered. His Adam's apple plunged up and down in his strong throat, like a prisoner tearing at close-set bars.

One of the fishermen cursed and cut his net free with an immense knife. Silvery fish flashed out of the water then dived into the Bosporus's blue depths. His fellow dropped onto the bench and began to row rapidly, the muscles of his back bunching and pulling against his thin shirt. Steering did not seem to be important, only speed.

The first man turned his back to the palace, now only a few boat lengths away. He dropped onto the other seat and, soon, he too was rowing hard.

"How much money did they lose?" Portia wondered, her heart aching. "All those fish and their net, too."

"The seas will offer more mackerel and bass tomorrow." Adem's mouth was a thin line, despite his words' insouciance.

"They also have their lives." Gareth shoved his long legs hard against the carriage's frame. "Unlike Murad, who still had music left to write."

Portia closed her eyes. She might have refused to help St. Arles—but that didn't mean he couldn't find another way to cause trouble.

Chapter Twenty-eight

"What beautiful tulips!" Portia exclaimed, more than willing to feast her eyes and soul on innocent delights. "Hyacinths and daffodils, too! You never mentioned them to me."

She tried to glare accusingly at Gareth. It was difficult when all she wanted to do was turn around and stare out the window again at Yildiz Palace's glorious gardens. So many tall panes of glass allowed the midday sunlight to pour in, until the garden seemed only a breath away.

"They are beautiful, aren't they?" Adem agreed smugly. "My father says our Sultan kept the best of the old hunting park when he built only a small palace—"

"Small?" muttered Gareth.

"Plus scattered pavilions for himself and key government functions," Adem finished, and made only the smallest of rude gestures at Gareth.

"It's truly, truly lovely." Portia sighed happily. "Thank you for bringing us to this isolated corner. After traveling in Egypt's deserts, these gardens are especially wonderful."

"Anything to make a lady happy." Adem bowed, adding a flourish he must have learned in France.

She strongly suspected he'd actually brought them there to show off the room's martial decorations. But she nodded back to him and returned to happily eyeing the spectacular blooms. Even this wilder section must be tended by an army of gardeners, to achieve such perfection.

This pavilion at Yildiz Palace was part of the administrative offices, not the Sultan's personal quarters. The second floor room was apparently designed as a minor functionary's office but dusty and unused at the moment. Even so, the walls were elegantly paneled and the doors so beautifully made that it was hard to see where one began and the other ended.

The room's biggest distinction was the knives and daggers spiraling around the corner pillar like scorpions on the alert. Centuries and continents had combined to build the collection into spikes and curves, a rippling river of potential murder from Asia to Africa, Europe to America.

Gareth walked his fingers up to another sharp-edged toy and slid sideways, wiping his reflection from the window in front of her.

Portia rolled her eyes. Gareth would probably still be playing with knives in his coffin.

"What do you think of them?" Having satisfied his excuse for being here, Adem headed toward his friend. "Have you seen all of these before?"

The door slammed open, banging against the wall like a drum. Almost simultaneously, another door slid open in the paneled wall like a glimpse into hell.

A half dozen, masked young men poured into the room. They had the thick muscular bodies of men willing and able to use their strength, not cheapened by wealth or alcohol.

Adem whirled to face them. Before he could even shout, two of them charged him and brutally, efficiently, knocked him out with small wooden clubs.

Her skin froze onto her bones.

"Portia! To me!" Gareth was free of the pillar, a weapon flashing in each hand.

Her feet took her to him, not her mind. Safely behind his back, her heart slamming against her chest, she tried to think.

She could help. She had to help. But how? Attack some-body—but with what? Call for help—but who would hear?

"What do you want?" Gareth was speaking French, his tone as rigidly precise as an executioner's blade.

She had to watch so she slowly turned around, grateful her walking dress didn't drag on the floor to kick up much noise.

"Give us the trunk and we'll let you live," ordered the one wearing a red mask.

"If I do not?" Gareth sounded calmer than when he was cutting cheese.

"We will kill you then seize the woman and the trunk."

"Oh no, you won't, my friends." Gareth shook his head slowly. His expression hadn't changed at all.

"You are only a puny westerner and we outnumber you six to one. You have no hope of defeating us."

"What do you know of me?" Gareth countered—and spun the knife and tomahawk in his hands. Her bowie knife, which she'd given him so many years ago, and a tomahawk snatched from the wall. Bright blades flashed in front of his fingers then came to rest once again, ready to kill.

Only long familiarity would permit that move. He'd marked his turf and announced how nastily he could defend it.

Their attacker stared at the tomahawk's broad head, good for both crushing and cutting. Several of his followers backed up a step.

"The chest is our path to the future." Their chief attacker snapped his shoulders back and popped a knife out of his sleeve. "We will do whatever is needed to obtain it."

"Blood feud?" Gareth inquired. Icy shadows lurked in his eyes.

Portia's knees were shaking. He didn't sound or look as if he cared, at least not for himself.

One attacker crept closer to him and Gareth whirled his tomahawk over his finger toward the fool.

The young man froze, his eyes very wide. Then he slid back into place, tidy as a sardine tin being returned to the cupboard.

"Blood feud," the leader asserted and sneered at Gareth. "You westerners know nothing of the fighting which comes from the heart, not the mind. If it takes every man in my clan, we will win."

"You can try." Gareth's lips curved into something a shark would have admired. "When you do, be sure to remember I come from two centuries of war between tribes. When I was twelve, I saw my mother and sisters burned alive—yet I alone survived."

Portia's heart wrenched in two. She started to reach toward him to comfort him then yanked her hand back.

Oh, my poor darling, no wonder you never talked about your parents.

"I killed every murderous bastard in the other family and became my clan's only survivor." For the first time, Gareth's expression turned lambent with the need to fight. "I was adopted by a far greater clan of warriors, to which this lady belongs."

Appalled realization swept through their enemies' eyes and made more than a few feet shuffle.

Gareth's chuckle held more anticipation than mirth.

Dear God, she couldn't allow him to be hurt.

Portia frantically looked around once again.

"You are welcome to try to kill me."

Surely Gareth didn't want them to, no matter how careless his shrug.

"Even if you do, I will take many of you with me to my grave—then laugh when her family tramples on your remnants."

Portia snatched a massive bronze lamp off the desk next to her and hurled it through the window, which exploded into a glittering cascade.

Two uniformed gardeners strolling past outside, with baskets for flower cuttings, looked up in amazement.

She shrieked, hurling her terror for Gareth into the note.

The men yelled something in Turkish at her then ran toward the building.

Their chief attacker glared at her then saluted both her and Gareth with his knife. An instant later, he and his band disappeared as invisibly as they'd entered.

Only Adem, barely stirring on the floor, proved the thugs had existed.

Plus, the sickening lurch in Portia's stomach whenever she remembered how Gareth had terrified even those brutes.

Chapter Twenty-nine

Gareth rubbed the back of his neck and reluctantly studied the bathroom again. Logic said he had to leave Portia alone sometimes, such as now. The prospect made his gut turn itself inside out, faster than anything from the Apaches.

Worse was the certainty that mentioning his mother's and sisters' deaths out loud was always followed by nightmares, not that his problems mattered tonight.

Portia's courage that afternoon simply made him want to cherish her more. She'd never screamed, turned hysterical, fainted—done any of the nonsensical tricks a girl had a right to pull when faced with six armed kidnappers. She'd been as brave and quick-witted as ever.

Damn, she'd even been the one who'd defeated the brutes. Maybe someday he'd laugh when he remembered how their expressions had looked when the window shattered. For now, his hands were still shaking at how close she'd come to dying. They could never have afforded to let her live, once they had the chest.

Christ, what the hell would he do without her?

She'd always been important to him, but he'd spent years thinking of her as William Donovan's niece. Now she was more important than what little soul he had left.

Ice scuttled over his skin, faster than any poisonous scorpion.

He passed his hand over his eyes and sank into the tub, letting the silly bubbles splash over his knees and chest. Kerem Ali Pasha's bathroom had enough marble on the walls and floors to allow a herd of elephants to splash without harming anything.

Maybe the hot water would relax him. It would certainly remove the reek of fear.

Gulls sang to each other in the distance about twilight and last meals. Water splashed against the yali, in a siren call to take a boat and go somewhere, anywhere else. Europe, Algeria, Indochina, even back to Arizona where he'd ruined her life.

He'd always run whenever anybody got too close. But he couldn't do so now, not when St. Arles was still in town, hunting Portia.

Somebody scratched on the door and he frowned. "Enter."

"Hullo." Portia cautiously poked her head inside the room. "May I come in?"

He started to sit up, caught a draft on his belly, and shoved his hips back under the scented water. His eager cock complained vehemently, more interested in shoving its heated length into her than in frivolities such as the air temperature.

"Would you like some wine? It's a good Riesling, the same vintage we always drank in Arizona." She offered a silver ice bucket on a tray with two glasses. More importantly, he'd swear she wore nothing underneath her silk kimono.

His heartbeat lurched into a fascinated trot.

Her smile came and went between her small teeth nibbling on her lower lip.

He dragged some air into his lungs and tried to regain his wits.

"Of course I would." He waved vaguely toward a corner or two. "Please have a seat and join me."

"Thank you." She carefully set down the tray on the small rolling cart beside the tub. A moment later, she sat down beside him on a stool originally meant for servants.

She poured the wine with the concentrated attention of someone who'd rarely done so, measuring the exact angle from the bottle's lip to the glass as if one false move could send a fountain pouring onto the floor.

Her frown called to him to be kissed away. He closed his eyes and recited long-forgotten multiplication tables.

"Here you are."

His eyes snapped open to find the fragile crystal only inches away from his fingers. "Thank you."

"Did I do it right?"

He almost dropped the delicious beverage into his bath. How the devil could she do it wrong, assuming nothing broke?

"You did it perfectly." He tried to fill his voice with the same robust assurance he'd give a tenderfoot just starting to learn how to drive an eighteen mule hitch.

"You didn't watch."

Her foot swung back and forth, betraying her naked calf. Good God almighty, she truly was wearing nothing underneath the kimono except possibly a chemise.

His chest tightened as if baked in the devil's own oven.

How did he tell her that if he had observed her, she'd be in the tub with him right now, soaking wet and very thoroughly fucked?

He opted for tact and discussing only her question, not his endless hungers.

"You were just as slick as when you told the Sultan's guards this afternoon our attackers were radical revolutionaries, determined to make an example of the old office."

"It was the first excuse I thought of." She flushed and hid her face.

"They believed you."

"Especially when you mentioned Adem's valiant defense of the Ottoman crest."

"Which he was clever enough not to deny, thank God," Gareth agreed. "After he finally came round, that is."

"Making him the true hero." She took another sip of wine. Her kimono slipped down her sweating shoulder, revealing bare skin.

No chemise at all.

Most of his wits dived for his cock and started a raucous clamor to taste her.

He gulped his wine and tried to remember when dinner would be served. Would they be interrupted?

What would Portia think if he tried to seduce her? She certainly seemed to have enjoyed last night, although they hadn't discussed it. Or had he behaved too much like St. Arles?

"Of course, you were the true hero this afternoon," she remarked. Her eyes trapped his, blue as diamonds, blue as truth, blue as hope. "Just the way you were back in Arizona, when you knocked me out to save my life."

He could only stare at her. His heart was caught like his breathing, somewhere between now and forever.

"I'm sorry. I wish I'd told you that long ago, when I first realized it."

He managed to shake his head, refusing to step onto a new path.

"I knew before I left on my wedding journey with St. Arles."

"But I didn't stop you." The damning words hung in the air yet again, as they'd haunted so many nightmares.

Her eyes were soft with forgiveness. "You couldn't save me from myself. Nobody could."

She planted little kisses along his forehead and the bridge of his nose, like a gardener cherishing his favorite fields in the springtime.

Then her mouth found his, awkwardly at first.

Shock that she'd be this generous froze him in place.

She angled her head and shaped her lips to match his. Her breath melted into his, warm and spicy like life itself.

He caught her by the shoulders and claimed her.

His tongue swept deep. She gave a low moan and moved

closer still, rubbing herself against him. He scooped her into his arms and held her tight against his heart. His chest was rising and falling faster than when he'd fought Victorio's army.

She was all hot, wet, living silk, branding him with life and femininity everywhere she touched—from her fingers threading through his hair to his scalp, to her breath sighing his name against his cheek when he turned his head to nuzzle her throat, to her breasts plumping to fill the crook of his arm.

Dear Lord, how her kimono thinned into transparency then dived off her shoulder when wet. How could a man resist such a display of fragrant temptations, especially when they belonged to his wife?

His wife, the only one he'd ever have. For the few days or weeks their marriage would last, she was his alone.

He yanked her sash open and was fiercely grateful he hadn't had to exert force on the supple fabric. God forbid he frighten his darling in any way.

"Ah, Gareth." Her fingernails scratched his shoulder until they drew a few crimson drops.

Hunger surged deep, stampeding his blood through his veins. He rolled her out of the tub and onto the floor, landing on the mat with a splash that sent water cascading across the marble.

Portia stared down at him, her blue eyes enormous with excitement—or fear?

Gareth paused, still holding her by the waist. He would never use force—but, damn, how he needed her.

Mischief teased her mouth.

He frowned, his cock still straining to reach her.

Both hands on his shoulders, she leisurely undulated down his front. Every movement's friction forced open her kimono more and more until she was completely naked. Her nipples were small, fiery diamonds firing his lungs into cauldrons of lust, her supple ribs continually caressed his core, and her belly—Dear God, his cock rested against her belly in the smug assurance it would be warm inside.

Still holding his eyes, she rocked her hips against him again, painting herself with his dripping shaft.

He bit down on his lip hard enough to draw blood, forcing pain so he wouldn't seize her.

"There are condoms in the cart." She caressed his cheek. "If you still want one."

She was willing to take the chance of a child?

The habits of a lifetime sent his hand into motion long before his brain caught up.

Her eyes flickered and she silently shifted to give him room.

But he couldn't read her expression, didn't give himself time to, before he'd rolled the damn contraption on.

She wrapped her hand around his shaft an instant after he'd tied the condom on.

He strangled himself with his own breath.

She pumped him a little, very gently. "Do you like that?"

"Hell, yes!"

She chortled softly, her eyes dark. While he'd been donning the preventative, she'd doffed the silk robe to become more enticing than ever. Her breasts were cream and rose confections, tipped with nipples perfectly formed to be suckled. Her waist was a narrow enticement above her mons' golden curls and her legs' long ivory lengths.

Ah, the hours he could spend exploring new ways to tumble her into ecstasy using every inch of those delights . . .

He slid his hands over her hips and allowed himself to blatantly enjoy her sweet rump's curve.

She arched her back and purred—then squeezed him lightly.

Blood and seed lunged upward to meet her.

"Portia, how long do you want me to remain polite?" Amazing that he could still speak.

"I don't."

Truth blazed in her eyes, a step behind hunger.

He flipped her under him and she clung, warm and completely willing. Mouth met mouth once again in a mating dance older than time, truer than recriminations or apologies. None of that mattered, not anymore, not with her sweetness to keep the nightmares at bay.

He knelt above her and she spread her legs, stroked his back, arched her hips to make his possession easier.

His woman, his.

He surged into her and their bodies knotted together like a lock and key.

His blood screamed at him yet his heart told him to stay precisely here.

Time could stand still for only so long.

"Gareth." Her voice was a beacon in the night.

He began to move, slowly at first then faster and faster. She hissed at him to hurry and gripped his back in ecstasy. Lust perfumed the air and sang in the heavy music of their bodies straining against each other.

His finger found Portia's back entrance and she shouted in startled delight. Ecstasy seized her and her inner muscles clamped down on him, irresistibly demanding that he too tumble over the precipice.

He gave himself willingly, spinning into an exuberant orgasm that pummeled his senses like running the rapids. He extravagantly shot his seed into Portia's warm depths again and again.

Afterwards, he had barely enough sense to carry her to bed and tumble in to join her. Thinking about what had happened, especially what she knew of his background, was a nightmare more distant than those her sweet loving had banished for the moment.

God forbid those specters—of all the men he'd hunted down like animals, because that was the only way to slay his family's killers—didn't visit him tonight. He didn't want to wake up screaming with a red mist clouding his eyes and crimson dripping from his fingers.

Not here, not now, now with delicate Portia who'd already endured so much.

He turned his face into her hair and inhaled her scent, pure and fresh, inescapably hers.

She muttered something and her hand clutched at his hip, pulling him closer. Their lungs matched, sending air back and forth between them like the gift of life.

Obscurely comforted, he crept into sleep as if he was pulling a blanket roll around himself—pleased to be there and praying not to be disturbed.

Chapter Thirty

"We simply have to tell the authorities the truth." Portia set her shoulder against the door from the bedroom to the salon. "Somebody around here must be reliable enough to trust."

"I doubt it." Gareth tweaked his bowtie until it lay perfectly straight across his collar. When he raised his chin like that, she could see his strong jaw and chin muscles, but not the purplish bruise her teeth had left on his neck. That mark—and its brethren!—were hidden by his starched white shirt and collar.

Need sparkled through her, fierce and bright with the urge to touch him again, despite how often she'd held him last night. He'd woken her up more than once, raging with hunger for her, then slept equally fiercely with her.

She desperately folded her hands behind her back and fumbled for the latch. "We can ask Kerem Ali Pasha," she proposed. "Or I can sound out his wife or daughter. Women often notice items that men do not."

"You can try." He dropped his vest down his arms to where it molded itself onto his broad shoulders.

Why did she keep imagining him without any clothing when she'd enjoyed him so well a few hours ago? Or with his vest but no shirt, to tease her all the better by glimpses of his powerful chest? None of her teenage dreams had burned quite like this. And the Church strongly encouraged a wife to seek the company of her spouse.

Her husband who would leave in a few days or weeks.

"Thank you." She threw her weight against the portal's iron restraint and burst through into the salon.

"But not now, Portia," he ordered in the same instant.

Her few stumbling steps took her into the center of the great gathering place, lit by morning sunlight filtered through the garden's graceful trees and slatted windows. It shimmered on the rose-pink silk pleated over the ceiling and the graceful silk rug in matching shades of cream, gold, and pink. The walls were painted with soft murals of village life along the Bosporus, turning them into a radiant reflection of the world outside. Velvet and silk upholstered the divans, while the low tables had been polished until their brass and carved woodwork gleamed more than the textiles. A circular candelabra hung overhead, like a wrought iron spider web hung with glass bowls at regular intervals to offer flames.

She'd seen its loveliness before whenever she'd gone in and out of the harem. But she'd never thought much about it, except to wonder a little why so much money had been spent on a room used only to connect the men's and women's quarters with the outdoors.

She jerked herself to a stop in the middle of Kerem Ali Pasha's family gathering place. Three generations—or four, if she counted Adem's baby son—looked back at her with varying degrees of surprise. It was the first time she'd seen the beating heart of his family.

Small secretary desks and sheets of paper were scattered at every seat, accompanied by fountain pens and ink.

Horror ran livid across Adem's wife's face but Kerem Ali Pasha's mother looked as if she was studying a new chess piece.

"I'm sorry," Portia stammered and dropped a curtsy. She hadn't done anything this clumsy since finishing school.

"My wife has seen nothing." Gareth caught her by the arm. "I swear she cannot read your writing to understand what you have said."

Dear heavens, he sounded almost terrified and yet these people were his old friends. The women had freely showed their unveiled faces to him before, marking him as an intimate connection to their household.

Kerem Ali Pasha climbed slowly onto his feet, flanked by his two sons. Their faces were as stern as if they stood in an armory, surrounded by soldiers with naked blades, rather than at their home beside their wives and children.

"I apologize for any disturbance we may have caused." Gareth bowed formally, lowering his head almost in submission. "We will leave now and never speak of this incident."

What incident? Portia started to glance up at him but his fingers dug into her like talons. She dropped another, deeper curtsy to underline her complete agreement with her husband, even if she didn't understand why they were making the bargain.

Saril, Kerem Ali Pasha's mother, spoke briefly and arrogantly in Turkish, without taking her eyes away from Portia.

Kerem Ali Pasha argued vehemently but a brief spurt of words, sharp as a butcher's knife, silenced him.

He turned back to the two Americans, his expression an intriguing mix of anticipation and nervousness. "You are our guests. More importantly, you saved my son's life yesterday."

Adem inclined his head. His countenance had settled into a soldier's unreadable mask.

"That makes you family—and welcome to stay as you please," Kerem Ali Pasha finished on an emphatic note. "But as family, we ask that you keep family matters within the bosoms of your own robes."

"Certainly we will," Portia agreed, her words mingling with Gareth's assurance.

"Please sit down if you wish," Saril offered, indicating a

corner of one divan. "I'd thought we might see you this morning, since you enjoy the gardens so much."

"Thank you." Portia folded her skirts around her legs as tidily as possible, grateful her bustle was far smaller than most. Gareth sat down beside her, wary as a cougar in a rattlesnake den. "Everything I've seen of Constantinople's gardens has been delightful."

"I hope you won't let yesterday's alarm scare you off." Kerem Ali Pasha resumed his former seat.

"No, of course not." She wouldn't leave until she was sure her former servants were safe from St. Arles' malice or his capacity for mischief here was blunted.

"I was shocked members of a secret society could enter Yildiz Palace." Adem's wife Meryem leaned forward, her sleeping babe's innocence a fascinating contrast to her avid interest in dangerous mayhem.

"An isolated corner, never used by the Sultan, at a former hunting lodge?" Saril harrumphed and drove her pen through the last line like a dagger through the heart. "Not impossible to achieve, although I'm sure you'd never have seen the like at Topkapi Palace in my grandfather's day."

"Grandfather?" Portia whispered.

The matriarch overheard, of course.

"My mother was an Ottoman princess and my grandfather was a great sultan. The empire was twice as large in his day and dreaded to the northern seas." She sighed, the brilliance in her eyes fading slightly, and exchanged her letter for the sleeping infant.

Royalty? Yet she'd always treated Portia with great kindness, unlike the more snobbish British aristocrats.

"Could you manage a similar attack at Chiragan Palace?" Gareth asked and poured a cup of Turkish coffee for Saril.

"Never. A fish couldn't land unnoticed on that marble slab." Kerem Ali Pasha handed his writing to Meryem as well.

"It's why the attack on Yildiz Palace was so easy to accomplish," Adem supplied. "So many soldiers guard Chiragan and the Sultan personally that there's little to spare for other places."

"Plus, many of the barracks are outside Constantinople. It would take time for troops to respond to an attack." Kahil finished the longest speech Portia had ever heard from him. Then he handed his and his mother's letters to his sister-in-law.

"It's fantasy to believe those men would be of much use, exactly like the fiction we just wrote." The soldier slammed his cup down onto the saucer.

"Adem!" Meryem hissed and flung out her hand to her husband. Papers spun like accusing fingers across the floor.

"Fiction?" Portia questioned, fascinated. "Are you writing a novel together?"

Silence fell, like an executioner's axe.

"We should leave, honey," Gareth announced and came to his feet.

"No, although we've created enough words to supply a book." Saril looked around the room at her descendants. "I, for one, am tired of this sickening nonsense. Let us be honest with people who have known only truth and justice."

Gareth's hand tightened hard on Portia's shoulder but she knew better than to speak.

"They would know *everything*," Meryem whispered.

"Who would believe them? Does anyone care what is fact or fiction, so long as it does not affect the Sultan?" Saril retorted. "You are the novelist; you know how to spin tales so nobody trusts them."

"It would feel like opening a window and letting the sea breeze blow through our lives, before we are caught again in our unhappiness." Kerem Ali Pasha seemed to have aged five years in as many seconds. "Gareth Lowell has always proven himself above reproach. We have treated him as a son of this house for years. Let us openly tell him what he has undoubtedly already guessed."

He flapped his hands brusquely at Gareth, urging him to sit down.

Gareth obeyed slowly, reluctance written in every line.

"My family and I are writing our regular spy reports," Saril announced and rubbed the baby's back.

"Spy reports?" Portia's mouth fell open. She looked from one person to another, totally baffled.

"Who could you be spying on? You don't seem to know any criminals." *Or potential traitors like myself.*

"We spy on each other." Kerem Ali Pasha's lips folded into a thin line. "I on my wife and her in return, my sons on each other—as well as on me. Plus, my daughter spies on me, my wife, her husband."

"And her brother-in-law," Saril added, then cooed at the baby again.

"You sound as if such behavior is entirely to be expected!" Portia stared at the old woman.

"Such is the pass to which we have been brought by our current Sultan." Loathing ran deep in her voice, like butcher knives lurking in a kitchen drawer.

"That's rather unfriendly," Gareth remarked, his voice shifting into that warning Kentucky drawl. "Some families could turn it into treachery."

"More than one has," snapped Adem, "may Allah have mercy on them."

Would idiots with the customs official's hair trigger temper recognize truth? "Can you afford to be honest?"

"Truth is like a valuable elixir to be doled out in small quantities, lest it be trampled underfoot by swine."

"We write the reports together." Elma, Kerem Ali Pasha's wife, spoke up for the first time. "Meryem ensures that the pieces fit together."

"You have been questioned about our affairs," Gareth commented.

"What of it? We have told them nothing you need concern

yourself about." Kerem Ali Pasha shrugged. "There is no punishment for errors since any spy may tell the truth someday in the future."

That logic was insane enough to make sense.

Tension eased out of Gareth's long fingers.

"And so the very officials charged with stamping out spies"—such as those working with St. Arles—"actually encourage its growth," Portia said furiously.

"Exactly. Everyone in this city is spying on everybody else."

"That's detestable." It sounded like living in a sewer. Facing Apaches on the desert sands would be cleaner, even if just as bloody.

Chapter Thirty-one

In their room Portia cast an uneasy glance sideways through the mirror at Gareth. He'd sworn to guard her but staring through the shutters at the Bosporus for ten minutes straight seemed more abstraction than duty. His white shirt gleamed against the wood like a ghost, bereft of his coat and vest's stolidity.

She held her hand up, silently telling the very efficient Turkish maid to stop brushing her hair.

A conspiratorial gleam entered the girl's eyes, making Portia's conscience squirm uncomfortably. Even so, she winked back in agreement and waggled her fingers to say goodbye. Some things weren't worth arguing about, especially with somebody who didn't speak English.

The girl bobbed a curtsy and slipped silently outside. She eased the door into place behind her like a feather falling onto sand.

"Adem's family is very brave," Portia commented. A moment's thought convinced her to step out of her drawers—oh, scandalous sensations—and leave her dressing gown unbuttoned. She advanced cautiously toward Gareth, wondering what troubled him.

"Being forced to spy on each other, simply because they're important and well-known, must be horrifying. Yet they still use it to bring themselves together."

"By plotting their tales at the same time." Gareth finally turned to her, his expression shadowed against the setting sun.

"If anyone catches them doing that." Portia held out her hands to him, unconsciously begging for reassurance.

He caught them but didn't pull her close this time. "That's very unlikely, especially since the old pasha has tentacles placed in every major bureaucratic office. His mother's connections are even better."

"All of them used to protect the family." Portia sniffled, feeling slightly chilled. "I almost wish I'd headed west when I left London after the divorce, instead of east."

"Why didn't you?"

"I couldn't tolerate facing any more journalists, or bringing them down upon my family." She pulled a face, amazed she could discuss those days. "I spent months, unable to leave the house without artists running after me to sketch another picture, or reporters desperate to discover my new lover. Nobody would speak to me or even receive a letter."

"Greedy bastards!" Gareth's arms finally wrapped her close to his warmth. "They should have hunted St. Arles and his whore."

She snickered at the image, well aware of its impossibility. "Oh no, all his infidelity was forgiven as an expression of his manliness."

"Hypocritical fools. Did your family help with the American press?"

"No, the American newspapers were as bad as the British. They printed story after story, until my father also had to dodge reporters."

Gareth's expression shuttered, making it impossible to read. She frowned and finished her explanation in a rush.

"I thought if I sailed around the world, those yellow journalists would surely find another story to pursue by the time I reached San Francisco."

"I'm sure they will, and that all of your family will be very comfortable to have you home again."

Did Gareth place the slightest over-emphasis on *all* of her family? If he meant her father, it didn't matter. They'd never be truly close but at least now they could be relaxed together around her brothers.

Was this her chance to bring up Gareth's family? He'd brought up hers within a difficult context.

Wary as a quail creeping onto the desert from under a cactus, she offered him a question.

"Would you be glad to see your own family again? If you could?"

"For the love of God, Portia!" His gaze could have cut her heart out. "My mother and sisters were trapped in our cabin with a half dozen men during a shootout. The sheriff had arranged a truce but instead showed our enemies how to place an ambush."

"The sheriff was involved?"

"We always called him Robin Redbreast for his fancy waistcoats. I had no doubt who led the butchers, not that I didn't know who our enemies were."

"You could see him." Ice flowed through her veins, dragging her back to the moment when his heart had stopped beating.

"We needed food but didn't have many cartridges so I'd been sent fishing. I could see our cabin but couldn't successfully intervene, since I was too far away."

"You must have been frantic." *My poor darling.*

"I ran until my legs knotted and my stomach heaved. But I couldn't reach them in time to stop the sheriff from shooting my father and brother down when they went to tend the fields. That's when everyone else barricaded themselves inside the cabin."

"And the lead started flying."

"Yup. But our old enemy Gunnison was never the patient type so he threw some lighted brands onto the roof. It had been a hot, dry year—"

"The cabin caught fire quickly."

"Too damn fast. The bastards refused to shoot our hogs, saying they were valuable. But they were lying in wait to gun down everyone who tried to make a break out of the door or windows."

She bowed her head, wishing she were an angel to heal his heart. "What happened next?"

"The womenfolk came out first and were butchered before they could make it onto the porch."

Grief, for Gareth and his family, tore through her throat.

"The remaining men used their last shots for themselves. The only reason I could tell the women apart was their heavy calico skirts—because I had to dig their graves."

"Oh, my poor darling." She caught his face and rained little kisses on his jaw, cheek, everywhere she could reach.

"Did you hear everything I said yesterday?" He shackled her wrists with his hands, his grip like hot iron. "I killed Gunnison and all the other men involved. I ended the blood feud *before I turned fourteen.*"

"Good." She stopped struggling to free herself in order to give another consoling salute to that twitching muscle in his cheek. "I hope you shot them down like dogs, the murdering heathens. They shouldn't have burned your family."

She glared at him, almost vibrating with rage and sympathy. To lay such a burden on a young boy was monstrous.

"Portia, I was nothing more than a savage animal myself. I forgot how to plow and tend cattle. All I thought of was death and killing."

"Those men would have slain you, too, if they'd known you were alive."

"I could have walked away." He shrugged impatiently. "By the time I was fourteen, I had more notches on my gun than years under my belt."

Agony staggered her knees for the first time, for all the men he'd killed—and the isolated fourteen-year-old kid who'd done a man's job but paid more than a man's price.

"That doesn't matter to me." Except for the strong desire to burn some ghosts in Hades, the way an ancient Greek would. She rubbed the knotted muscles at the back of his neck for several minutes before she could speak again. "Please, let's go to bed and hold each other, husband."

"Portia!" His bellow almost staggered her and he removed himself from her clasp. "How can you say that, when you know what I am? I will never free myself from the blood on my hands."

Was that what his nightmares were about, all those times he woke up during the night?

"Gareth, please—"

"Do you think I haven't tried? Even the wildest games and the greatest charities haven't helped. I can still see all the men I destroyed." He stopped, his chest heaving.

"You deserve better," he whispered.

But you are mine. The unspoken words echoed through her heart, as they had when she was twelve, the first time she'd seen him. His hair had been windswept and dusted with snow from an early winter storm. He'd looked like an angel—a very special, rugged angel.

She'd fight with every weapon she had to claim her love, no matter what the cost.

"When I was twelve, some coals popped out of the fireplace and landed on my mother's train, catching it on fire." Try as she might, her lips didn't work very well on these sentences. Of course, this was only the first time she'd tried to tell anybody the full story.

"I screamed and tried to put it out with water. But Mother ran and ran as soon as she felt the flames on her legs and back."

"Dear God, Portia." Gareth took a step toward her, linked by the same raw agony which racked her.

"Her dress burned so fast she looked like Fourth of July fireworks." Portia choked back memories of the awful smell.

"Hush, dearest, hush." Gareth rocked her in his arms, his head resting on the top of her head.

"She screamed and screamed until the doctor came with laudanum," Portia whispered into his shoulder's safe haven. "I prayed for her to die so she wouldn't hurt anymore. But she lingered for days. I thought it was my fault."

"Never that, Portia, never that." Ferocity lit his eyes, too savage to be doubted. "You couldn't have stopped those embers, any more than you could have rescued her."

"Are you sure?"

"Completely."

"Then promise me you'll believe you had to obtain justice for your family, because nobody else could."

He hesitated, his eyes flickering to find an escape from the trap she'd set.

"I believe it," she added, providing the strongest seal she could.

"I may believe it was the only road to justice, Portia."

She almost cheered but the hard set of his jaw made her wary.

"But I'm still a man who'll turn killer far too easily. I'm no fit husband for any woman, especially you, because I will never escape that taint."

"You are my dearest friend, Gareth, and have always protected me. We're already married."

"Not for long."

Nightmare glimpses of agony to come racked her bones. Dear heavens, what would she do when he truly took back his ring and the joy of his presence?

She would not let that happen; she could be strong, too, and cunning. She still had a little time to play with and he did care for her, beyond their old friendship.

She would have to use a woman's weapons in this battle, little though she believed in them after her marriage to St. Arles.

Now she would have to open herself up freely and rely solely on what Gareth had taught her about herself in the past few days. It must be successful because it meant everything.

She managed a smile, matched by a hopefully seductive shrug to emphasize her dishabille.

"Do you want to stand in the middle of our bedroom and

argue paperwork? Or would you rather come to bed and play for a few hours until St. Arles proves again that he's an ass?"

"You want to sleep with somebody who's killed so many people?" her husband questioned unsteadily.

"I want to sleep with Gareth Lowell," she corrected him firmly. "The man who makes my pulse melt in anticipation of every hour alone."

Gareth's gaze swept over her once again, like burning silk caressing every inch of her skin. He had to wet his lips before he could speak.

"It would be an honor, ma'am."

Slowly, like the first sight of approaching rain across the desert, he held out his hand.

When he made no move to come closer, she lifted it to her mouth and gently kissed it, rubbing her cheek over his scarred knuckles.

A choked gasp broke from him and she waited hopefully. When he still didn't reach for her, she turned his hand over and laid gentle kisses on each callused fingertip. Finally she drew it against her breast and curved her head over it, until her hair poured protectively over his arm.

He shuddered, like a colt ready to bolt for freedom.

She waited, her breath suspended somewhere between heaven and hell, certain he must be able to feel her heart clamoring for him.

An instant later, his free hand stroked her cheek. The tentative touch sent warmth curling into her throat. She leaned closer to him and his fingers opened up to welcome her. His palm cupped sweetly around her head, rough with calluses yet strong and supple. She was perfectly safe from everything except her own desire for more contact with him.

Humming approval slipped out of her mouth and she nuzzled his fingertips.

"Portia, you are a wicked woman." His voice was hoarser than usual. "Do you know how little sleep we'll have if we spend the night enjoying each other in all the ways I can imagine? For starters, I'd like to lick you all over like a champagne ice, indulgent and intoxicating at the same time."

His every syllable singed her veins until she quivered, her knees barely able to hold her.

"I could drink your kisses' wine for hours," she whispered. "Or stroke myself over you again and again, like a cat who knows where the exact combination of curves and textures always brings ecstasy."

"You temptress." He snatched her to him and she came eagerly. His fingers bit deep into her shoulders but the momentary pain only reminded her of the joy to come. Her heart pounded sweet and strong, her core pulsed fiery hot and wet for him.

"Sweetheart," he growled and his mouth came down on hers.

Surely this night was the harbinger of a bright future together, when St. Arles' plots would be vanquished and Gareth would stay with her.

Somehow.

Chapter Thirty-two

'Abd al-Hamid pounded his fists against the plaster wall, trying to make the cacophony stop before the Italians next door decided to see why Turks were massacring the French language.

Yet still his cousins continued to argue. One would think the sons of donkeys were penned with the beasts, from the way they shouted, instead of merely descended from them.

No wonder his wise uncle—may Allah bless him with many more years—had banished them to the European City to finish their education. Surely it could not have been for any other reason, such as the matters which had driven Abdul's French mother to flee with him to Paris.

He shouted again but could not make his voice heard above the racket.

Finally he gathered his crutches and hobbled into the other room. "Enough! Enough of this, I tell you!"

They fell silent, staring at him as if he were a ghost. As well they should: his visit to the Customs House guards had depleted a bit too much of his vital humors.

"You should be ashamed of yourselves." He waggled his finger at them sternly. The effect was unfortunately marred when his torso started to sway sympathetically on his crutches.

"You should behave with dignity and propriety, as befits members of our honorable clan."

He touched his free foot onto the floor to steady himself. Pain, blinding hot, ricocheted through his leg and into his teeth faster than any festival fireworks. He yelped and wavered.

His giant cousin Areef grabbed his arms and lowered him tenderly into a chair. "You fool, you should not have risen so soon. Tabib, brew more of Grandmother's cordial for him."

Abdul closed his eyes and willed the dizziness to depart faster than their solicitude.

Finally he could turn the warm glass of tea around in his hand without wanting to heave his guts every time he sniffed it. His ankle was carefully propped on pillows, lifting it to a comfortable height above his chair.

Best—or worst—of all, his cousins were clustered around him like stray cats waiting for the farmer's offering to disappear so they could resume their true identities as unlicensed predators.

He rubbed his thumb over the glass's rim.

"Remind me what the trunk's owners look like," he ordered very softly in French.

His cousins stared at each other and not their food.

"I am not entirely stupid and I am certainly not deaf." He assembled them remorselessly with his eyes. "You are determined to obtain a European-made steamer trunk from an American man and woman."

"A British noblewoman!" Tabib corrected before falling silent under Areef's glare.

"Ah." Abdul allowed his teeth to show. "How many women can name themselves both a British noblewoman and American? Does this lady have golden hair like the sun, blue eyes brighter than the Bosporus, and a smile to make the birds sing?"

"What if she does?" Areef slapped his chest. "Foreign women mean nothing to our country's future."

"Only your father was present so you would not know." Abdul slipped into the deadliest legal examiner's voice, used just before final judgment came down. "This one and her man saved me from the guards at the Customs House."

Hideous realization swept over their faces and destroyed their appetites for bread and cheese.

Areef thumped the table, jostling Abdul's leg. But this time, it felt like a call to unity.

"We must set matters aright with her," he declared. "Even so, we cannot go back on the revolution."

Abdul closed his eyes and reminded himself that prayer had many benefits, especially to protect the great-hearted.

"But we will do what we can to protect the woman and her husband," Areef finished.

May Allah grant enough angels to protect all of them from danger.

Still watching Gareth, Portia shoved another button through a loop on her jacket's front—and cursed silently. It too was out of sequence.

Sleeping with the man might have granted her a good night's rest and a delicious rising in the morning. But it also seemed to have freed him from any previous constraints regarding her business affairs.

He was circling St. Arles' trunk, over which they'd draped an embroidered tablecloth. Despite its now innocent appearance, she'd never been able to entirely relax around it. Gareth stalking it like a panther eyeing a wolf's den made her long for her old rifle, rather than more trousseau linens.

She undid every button she'd fastened, considered starting from the beginning, and instead went to her problem's root.

"Why don't you sit down? Or take a walk in the gardens instead? I'll need a few more minutes to finish dressing."

"I thought you trusted me, honey." His left eyebrow lifted a tad.

"Oh, I do but—" She stopped an instant before going too far.

"If you can trust your body to the murderer," he mused, silky as a rifle's polishing cloth, "surely you can at least consider my questions for this item."

"It's very heavy. What else could it contain except gold for bribes?"

"Are you certain? If so, then it's easily replaced. But if not—"

Her mouth went very dry. "It's certainly big and heavy to hold enough sovereigns to buy a new sultan."

"True. But bribes are a dime a dozen in this town. What if St. Arles has something else in mind, something that can't be argued with?"

"Like what?"

"Let's look." He whipped the cloth off and flung it carelessly over the divan. The solid oak trunk stared stolidly back at them, its ink-black straps as remorseless as a rattlesnake's stripes.

"He'll know in an instant if you force the lock." Her voice came out in a wail from the heart. "The metalwork is very freshly painted."

"You already told him you won't assist him. Given that, what does it matter if we pick this lock—or do you worry that he'll hurt your friends even more?"

She hung her head, unable to answer.

"We can't help your friends, honey, until we know what we're fighting against."

"Go ahead," she whispered. "If it's worse than gold, we can't let innocent people get hurt in a revolution, like Kerem Ali Pasha's family."

Gareth lifted each end by the padded strap to test its balance, while Portia pretended nonchalance. Afterward, he squatted down on his heels before it.

"What do you think?" she asked, too unsettled to stay quiet.

"I don't think it's gold. At least, it's not how I'd pack gold." He reached inside his coat and came up with a small roll of silk, unlike any she'd ever seen.

"What is that?" She dropped onto her knees beside him.

"Burglars' tools. Please don't remind your uncle how many I have, okay?"

"Thanks to your misspent youth?" It felt good to smile, however flickering.

"Yup, although I've added to the collection since." He studied the lock and she held her breath, unsure how much success she wanted. Muttering to himself, he finally chose a single iron key and slid it into the lock. He turned it very delicately, there was a loud *click!,* and the trunk seemed to settle back onto its rollers.

Bile touched the back of Portia's throat.

Gareth glanced over his shoulder at her and gripped her hand. She squeezed it back, as ferociously as she could, to tell him that she was in this with him.

He lifted the lid and they looked inside.

"Hell and damnation."

Portia could hardly argue with her husband.

A half dozen Winchester '73 rifles rested comfortably on the tray, custom-made appointments an obscene counterpoint to the cartridges loaded neatly into the tray's center compartment.

The yali's sea-washed murmurings suddenly sounded like souls diving into hell.

Portia dropped her head and tried to recover her wits. "How many men do you think St. Arles plans to equip?" she croaked.

"A dozen rifles plus fifty rounds each." Gareth finished emptying the chest. "Put these lever-action beauties up against the muzzle-loaders the guards are carrying, and you've made a massacre."

She measured one against her arm. "They're all carbines, too. They could be hidden inside a man's coat or robes."

"And still provide the same firepower as a rifle, at least from close range." He shook out a few cartridges into his hand and his face darkened still more.

"We can't tell the Sultan."

"No, even if he believed we were innocent"—Gareth's voice

almost snickered at that possibility—"he'd still leave us dead before he was sure we'd told him everything we knew."

Portia shuddered but didn't argue the point.

"We must get rid of them."

"How? That bastard St. Arles chose very well when he put all the guns in a single trunk. It's damn awkward to move and even harder to conceal. Plus, we don't know when he'll want them back."

"This Friday for the festival?" she suggested.

"Or two weeks later when Ramadan starts. Then he'd have an entire month to overthrow the government, during a time when people are becoming weaker and weaker from fasting."

"Even the guards?"

"The guards are more often Moslem than Christian."

She closed her lips against a protest based on the city's cosmopolitan atmosphere and returned to basics. "Where do you think he plans to use it?"

"An inside attacker somewhere, or perhaps two. These rifles would be lethal at close range."

"Where? How?"

"Mow down the Sultan himself? Inside the Sublime Porte and take over the Grand Vizier's offices? Kill key generals at the barracks before they can stop a revolution?"

"We can't let anything like that occur."

"No."

The rifles sneered.

Chapter Thirty-three

The wind dived and tore Gareth's clothes, fast as a hawk striking at a dove. Sunshine might make the day warm and bright, but it also gave predators far too many advantages.

"It's a beautiful mosque," Portia commented.

"Even more so, on the inside," Gareth agreed absently.

Perhaps if he craned his head a little more, he might spot something which would reveal St. Arles' intentions, here at Constantinople's highest point. Or was he on a fool's errand, looking for clues amid the chaos of an old bazaar quarter?

"To have an ancient Greek church next to it, plus the ruins of another, is grand," Portia cooed in a splendid impersonation of sightseeing awe. "Where else could I see such wonders in one place?"

He grunted an acknowledgement, far more interested in that British warship. Had she moved out into the harbor a little more?

"And this Roman wall." Portia clucked her tongue. "Did it truly stop invaders for more than a thousand years?"

Gareth pulled his attention back from the distant Golden Horn's waters to his very close wife and the pile of rubble beside her.

Portia. His beautiful, courageous, stubborn friend, who insisted on calling him her husband. Even though she knew what he'd done in the past and that he planned to walk away from her in the future. Somebody to ride the river with, as his father would have said.

Portia, a woman he didn't deserve.

"Do you believe this wall could stop invaders again?" she asked, her cheeks nicely flushed by the wind.

If he bent his head a little more, he could pretend the single cypress tree concealed them from passersby and kiss her.

"Yes, it's Roman," he said softly, his lips very close to her ear.

Most importantly, he could pretend they had a future together.

"Yes, it did stand for more than a thousand years, including through multiple earthquakes."

Her lips trembled in a large, round O.

Movement beyond her shoulder caught his eye.

Gareth lifted his head—and reluctantly thanked God for the interruption. Kissing Portia rattled his wits far more than gunplay ever had and he couldn't afford to lose any edge now.

"But our Ottoman overlords let it fall into decline two centuries ago, Lady St. Arles," said a French accented voice. Familiar but not extremely so.

"In the same manner as they themselves forsook all manly pastimes and sank into the pits of degradation," growled another, far too well-known voice. The revolutionaries' leader at the palace, dammit.

The intruders stopped several paces away and well within sight, holding out their hands. At least they weren't trying to sneak up on him and Portia.

"What a pleasure to see you again, 'Abd al-Hamid," Portia exclaimed. "But, please, you must call me Mrs. Lowell now. I married this gentleman several days ago."

"Congratulations, monsieur, madame!" 'Abd al-Hamid looked genuinely pleased, rather than green from puppy love gone awry. "May Allah bless you with many years and children together."

Gareth hoped his smile seemed genuine.

"We have come to apologize for disturbing you yesterday," said the large revolutionary.

Why the devil would he want to do that?

"Indeed?" Gareth inclined his head, indicating willingness to listen, and strolled closer to the church. They'd be less likely to find an audience there who'd understand French, unlike the Francophile Turks.

"Both of you have done much good for my young cousin," the big man said, lowering his voice to a remarkably soft bass rumble. "We owe you much in recompense."

"Therefore we have come to warn you what St. Arles' chest contains." Abdul suddenly sounded very decisive and Portia stared at him.

Gareth frowned slightly, old nerves firing up for battle.

"Yes, that is why I found you—or allowed you to think you discovered me, gracious lady. It has always been necessary for us to keep a close eye on that trunk and its contents."

"Go on," Gareth said curtly, unafraid to be blunt. After all, nobody could reach the priceless object without his and Portia's help.

The two men glanced at each other.

"There are at least two separate groups of revolutionaries," Abdul began. "One does what you might call typical tasks— demonstrations in the public squares, control of the news-papers . . ."

"Not to mention the army and navy?" Gareth suggested.

"Those, too," Abdul agreed, with a far too-practiced smile.

"Unless you're proclaiming a republic, you'll need a sultan to become a puppet. You'll also need to get rid of the current ruler," Gareth pointed out. "How do you plan to do it?"

"The chest will be smuggled," the big man's voice dropped even further, "into Chiragan Palace as a special festival gift."

"Where the former sultan is held?" Alarm strangled Portia's voice. Gareth patted her arm, trying to give her a reassurance he didn't truly feel.

Good God, nobody would ever expect that kind of firepower inside the stronghold. It was designed to keep attacks out, not to shut down one coming from within. The villains would be able to escape within a few minutes, at most an hour.

He had to admire St. Arles for conceiving of such a bold stroke. He'd only have one opportunity to pull it off—but if it succeeded, he'd gain everything he wanted.

"At the same time, British Marines will land—"

"At Chiragan Palace and key points throughout the city," Gareth finished the scenario for the would-be rebuilder of his country.

"We will rescue Murad from him, as soon as possible," Abdul inserted.

"Do you realize that St. Arles doesn't give a damn if Murad is mad or not? In fact, it's probably easier for the British if their puppet sultan is mad." Damn, but even saying things like that made Gareth want to wash his mouth out.

Portia's sweet scent drifted past him and she brushed her fingertip over his hand.

Clarity returned and with it the hope of springtime and flowers.

The two Turks drew themselves up, dark eyes flashing like cannon muzzles. Then they seemed to collapse into a single being.

"We are aware of that," Areef agreed. "Murad was—is—a great musician. He will receive better care from friends than in a stone cage like Chiragan Palace."

"You haven't told us when the attack will occur," Portia prodded.

"We don't know. In fact, you're likely to discover it sooner than we do," Abdul said, his voice sugar sweet but his eyes ageless cold.

"When St. Arles summons the chest," Gareth supplied, his skin cold with the awareness of coming battle. His brain was searching, assessing, rejecting every tactic as too risky without any backup.

Dammit, if he only had one other member of Donovan &

Sons here, he could do so much more. Temporary hirelings were all well and good but they weren't the same. They weren't men he'd already gone into battle with and could already trust to watch his back.

"Exactly. Peace be upon you." Areef bowed, his expression troubled.

"And upon you be peace," Gareth returned.

It would only happen if they stopped St. Arles.

Forests of white marble rose out of the floor and upheld the ceiling as far as the eye could see. Long dead faces swam amid curled hair and tendrils of moss, their vacant eyes always searching for an escape. Black water rippled knee deep over the floor, offering early warning of any intruders.

St. Arles studied the last remaining piece of the puzzle from a small ledge overlooking the ancient cistern.

Whitehall had promised competent help to take the chest into Chiragan. Having dealt with those London chaps before, he'd hardly dared hope to find tolerable assistance.

But these blokes promised to be quite efficient indeed.

A half dozen cold, calculating men looked back at him, with their arms crossed over their chests as if he mattered little more than their next meal.

"Gentlemen, the time has come to begin our attack's next phase."

Nobody moved, even though they were supposed to speak the Genoan dialect of Italian.

"Two of you must pose as porters in the European City to pick up a chest."

Tension swirled suddenly, more vibrant than the moss.

"Why should we care about a chest?" the eldest one asked in excellent Italian.

Ah good, they did speak the language.

"After you pick it up—and *discreetly* kill its current owners—you will deliver it to Chiragan Palace."

"For a bonus," the elder pressed.

Excellent: he hadn't hesitated at the mention of murder.

"A very large reward," St. Arles agreed. Whitehall wanted no witnesses left alive, of course.

But this bounty came out of his private purse: He wanted the slut dead.

"Mail," Gareth announced and dropped the damning little note onto the table. The embroidered cloth quivered but the chest underneath, containing all the rifles and ammunition, didn't move a hairsbreadth.

Dynamite would totally eliminate it—and Adem's home.

Beautiful Portia stopped brushing her hair, the golden strands gleaming brighter than fairy dust. Terror tightened her mouth before she started to draw the brush far more slowly over a single golden strand, again and again. "Did you open it?"

He propped his foot on the iron-bound beast.

"It's unsigned," he warned.

"Gareth, do either of us need trumpets and banners to recognize St. Arles' work?" she retorted acidly.

He grinned privately, pleased with her return to normalcy.

"Probably not," he agreed. "We're to bring the trunk tomorrow afternoon to a quay in the European City. Once there, we prop it on end and wheel it through the crowd. Another porter will bump into ours and—"

"Exchange chests in the confusion, since they're identical."

"Except for the monogram," he reminded her, very proud of her quickness.

She shrugged that objection off. "St. Arles had this trunk made; he probably has a duplicate waiting." She let her brush fall into her lap. "What should we do?"

"I'll deliver it."

"No!" Fear, more potent than liquid mercury, ran through his veins.

"Portia, I've delivered far more hazardous freight a thousand times and he won't be looking for me." *Plus, I'm expendable and you're not.*

"He asked for me, not you. If he doesn't see me, what if he calls everything off? What if he increases his attacks on my friends?"

"We've already asked your solicitor and Donovan's to help them. We must believe we've done everything possible and leave them in God's hands." He stopped to watch her expression, wishing he knew some magical words to ease her fear, wishing he could destroy St. Arles to remove its cause, wishing . . .

She wiped her hands over her face.

"We'll both do it."

"Portia!" How the hell could he stop her? By knocking her out again?

She stood up, her hips swaying underneath that frothy bit of clothing called a tea gown. All the lace and most of a gown's buttons, but no corset was how he'd sum it up.

His idiotic cock promptly sat up and saluted, abducting most of his brain cells.

"Portia." He tried to think of another way to dissuade her. "I, we . . ." His tongue was uncommonly thick in his suddenly dry mouth. He fumbled for words and stumbled upon the truth. "It's probably a trap, meant to kill both of us."

"Gareth." Somehow she scratched his chest when she gripped his shirt with her slender little hands.

He shuddered and closed his eyes. He would not pick her up and tumble her upon that big bed. He was not a heathen, so help him, God.

She ran her hands up and down his front until the starched linen rubbed his back and shoulders like a thousand little fingers, igniting every previously indefinable urge. Heat danced into his bones, pricking him with his lust that throbbed with every beat of his heart. His eyelids sank until she became a golden blur, as evocative of joy as the dreams he'd once known in the Kentucky mountains.

"Portia, my darling." Did he say those words? He caught her by her slender waist and let his fingers span her womanly hips.

"Gareth, my love, my life." She softened and swayed toward him, ageless and ripe as the ancient waters lapping the house they rested in.

Love? The two of them, united in heart? That was a prospect more terrifying than facing a desert sandstorm without shelter.

And yet his heart yearned for her as much or more than his blood did.

"Portia." He pushed back her gown to expose her white shoulders. "Sweetheart." He bent his head to her lips and thrust his leg between her soft thighs.

She answered him eagerly, her little tongue seeking his. Her taste filled his mouth, spicy and warm like the breath of life.

Somehow his fingers fumbled well enough to undo her buttons but he'd never know how. He only cared that Portia moved against him, her curves teasing him until his recalcitrant barriers of vest buttons and suspenders and trouser fly disappeared.

Portia. Her sweet breast filled his hand, her plump nipple swelled eagerly to meet his thumb's caresses, her pulse trembled in her throat when he nibbled it, over and over again until needy cries rose from her mouth. His darling.

Her hands swept over his bare skin as if every muscle, every scar was precious and beautiful to her. Lingered and coaxed until his bones turned to fire and liquid lust cascaded through his veins.

"Gareth." A single word yet it meant everything, since she spoke it.

He lowered her to the bed and knelt over her. Her eyes were wild and desperate, yet they saw *him*. They had always seen him, as nobody else ever did.

He lifted her hips and entered her, welcomed by her womanly cream.

His woman, nobody else's.

He thrust again, harder—and slid sweetly home, embraced and held to his root.

Portia moaned, rocking herself voluptuously against and upon him.

Pleasure wailed through him, too great and too familiar to

be snatched immediately. He began to move again, driving both of them toward a barely glimpsed destination.

And oh, how she encouraged him, with voice and hands and body. Stroking him, gripping him, singing to him of her lust and love.

Until the passionate drumbeat roared hot and heavy through his cock, fueled by the scent of musk and barely restrained by the slick grip of her fiery hot sheath.

"Gareth!" Portia cried out and tumbled into passion's whirlwind, climaxing with a rapturous energy that gave as much as it demanded.

He shouted and followed her, shooting jet after jet inside her. Ecstasy tunneled through him and rocketed out, rattling every bone and remaking every muscle in a coruscant torrent, like the inside of a waterfall. Rainbows pummeled his eyes until they rolled back inside his head.

He cuddled her afterward, linked by sweat, the raspy sobs of their recovering breaths, and the last sticky remains of their lust.

God help him, he was horrified he'd remembered to use a condom. But wanting to make her pregnant would prove he was in love.

He didn't, quite, hurl the damn thing through a window into the Bosporus.

Chapter Thirty-four

"I will accompany you to exchange the trunks," Portia stated again, far more forcibly.

"No." Gareth dusted a nonexistent speck of dust off his bowler hat. Fiddling with his clothing was far better than considering his wife or looking too deeply into his heart.

"St. Arles will never send his trolls out if he doesn't see me." She was dressed like a female admiral in a closely fitted blue dress. She sounded like one, too.

"We need to buy time, Portia, so your friends can escape."

Her sigh shivered his heart. "The last cable from my solicitor said he had some ideas."

"Many of your friends still remain at St. Arles' houses, despite how he's firing others. They're afraid of the unknown," he added more gently.

She leaned her forehead against his shoulder and he hugged her consolingly. This early in the morning, no gardener should disturb them in a corner of Kerem Ali Pasha's gardens.

"I wish . . ." Her voice trailed off, like how the sun was rapidly burning off the fog.

"Hmm?" he prompted, savoring her delicate scent and warmth pressed close to his heart.

"I wish Uncle William was here. Of course, you're grand"— her enormous blue eyes beamed up at him—"but it would be comforting to know my uncle could back you up."

"I understand, honey—and I feel the same." Gareth plopped his hat on her head. "But we'll manage."

"Wretch!" She batted at the brim, forcing the oversized hat backward. "You just want to blind me so you can sneak off."

"Would I do that?" Gareth drawled, pretending to be offended.

"Yes," she snapped, backed by the certainty which came from years of acquaintanceship, and triumphantly slung the offending headgear onto his scalp.

Ahoogaa! boomed a horn in complete agreement.

They both turned toward the Bosporus to listen.

"That's not one of the ferries, is it?" Portia asked.

"No, and it's not a local freighter either." He'd spent too many years around their ilk not to have learned their favorite cries. "Or a local navy ship."

Oars dipped and splashed rhythmically into the water, like the accompaniment for an unknown song. Very well-trained crew, too.

Gareth grabbed Portia's hand and headed at a dead run for the landing.

Sunshine painted the little dock until it appeared as vibrantly alive as the flowers behind it or the mansion rising solidly, if vividly pink, next to it. The sky was bright blue and even Constantinople's ancient stones were a golden cascade beyond the Bosporus's rippling waters.

A very long, sleek, black boat lay at anchor off the yali. A single golden stripe ran down her side and the Stars and Stripes waved gently above her, near a golden pennant.

Portia whooped and hugged Gareth.

Servants clustered at the garden gate and even the women-folk watched from the windows.

A rowboat, white as the gulls circling overhead, nudged against the quay. The uniformed crew rested on their oars at a single command, every one of them careful not to cast a single glance at the veiled women observing their every move.

Who the hell had disciplined them that well? More importantly, who the devil had taught them such good manners?

A tall, well-built man in naval uniform leaped deftly out of the rowboat and onto the dock, showing the cat quickness which only long years around the water confers upon land mammals. Another man followed, similarly outfitted and equally graceful.

Gareth would have far preferred to fight alongside, rather than against, either of them.

The first, and considerably more senior, fellow had already assessed his greeters with a born commander's ease. He turned his gaze upon Portia.

"Mrs. Vanneck, I believe?" he asked, in the purest of South Carolina accents.

"Mrs. *Lowell*," she corrected, her voice only slightly tinged by a note of *thank God!* "This is Gareth Lowell, my husband."

"Sir." The newcomers bowed to them both.

"I am Captain Elliott Pendleton of the SS *Naiad*, and this is my first officer, Theodore Barnesworth. Our services and the *Naiad*'s at your service, ma'am, while you cruise the world."

"I-I don't own a yacht," Portia stammered.

"Mr. William Donovan thought you might be more comfortable in your own vessel than if you were dependent on hired accommodations."

Kerem Ali Pasha, flanked by both of his sons, could just be glimpsed coming through the gardens.

"However, his yacht was not readily available, since it cruises in Pacific waters, ma'am. He sends his apologies for any disappointment," added Barnesworth.

"Quite all right," murmured Gareth. He'd swear the fellow had lost his earlobe to a knife, although it was well-hidden in neatly barbered hair beside his black eye patch.

"Mr. Donovan therefore acted with your grandfather, Commodore Lindsay, to find and purchase a suitable yacht. The *Naiad* was commissioned for Mr. Gould, but he had expressed some concern that the designers had sacrificed comfort in favor of speed."

"Do you agree with Gould?" Gareth asked.

"I believe you will have no complaints in either quarter, sir." Pendleton allowed himself a small smile.

This changed the game. If he could get Portia out of here . . .

"How big a crew?"

"Slightly more than fifty, sir, and all of the officers are former Navy. The Lindsay family brought each of us in."

Portia beamed as if the sun, moon, and stars were floating out there upon the water.

The two naval officers looked her over protectively, proud as if they were watching a race horse run for the first time.

Kerem Ali Pasha stepped onto the quay and Portia, as the closest, turned to make introductions. But Pendleton stepped back for a last, more private word with Gareth.

"I served with Hal Lindsay, your wife's uncle, in the Mississippi Squadron during the war between the States, as did Barnesworth and Murrah, the engineer. We'll protect any member of his family, as well as we did him."

"Thanks. I'll remember that."

The first genuine grin touched Gareth's mouth in far too long.

"My old friend." He bowed to Kerem Ali Pasha. "May we borrow your house for a very private conversation with our newfound friends?"

The delicate pink salon was almost overwhelmed by so much masculinity crowded into it. The yacht's two officers, Gareth in his formal business attire, Kerem Ali Pasha wearing the fez and black robes of a high ranking state secretary. Even Adem's military uniform with all the gold braid and Kahil's simpler student tunic added to the impression of men gathered to do battle.

"Gentlemen, do you speak any French?" Gareth asked the yacht's two officers.

"Reasonably well for technical matters," Pendleton admitted, "although you'll not catch me spouting any poetry."

"Barnesworth?"

"I can't write it but I can understand it well enough," the younger man admitted warily.

"Good; we'll converse in French. Kind sir, are we assured of privacy?" he asked their host.

"My mother has guaranteed it and my wife has promised to enforce it." Kerem Ali Pasha folded his hands across his middle, like that of a man who prefers not to be aware of any details.

Portia started to question him and then decided she too didn't want to know. No government spy was a match for those two ladies.

"You are a great and powerful man in the Empire, as your father and grandfather have been before you. I brought my wife here for protection from burglars, which you have generously provided, and for which we thank you."

Gareth bowed deeply, adding courtly flourishes. Portia echoed the movement, careful not to say anything. They needed the Turk's help and one wrong word from a woman could curdle their chances.

She sensed, rather than saw, the two officers glance at each other but they too remained silent.

"But matters have grown worse. We have learned that evil men intend to break into Chiragan Palace and restore Sultan Murad to the throne."

"No!" Kahil came to his feet. His father snapped his fingers and pointed. The young man slowly resumed his seat, his expression thunderous.

"What do these evil men desire?" the state secretary inquired, calm as if they discussed the latest popular play.

"They believe that my wife's luggage contains a large enough bribe to make the palace guards disappear."

Portia barely stopped herself from going slack-jawed in surprise. That was one description of a dozen rifles and their ammunition—but hardly the most accurate. It might be the most polite one, though.

"Bribes. Faugh!" Adem made a violent gesture then pounded his fists together. "They will be the death of our country."

"Adem!"

Dark eyes clashed with darker before the sire won.

"Continue, please." The saucer shook slightly in the old bureaucrat's hand but his voice was completely steady.

"We believe they will take action tonight, sir, on the Night of Absolution," Gareth said. "I have some ideas on how to stop them but doing so will require all of our assistance."

"What is the Night of Absolution?" asked Pendleton.

"It's one of five religious festivals when the mosques are outlined in lights," Adem answered, his mind clearly elsewhere. "Many people spend the night outside in the streets, praying or visiting friends."

"But why is it called the Night of *Absolution*?"

"Allah comes closest to Earth at this time and settles the destiny of each believer for the coming year. Some describe it as being similar to a court of law, where decisions are handed down," Kahil explained.

"Court of law?" Pendleton shook his head and settled back.

"What does that have to do with snatching a former sultan?" Barnesworth queried. He leaned forward, his single eye alight with curiosity.

"The streets will be lined with soldiers for the Sultan's procession to the mosque," Adem said crisply. "It usually weakens the forces at Chiragan Palace."

"Can't they get enough from elsewhere?"

"Too many disciplined troops are needed. Turkish soldiers aren't fed or clothed by the state, except for those stationed within Constantinople."

"Such as at Chiragan Palace," Portia gave the example, feeling rather hollow. Soldiers who weren't reliably fed? Good heavens, how trustworthy could they be?

"We need to stop the attack." Gareth watched his host, whose fingertip was endlessly circling his coffee cup's rim.

"Can you identify them?" Ancient eyes contemplated the Bosporus's glittering waters floating past.

"Yes—and ensure they're arrested for stealing from foreigners. But only with your help, sir."

Kerem Ali Pasha looked at each of his sons. His grandson wailed in the distance and he flinched, growing decades older.

"Very well. What do you want us to do?"

Chapter Thirty-five

Kerem Ali Pasha bowed politely, but not too deeply, to Qadri Bey, the new head of the secret police. One had to remember all of the nuances for why one was supposedly here—and not keep thinking about exactly how Qadri Bey had gotten his blameless predecessor exiled to Aleppo. A western fan whirred overhead, incapable of eavesdropping through the shadows unlike old-fashioned slaves.

A single sheet of paper, covered in Kerem Ali's handwriting, glittered balefully from the official's blotter.

The entire family had worked on their reports with Meryem's aid. Even his mother had contributed a note obliquely urging an investigation of strange doings in the old palace.

"You state here that a group plans to attack Chiragan Palace." Qadri Bey picked up the page and pretended to exam it more closely.

"Yes indeed, sir." The honorific rasped his throat worse than all of a mackerel's bones.

He owed Lowell his son's life and he trusted the man. If Lowell said there was a threat, then the dagger was poised, ready to fall sooner than his family had guessed. That certainty alone kept his face calm.

He stretched his legs out, in a casual assumption of authority designed to prod the other into action.

"They are driven like sheep by the British, Qadri Bey," he added. "If you reach out your hand, you could cut their throats."

Flat black eyes turned inward and the overly polished hand slowly waved the sheet back and forth. Finally a snake's obscene spark of life returned to them.

"The Sultan wishes to thank you for your concern."

Kerem Ali gratefully recognized the dismissal and rose, gathering his dignity around him like a cloak.

"A token of his gratitude will be delivered to your home." For a moment, naked envy blasted the secret police chief's face.

Kerem Ali bowed very fast before he saw too much then left as rapidly as possible.

Everything Lowell had said was true—and more? They must have already suspected a plot, for which his words provided the evidence and a chance to catch the devils behind it.

Allah willing, the same brutes who'd so swiftly knocked out his son would not eliminate Lowell and his wife.

Portia longed for an enormous hat, or two, or three. Or maybe a half dozen brocaded kaftans with matching pants. Anything to drip convincingly from the corners of her enormous trunk, which was now being propelled by a uniformed porter down the busy quay in Constantinople's European City.

Some trinket to make her and Gareth look as if they belonged, so he wouldn't need the knife that had brushed against her, from inside his sleeve. Wouldn't need to use the coiled tension behind his amiable gaze, with which he surveyed everyone who walked past.

If something happened to him, her world would end.

Dogs scampered by, vendors hawked a variety of foods to tease the senses, and men rushed onward as if their lives depended on being aboard the next grubby steamer.

She wet her lips again, wishing she could clear the dust from her mouth or open up her lungs to the tangy air. Maybe if she could avoid looking at that blasted British cruiser and its tea party for the ambassador. Half the European population had to be aboard under that canvas awning, including no doubt St. Arles.

They hadn't been able to talk to the police before coming here. If anything went wrong with the plan, there would be only the two of them to deal with St. Arles's blackguards.

No matter how much Barnesworth might boast of his ability to act in disguise, he was still acting as a porter and that heavy trunk would keep his hands busy.

Her stomach wrenched into an incipient sob but she ignored it. To protect Gareth, she'd use every lesson she'd ever been taught in finishing school or those years of duplicity and vitriol called international diplomacy.

This was the moment to show only her appreciation of the crisp breeze and lovely view of Hagia Sophia to the south from across the Golden Horn.

Very well, she could manage that, no matter how much the little hairs shivered on the nape of her neck.

Maybe if she imagined that she was strolling alongside San Francisco Bay, the salt breeze teasing her hair, and no greater concerns than the perfect folds of her parasol—and how quickly she could coax her beloved husband to take her home. His strong arm under her hand, his thigh propelling her forward, his warm breath teasing her cheek when he bent to answer a question—Oh yes, she could saunter like this forever.

And if she imagined that Barnesworth was merely a silent banker, not a porter . . . Yes, that would do.

She elevated her chin a little higher and strutted a little more emphatically, using her parasol to emphasize her pace. At least her hat and parasol were the latest fashion, bought during a whirlwind visit to Paris when she'd freed herself of anything which smacked of St. Arles' taste.

Gareth patted her hand approvingly but said nothing. His beautifully tailored suit became him admirably, although she suspected it hid more than the single weapon she knew of.

Another porter stepped out of the crowd, also pushing an expensive trunk. A trunk which exactly matched Portia's, down to the same number of black, wrought iron bands circling it and the heavy lock on the top. The porter was dressed as they'd been informed, in a dull maroon livery.

Her foot skidded on the uneven planks but her parasol's rhythmic *tap, tap* never faltered. Tension swirled like an opera cloak and settled into her bones, cold and surprisingly calming.

The two porters came abreast of each other and Barnesworth stepped toward the newcomer as he'd been instructed—and they'd planned—ready to exchange one set of handles for another in mid-stride.

A second man, dressed in a well-worn suit, abruptly stepped out of the crowd and brutally clubbed Barnesworth down. Then he grabbed the trunk's handles and started to run for the nearest boat.

Gareth slammed into his back, driving him onto the chest. The attacker twisted and rolled over with a trained wrestler's speed until they came snarling to their feet.

They circled each other, both clearly more ready to kill than talk. Knives flashed in their hands, pitiless as serpents' teeth.

Portia's heart was bouncing within her ribs.

Whistles blew shrilly from behind her back, too far away to help her husband.

She looked around for a gun, a weapon, anything to aid Gareth. Anything to stop another threat against him.

The original attacker started to run, pushing his trunk past Barnesworth's limp body.

Portia shoved her parasol between his legs and twisted it, the tendrils of ribbon and lace wrapping against his ankles in a foaming torrent of feminine wrath.

He screeched and tumbled head over heels into the uniformed policemen finally running toward them down the quay.

Portia retrieved her parasol and quickly turned around, ready to assist Gareth.

"Well done, my dear, well done." Her beloved nodded to her above a very grubby, infuriated villain. Gareth had painfully twisted the fellow's arm behind his back, thereby winning the bout.

"And you, my love." Her heartbeat slipped slowly back into normalcy. He was alive, with her, for a little longer.

Barnesworth stirred and she stooped to check him.

Together they awaited the forces of the law, who'd perform the cleanup—and make sure none of St. Arles' packages entered Chiragan Palace.

At least on this Friday night.

Chapter Thirty-six

Constantinople, night of 7/8 May 1887

The moon glowed golden and ripe with mystery, just above the horizon, as if the rippling waters were a road leading to undreamt-of delights within its portals. Dark woodsy scents and sweet flower aromas sifted into the air to tease the nose from the quiet western shoreline.

But the Old City, on the eastern shoreline, was very different. All of the great mosques which dominated the city's backbone were bedecked in light, from ancient Hagia Sophia to the immense Blue Mosque. Gareth could even see Mihrimah Sultan Mosque far to the east like a beacon of hope, where Abdul Hamid had warned Portia and him about St. Arles' plans.

Horses' hooves, plus the heavy metallic clank and rattle told how thousands of soldiers returned to their barracks, after lining the streets while the Sultan lighted the first candle.

The Sultan was safe and Portia had finally consented to depart for England.

He should be glad. He could leave her now and let her have a quiet annulment. Nobody need know about a marriage contracted in a foreign land, which had only lasted for a few days.

"Are you sure it's safe?" she asked again. Her face was very white in the moonlight. No lights showed where Kerem Ali

Pasha's yali slept within its sheltering gardens on the Bosporus's eastern edge.

"St. Arles will have to lie low here until the furor dies down. That should give you more than enough time to return to London and look after your friends, no matter how cautious they are." His cheeks were too stiff for an encouraging smile. Stupid idea, anyway.

Her family's men started to lower her last trunk into the *Naiad*'s launch and they both turned to watch. He, at least, was grateful for the distraction.

The northern wind, a harsh counterpoint to the evening's festival, shoved the small boat sideways, away from the pier. A sailor's foot slipped and the fellow lost his grasp on the damn chest.

Gareth lunged forward to help prevent the rifles and ammunition from crashing through the boat or, worse, into the man's leg. His fingers closed on the padded handle just as two other sailors caught the damn heavy thing, and their helmsman brought the recalcitrant vessel well under control.

Portia let out a long, almost inaudible sigh.

Gareth flashed them a quick thumbs up and stepped back.

"Sorry, sir," the helmsman said. "Very choppy seas running tonight and I wasn't quite prepared. We'll do better when the lady comes aboard, I promise."

His heart, which had dropped back into its normal rhythm, rocketed into something far closer to a bullet's hungry search for mayhem.

They'd damn well better look after her or he'd tear their eyes out for frightening her. If anything happened to Portia, he'd . . . he'd . . . he'd be better off dead. He'd found a way to keep on living after his parents died. But he didn't think he could do that if she wasn't in the world.

He didn't have to see her every day because he didn't deserve that. He only needed to know she was happy.

He loved her.

The truth hit him like a stampeding longhorn bull, closing his lungs and taking the strength from his knees.

He swayed slightly, unable for the first time in years to find his knife against his wrist.

Portia tugged on his sleeve and he looked down at her. Dear God in heaven, she was beautiful. She'd been a damn smart fighter when she'd tripped up that fellow with her parasol, too.

"So you do think St. Arles is still a threat?" she hissed, a distinct note of triumph in her voice.

He tried to remember what she'd just been saying to him, after she'd dragged him away from the sailors. "Could be."

"He'll certainly be furious when we dump the rifles at sea."

Was she having second thoughts now?

"There's no other sure way to destroy them, unless we sail them all the way back to London. A ship's the only way to keep them far from St. Arles and his hirelings."

"But I have to catch the first possible train back to London so I can reach my friends. I can't stay with the boat."

"We're back to the beginning, honey: The rifles will have a decent burial at sea."

Even so, St. Arles could follow them, hoping to regain his box of tricks, and revenge himself on Portia in the process.

Gareth could escort her and make damn sure the brute didn't lay hands on her again. But that meant drawing close, far closer than he'd ever dared before, to home and family, everything he didn't deserve and couldn't have. Everything that sent him back outside with the wind, where it was safe, or at least less dangerous.

No matter how many of her family's men were on that boat with her, they wouldn't be willing to die for her.

"I'll come with you," Gareth said.

"To London?" Her voice rose.

"All the way to England," he affirmed, putting his neck in the noose.

"Thank you, Gareth!" Tears welled up in her eyes until they sparkled like diamonds.

HMS *Phidaleia* rolled hard, jolted, and twirled in the opposite direction like a Cockney flower girl pretending she still possessed her virginity. A man's voice rose from below decks, cursing his once-neat equipment.

Waves smacked against her sides, promising a long, bitterly uncomfortable night. Thank God the charts for these waters were younger than the Christian Church and showed every lee shore where a ship might run aground, given these high winds.

St. Arles dropped the telescope down to his side, enjoying the salt spray crystallizing on his hair and wool coat. For a few minutes, he could pretend he was at home, no matter how bad the news was.

As he'd suspected, the silly little house contained no traces of his former wife and her paramour. Or new husband, to give him due credit for an English wedding, at least.

He still needed the damn chest with its rifles and cartridges to create a puppet Sultan. And the sooner the better, too, for both Britain and himself.

"What do you want, St. Arles?" Southers asked.

"Can you see the American yacht which just got underway?"

"Very pretty lines," the British captain commented, "but she's having a hard time of it, with this sea."

"Aren't we all?"

"True, we're all fighting the wind. But she's cutting very close to the Asian side, rather than staying more toward the center of the channel."

A bit of over-caution which would give him time to catch up with her. Of course, British ships didn't have to worry about coming close to Chiragan Palace's bloody-fingered jailers.

"I want you to put me aboard her."

"Unnoticed, St. Arles?"

"Of course."

"A little tricky, given the full moon and these sea conditions, but I'm sure the lads will consider it a pleasant break from the recent monotony. What else?"

Life held few pleasures greater than rejoining the Royal Navy, even for a few minutes.

"I will create a distraction and then signal for assistance. At that time, I want two men to come aboard and assist me in taking off the chest lashed down behind the aft wheelhouse. Do you see it?"

"The large oak one, old chap, with black bands?" Southers fiddled with his own spyglass for a moment before nodding with satisfaction. "Yes, of course, the lads will be ready the instant you need them."

"Thank you, Southers." He'd have to give the young captain a longer mention than planned for this assistance in his despatches back home, possibly even enough for a medal. Damn. But it would be worth it, to regain the rifles—and ruin the bitch's happiness.

"Good luck, St. Arles." For an instant, Southers' voice darkened to a warning note deeper than the wind's hungry howl.

St. Arles's eyes flickered then he shrugged off the comparison as nursery rhymes' rubbish. He had far more important matters to think about, such as how best to destroy his ex-wife's new marriage.

Chapter Thirty-seven

The *Naiad* hit another wave and jounced before settling back on course. Crockery rattled as if all the fiends of hell were trying to escape their bounds. The gas lamp swung, bouncing its light through a blinding arc of reflections.

Portia's stomach leaped for her mouth, somersaulted, and started to slowly settle.

The steward lifted a cup of hot tea off his tray, moving as carefully as if he were gliding over hot coals. In the same instant, the yacht jolted and rolled again, restarting the hellacious racket.

"I believe I need a bit of night air," she said firmly, to the world as much as to herself, "to refresh myself."

"But, ma'am," the steward started to protest.

"I'm sure I will be more comfortable there, sir." Plus, she'd have the freedom to be alone with her husband. Dear Lord, how she needed every minute of that which she could grab.

The stern deck was deserted and its usual canvas awnings rolled up, due to the heavy wind. But she could adapt a little better to the ship's motion there, since she could see the waves' choppy pattern.

Gareth was silent, stumbling a little bit when the ship's awkward motion caught him unawares.

But her heart was happy to watch him and save up memories of how he looked—his profile against the moonlight, his quick grace when he pivoted, the warmth of his hand when he caught her elbow . . . Every small detail that might be fodder for a thousand future dreams.

The trunk—St. Arles' blasted mass of iron and oak which had started everything—was lashed beside the waist-high deckhouse. Stolid and dangerous, it commanded all eyes the same way the judge's bench had in that British courtroom. It creaked and groaned, straining against its restraints like a living being. She'd have to ask Captain Pendleton to secure it more firmly.

A stench drifted back from the ship's bow and Gareth's nose twitched. Portia sniffed, too.

Faint but unmistakably foul, it was—fire?

The alarm bell broke out, tolling the cry more dreaded than any other at sea.

Fire! Men shouted, doors slammed, and feet pounded toward the bow. The yacht could sink within five minutes if flames reached the boiler, fifteen if they reached the coal bunkers.

Portia stared at Gareth, her heart leaping in her breast. He alone hadn't moved.

"What are you thinking?" she asked softly.

"Go to a lifeboat, honey." His face held the hard determination of an Arizona gunslinger and he scanned the deck.

She glanced around. But all she could see was a thin plume of smoke rising from the *Naiad*'s bow.

Fire, ready to kill them all.

"Darling." She bit her lip, forcing herself to find a steadier note.

Bang! A shot whizzed from behind the deckhouse, past Portia's head, and into the capstan. Its hot trail scorched her ear and she yelped, then dropped flat on her face.

Bang! The second shot nicked Gareth's shoulder, singeing his linen jacket as if the hounds of hell had bitten him.

He whirled, just in time to grab St. Arles' revolver before the dripping wet brute could get off another shot.

They struggled for it, both pairs of hands wrapped around the gun. The sea flung them back and forth against the deckhouse until they stumbled and fell. They rolled a few feet more and then St. Arles slammed Gareth into the mast.

What could she do to help? Everyone else was fighting the fire.

The Bosporus roared and shook itself like an angry beast, until taking even two steps unaided was a miracle. Her life turned to ashes in her throat, Portia reached for a handhold to steady herself.

Gareth beat St. Arles' hand against the deck again and again but the Englishman's grip was too strong to break.

The great moon hung golden and unmoved above and the wind howled around them like Apache war cries. The sea hissed and flung itself against the *Naiad* in a portent of hell, while the chest pivoted like a tiger under its ropes.

Two shots fired, four to go. If she grabbed the gun, she could be injured, too, even if she managed to grip it.

St. Arles forced the revolver back toward Gareth—and fired it again.

Bam!

The wind blew the acrid smoke away, as if the gates of hell had opened.

Gareth's face was black with smoke and red streaked one side of it. But his silver eyes, lethal as any wolf's, promised revenge.

Slipping and sliding on the wet deck, Portia ran for the only other weapon—the fire axe inside the deck house.

A second later, far too few paces separated Gareth from St. Arles and the damn revolver. Her knife gleamed in her lover's hand but how much use was it now?

What could she do with the heavy axe? She could lift it but throwing it was beyond her strength.

The *Naiad* heaved again, as if the sea mocked their tribulations. In the distance, the Sultan's palaces glittered like undisturbed fairy tales—Yildiz, Dolmabahce, Chiragan with its blood-soaked prisons.

"I used to think I'd make you pay for his life, Portia," St. Arles remarked, as conversationally as if they stood in the center of Regent's Park. "But now I believe he's caused so much trouble that I'll simply kill him out of hand."

You hellspawn fiend.

Portia crept forward until she came out into the stern deck, away from the deckhouse. She had two possible targets from here—St. Arles' damn chest or the beast himself.

For a moment, she teetered, fighting the wind. Her skirts tried to become sails and manacles, while she had nothing nearby to hold on to.

But she'd manage this. Somehow. For Gareth and everyone else whose lives St. Arles had carelessly wrecked.

Calling on all the Lindsays in her blood, she created a balance between herself and the ship and the sea. Then she took a firmer grip on the axe.

One long step to the trunk and the weak rope holding it—or three paces to St. Arles.

Gareth's eyes widened slightly, even underneath the salt spray and the blood from his wound. His smile turned as sharp-edged as his blade.

"Perhaps you should look to your own defenses in this weather," he suggested to St. Arles. He feinted, moving forward, pressing his opponent as if he had full advantage.

He'd attack a man with a gun—when all he had was a knife?

The Englishman laughed, the sound's gleeful triumph resonating through the sudden absence of bells and shouts from the *Naiad*'s bow.

"You fool. You bloody, glorious fool." He shifted and circled, keeping his gun pointed at Gareth's chest. Then he cocked it.

Her heart leaped into her mouth. She swung down the same way the judge had wielded his gavel on the bench—and sent the axe's full weight into the hemp strands. The blade thudded into the solid oak, final as the gavel's slam. The strands snapped in an instant and the trunk hurled itself forward to slide free.

The big, heavy chest roared across the deck toward the two fighters. Gareth sprang for Portia and knocked her away from it.

St. Arles turned to dodge it but slipped on the wet deck. The *Naiad* continued to roll, sending the iron-bound oak chest thundering down upon him. He fell, screaming curses, and skidded into the ravenous seas through the open gangway only inches ahead of the great chest.

Gareth and Portia raced to the rail.

"Where is he?"

"There!" Gareth pointed. "Can you see him swimming?"

"If you say so but I'm not sure I want to." She leaned against her husband and tried to find merciful thoughts.

Others joined them, smelling strongly of smoke. Someone handed her a telescope.

"He's heading for the small white palace to the north. With the large terrace," Captain Pendleton reported.

"Chiragan Palace," Portia said. A very hollow feeling began to grow in her stomach. "Where the former sultan is held captive."

"All unexpected visitors to Chiragan Palace are always interrogated by experts," Gareth murmured. "I understand it frequently involves having your rib cage bound so your spinal column can be extracted."

Neat as any marshal, she and Gareth had delivered St. Arles to the only tribunal where his nationality and rank meant nothing, compared to his crimes.

Portia hid her face against Gareth's shoulder and he hugged her. She'd have to go to church and pray for forgiveness, because she had no regrets.

St. Arles hadn't gone to court for adultery but he was standing in the dock now.

In a Turkish court, on the Night of Absolution, may Allah have mercy on him.

Chapter Thirty-eight

St. Arles staggered onto the rocky shore, his woolen coat streaming water from the howling gale. Wind beat at his back and waves tore at his knees and ankles. The golden moon sailed above, barely visible through the pounding spray.

He hissed with pain when the first boulder cut into his feet but kept walking. He'd quickly sacrificed his boots when he first went into the Bosporus, lest they became sea anchors dedicated to locking him onto this foul place.

White steps glimmered ahead of him, probably from somebody's seaside mansion on the Asian side of the Bosporus. A few bribes, the mention of the British Ambassador, and he'd be able to fight once again, ready to destroy his ex-wife and that cur Lowell.

Once he had his revenge—and silenced their yapping mouths, no doubt—he could decide how best to bring rifles into Constantinople. The filthy Sultan still needed to go to hell.

He caught the railing and started up. Another wave crashed into him and snatched his breath away. He clung, panting, to the heavy marble balustrade until the swell slunk away.

Dammit, any house this grand should have servants to help unexpected guests. Where were they?

He spat out more saltwater and pulled himself onto his feet. Water swirled below the stairs, green and black with debris beneath the angry foam.

Now—finally!—boots pounded toward him across the marble terrace.

St. Arles shoved his streaming hair off his forehead and wiped his eyes so he could better gauge his greeters' social rank.

But behind them rose the immense white marble block of Chiragan Palace, more dangerous to the unwary than the Tower of London. The etchings around its windows and doors seemed to writhe in the fitful light and pour water like demons grasping for his soul.

Two big brutes grabbed his arms and half threw him onto the terrace.

"I say, now!" he protested. "I'm a British diplomat."

A boot on his neck ground his face into the tiled surface. More enormous ruffians pinned his legs and back against his attempts to rise.

He yelled again. Surely they wouldn't treat a foreigner like one of their own ignorant heathen.

They rolled him over, two men on every limb and others on his torso. The indignity was more than any St. Arles had tolerated since Cromwell's time.

"Release me, you filthy buggers!" He bucked, outrage washing away diplomatic platitudes.

A boot smashed into him, precisely between his legs.

Fiery pain ripped him apart, more crippling than anything he'd ever endured. Fierce as the worst agony he'd seen in a bed partner's eyes before she died.

His scream came from the bottom of his soul. He tried to jackknife but the fiends held him still, even piled on more to hold him down.

When he could speak again, cold black eyes watched him above a gold-braided uniform, lit by an equally impassive golden moon.

"You will speak politely of my men, English," the officer remarked, "or you will regret it. That is, if you are English."

His accent was barely understandable.

St. Arles spat. "You fool—"

The officer kicked him in the ribs.

The pain wasn't as foul as its predecessor. On the other hand, St. Arles was certain he had at least one broken bone.

He lay on the terrace, sweat streaming down his face, and stared up at a dozen foreign heathen. All of them were big, strong, and clearly ready to use their big knives on him.

For the first time in his life, terror crystallized his bones, not his bed partner's.

"Why are you here, English?" the officer asked. "The truth please, or you will speak only to the torturer."

"I was—" He stopped to wet his lips. He was a diplomat; where had the clever words fled to?

"Explanation, English." The officer's tone hardened.

"Visiting a lady." Surely they wouldn't ask him to produce her as his alibi.

"So you went swimming during a storm? Fully dressed? Here at Chiragan Palace, which is close to nobody's home except the Sultan?" The Turk put one hand onto his sword hilt, a gesture echoed by all of his men.

All the water St. Arles had swallowed surged into molten poison inside his belly.

"Liar!" Another kick hurtled into St. Arles' ribs. "You are only disguised as an Englishman."

"No," gasped St. Arles. How could he get a message to the Ambassador?—if the chap was even at home to receive one in time.

"You are a traitor who hopes to steal the former sultan and replace our glorious master."

St. Arles stopped writhing and stared at his interrogator. How had the fellow guessed the plot? An instant later, he pulled the old diplomatic mask back on but the damage was done.

"So—you are a traitor! Guards, take him to the torturer. He will extract the truth."

The brutes started to lift him up and St. Arles kicked out

wildly. He could not let them interrogate him and discover the British network here in Constantinople.

His hand slipped free, then a leg. A wrestlers' twist, learned on a Portsmouth dock, left them holding only his coat.

He raced for the terrace's railing.

"Grab him!" shouted the officer.

Twice as many thugs leaped upon him this time and his head banged against the paving. He threw off some of them but more came until every inch of him was weighted down. His ribs slashed into his chest, a fiery reminder of past pain and future torment. Fiery stars blurred his sight.

"Take him away."

Prayer was for weaklings. Instead, St. Arles offered them a golden bargain.

The senior Turk belted him in the side of the face and St. Arles's teeth ripped free into the wind.

The last fresh air St. Arles ever breathed was tainted by the officer's contempt.

From *The Times* of London, 10 May 1887:

> We regret to announce the sudden death of the Earl of St. Arles at the shockingly young age of thirty-eight. His lordship had been visiting Constantinople in pursuit of his photographic hobby, a pastime he first embarked upon while commissioned into the Royal Navy. He was suddenly overtaken by a tropical disorder, sinking rapidly into a decline from which no doctor was able to rouse him.

Chapter Thirty-nine

Dover, England, late May 1887

Gareth reached under his coat and tucked his vest down, striving again for sartorial perfection. Idiotic thing to do, since he had no intention of being present when William Donovan boarded the *Naiad*. To say nothing of anybody else Donovan saw fit to bring along, like his wife Viola or maybe his right-hand man Morgan Evans. Or Mrs. Donovan's brother and Portia's uncle, Hal Lindsay.

Or all the other family Portia had, which he didn't.

Spilled milk, boy. Spilled milk. Don't fuss about it, just move on.

He'd left a detailed letter explaining everything he'd done for Portia. If—when—Donovan wanted to know, they could discuss it in the fall, when he went back to California.

Six months should give her plenty of time to get an annulment or a divorce started without scandal, since she had his lawyer's name.

But he'd kept his word: He'd stayed with her until she reached England, despite the slowest boat trip he'd ever taken. Now it was time to leave.

One way or another, he'd make sure she was happier the next time around. She deserved somebody far better than St. Arles or him.

Maybe, if he was very lucky, she'd still think kindly of him, enough to let him stay in touch if she had children. He'd happily dote on her daughter.

"Good morning, sir. Newspapers for Mrs. Lowell." Barnesworth offered him an enormous market basket overflowing with newsprint, like a gray and white fountain.

"Where on earth did you find so many?" The heap looked as if it might heave and throw out offspring at any minute.

"Mrs. Lowell gave us a list."

"Really?" While Portia liked to read, she'd been more interested in books than newspapers lately. But perhaps she wanted to lay in a supply for the long voyage back home. Or maybe she was looking for a more accurate obituary of St. Arles than what the *London Times* had written.

Tropical disorder, indeed. British government lies, more likely.

At least all her friends, St. Arles' old servants, were happy with the new Earl of St. Arles. He'd hired them fast as St. Arles released them, even before he inherited—probably to infuriate the cousin he openly loathed. Now he had a staff whose loyalty he praised and which Portia was eager to meet again. They'd certainly have a great deal to say, just like the damn newspapers did.

"I'll take them down to her."

They might also give him a graceful topic to ease his way out the door before Donovan arrived.

"Portia?" He rapped lightly on the stateroom door before entering, then stopped. God help him, he could live with her for a century and still be amazed by how beautiful she was.

Or still be scared spitless when he remembered how she'd stood there with that damn big axe over her head and a boat rocking wildly around her, ready to bring it down to save him.

Today the spring sunshine gilded her hair like a halo before the mahogany paneling. She wore a simple pale blue dress, embroidered with white flowers, and her mouth was still swollen from his kisses.

If he looked closely, he'd see the bruise at the base of her neck where he'd marked her and he could probably smell himself on her. She swore she loved that scent as much as he loved hers.

Through the door on her left was their bedroom, which contained a bed more than large enough even for him.

He formed his face into a vaguely social expression and edged toward her.

"Newspapers, honey?"

"Why don't you read one to me? The social page first, if you please?"

Was she wearing a corset? No, her breasts were definitely unbound.

"Certainly." At least his voice hadn't cracked.

He managed to pull one out of the stack without ripping any pages. It was from a town he'd never heard of, that seemed more interested in industry than society.

"The marriages," she prompted, her cheeks a little pink.

He frowned and ran his finger down the brief list, looking for names he knew.

"Married. Gareth Lowell and Portia Vanneck. At Constantinople, 30 April 1887."

The sheets dropped onto the floor.

He cast her an incredulous look, which should have sent her shrinking back into her seat.

Instead, she fluffed out her hair and toyed with his mark, as if well satisfied.

Air started to disappear from the elegant stateroom. If all England knew they were married, a quiet divorce would be impossible. Her good name would be ruined if he left her.

He scrabbled through more newspapers but every one of them contained the same announcement, the same golden manacle: his marriage to his darling.

He stared at her, his heart beating in circles somewhere around his ears like a bird taking wing.

"Portia, what the devil is going on here? A dozen or more

newspapers are touting our marriage. You'll never be able to have a quiet divorce from me."

"You spoke of love—but you also spoke of leaving."

"You deserve better than me." The old cry was a shout from somewhere in his past.

"I am proud to be your wife because you are the finest man I know. I have wanted to call you *my husband* since I was twelve years old." Glory shone from her eyes.

"All these years?" He couldn't reach for her.

"Ever since you walked into Rachel Grainger's kitchen on Christmas Eve, I knew you were meant for me."

"That's madness. Nothing lasts that long."

"You healed me from St. Arles' tortures and taught me how to believe in joy again. Of course, I want you."

"Portia, any man who loves you would have given you that."

"You admit you love me." Her face lit up, brighter than the sun dancing on the water.

"Yes—no!" He slammed his fist down on the table. "But it does us no good. We must part."

"If you want a divorce now, you will have to fight for it. I love you and I want you more than my life. You must create a scandal in order to end our marriage."

When would she see the blood dripping from his hands, the trail of men he'd killed, the taint he'd pass on to his children?

"Portia, nobody in California knew you were married. All you had to do was get an annulment."

"Gareth." She knelt before him and kissed his hands. "You are the best man in the world. Why can't you see that? If you leave me this time, I will follow you, no matter where you go. 'Whither thou goest, I will go. And thy people shall be my people and your God my God', as Ruth said."

"Portia—"

"Gareth, you know you brought justice to your family's murderers, no matter how bitter the price. Please believe I understand that, too."

Christ, when he thought about all the nights when all he could see were the faces of the men he'd killed. But he never saw them with her.

"Come down here and love me," she pleaded, sliding her fingers around his wrists as if desperate to tie them together.

Instead he lifted her up and held her against his heart. He started to blaze a trail of kisses over his wife's cheek and down to her lips.

"Sometime soon we'll have to go above deck and greet our family," she reminded him.

Our family.

He began to grin, enthusiasm for the future bubbling up inside him for the first time since he was twelve.

Chapter Forty

Santa Barbara, California, August 1892

Rays of sunlight heated the lemon grove's dappled shade. The woodsy, sharp scent of citrus wood brightened the air until a breeze brought the headier aroma of jasmine from the banks by the irrigation ditch. A haze of lavender grew contentedly high along the ridgeline, in one of the few hillside fields not full of cattle or vineyards.

The Pacific Ocean sparkled beyond them, bright blue as a sailor's dream. Today it seemed to be on its best behavior as an avenue of commerce.

Gareth plucked a twig from one of his trees and began to examine it. Portia cast a suspicious glance at him then patted Juliet, their eldest child and only daughter, on the shoulder.

"Go tell Uncle William and Aunt Viola that Mother and Father will be along in a few minutes, please."

"Honest?" The little girl looked at them curiously, her clothing very clean for once. "But you're never late."

Gareth felt crimson steal into his cheeks and hastily adopted a stern mien. The attitude had grown easier since he'd been elected to the local city council. If nothing else, pomposity deflected questions about quick exits from official functions— and sudden reappearances with his beautiful wife.

Portia's skin was flushed, too, beside a very tight smile.

Their passion for each other had caused tardiness more than once—but not in front of the children.

Gareth came to his hapless darling's rescue, before her incurable honesty disclosed too much.

"Your mother and I need a few words together. In private," he added firmly, lest the little minx think to join them and thereby lord it over her siblings.

Juliet's eyes lit up. She started to wag both hands, the telltale start to a mischief-making campaign.

"We need to discuss some details about the ranch before we leave." Portia slammed the door on her interest in their conversation.

"For that?" The little tyke glared at them. "We could be in Uncle William's private car already!"

She took to her heels and raced off, every line blazing with indignation.

"I am properly put in my place," Gareth remarked and tossed aside his tree's leaves, satisfied they were healthy as his daughter. His father and grandfather would have been proud of this ranch, a worthy inheritance for future generations of Lowell family farmers.

The railroad had arrived in Santa Barbara the same year he and Portia returned from Europe, making this lovely port the western terminus of the southern transcontinental route. From here, travelers took a steamer to San Francisco, since the Southern Pacific had not yet conquered the coastal mountains' steep inclines.

He'd resigned from Donovan & Sons once he returned, determined to spend time with his wife instead of on the road. Portia, thank God, never wanted to set roots in San Francisco; she probably suspected the urban hurly-burly evoked his nightmares more rapidly than any other setting.

This delightful town offered the perfect compromise. It was only a few days away from her family, close enough that visits were frequent and casual. Yet the setting was quiet and bucolic. Their beautiful ranch had once been a Spanish land grant.

Many of the buildings' small details, such as the creamy stucco walls and red tile roofs, provided reminders of the Arizona towns and friends who'd sheltered him long ago.

Even his dreams were peaceful here, in his wife's bed.

Portia tucked her arm through his and began to stroll toward their private railroad siding, a wedding present from her grandfather.

"I sent a half dozen cases of our lemons ahead to my brothers," she remarked. Her golden hair gleamed above her white dress, showcased by the jasmine's glossy green leaves behind her. He never tired of telling her she was the most beautiful woman in California. "Their chefs apparently plan a competition at Newport showcasing their use."

"Bravo. Cynthia and her husband are judging it, aren't they, now that they're back from Australia?" He cast a longing glance back at his grape vines. This would be the first time he missed the harvest. "Do you think—"

"No," she retorted. "You have to leave the ranch sometime, instead of making everyone visit us here. Besides, this is a very important family trip and everyone will be there."

"Morgan and Jessamyn Evans, Lucas and Rachel Grainger, even Hal and Rosalind Lindsay will meet us in Los Angeles with all of their broods." He whistled softly at how far that steamboat captain and his lady gambler had traveled. Then he reached up and snatched a golden fruit from the highest branch. "All to see Neil Donovan, the firstborn son of an Irish clan, off to Harvard. Truly, miracles do happen."

Children's laughter swelled through the trees from up ahead. A man shouted something, more weary repetition than sharp warning.

Gareth offered the token to his darling, the lady who'd given him joy and warmth beyond measure. Her fingers wrapped his wrist in an unbreakable bond.

"Yes, truly miracles do happen," she agreed and trailed her fingers down the side of his face. "You are finally mine."

"We are both at home in each other's arms." He kissed her,

heedless of the clock or their proximity to dozens of family members. Only her sweetness mattered to him now—until the four Donovan boys ran past, hurling their usual insults at each other.

"Marlowe Donovan, where do you think you're going?" Neil Donovan shouted, his voice as effortlessly loud as his father's. At nineteen, he was already a fine man whose eyes were older than his years.

"To pick some grapes!" The younger boy's response faded along the path toward the orchards.

Gareth lifted his head to watch, his arms still locked around his wife.

"Dammit, Brian, why did you teach a ten year old how to make wine?" Neil snarled. Due to some trick of the landscape, almost any word said close to the working sheds could be heard by the stables and the railroad siding.

"I didn't—he stole the book," snapped the second son and redoubled his pace. Slimmer than his older brother with laughter tempering his eyes' alertness, Brian soon passed Neil on the lane but still lost the two younger devils, who'd disappeared into the packing shed.

"Do you think any of Marlowe's efforts will be drinkable?" Portia asked softly, her voice pitched in the husky croon which wouldn't carry to the sheds—but always traveled straight to her husband's groin.

His blood immediately answered her, as always, and Gareth cursed silently. Still, they'd be alone together again soon enough in their own private car on Donovan's private train.

He tried for a joke to cover his response.

"Perhaps we should let him make it and then taste the results. After that, he'll probably look for different mischief."

"Unlike us, who found the best during childhood." Portia drew a heart on the back of Gareth's hand.

He caught her fingers and stared down into her eyes, eternally amazed by the miracle of her love. Surely there was time for a quick detour into the house.

"Ahem." A man coughed softly and Gareth reluctantly looked up.

William and Viola strolled through the garden from the railroad siding to join them. Thank God Viola's eyes twinkled with laughter over her sons' antics. It was far better to see that than the coughing spasms which could attack her when she was anxious.

"How long do you think it will be until Neil rounds them up?" Portia asked, her tone light and jocular.

"Less than five minutes."

Gareth had never dared to disbelieve William Donovan before. But such a flat statement certainly begged to be contradicted.

The Irishman glanced at him, his arm locked around his wife's waist the same way Gareth held his lady.

"All of them know the chef has a fresh batch of raisin cookies in the oven."

"They won't miss those," Gareth agreed, awed by his friend's foresight.

"Every husband and father learns what bribes work and when to have them ready." William winked at him. "It's part of leading a family."

"Thank you for the advice—and for welcoming me into your clan."

"You always were a member of my family, from the minute you joined up in Kansas City."

Gareth's breath stopped in his throat, while all too many things became clear. His friend's casual but vital teachings, the protectiveness, the willingness to let him go his own way while always making sure he had friends and resources to back him. And, most of all, the unquestioning support whenever he needed it.

William held out his hand to him and they gripped strongly, while their wives beamed.

Author's Note

The *Al-Muqattam* newspaper of Cairo reported (in no. 1964, 7 September 1895) the imprisonment of a newcomer to Constantinople, whose only "crime" was having the same name as the current Sultan and staying at a hotel named similarly to the Sultan's palace. Poignantly, that gentleman had come to take up a job in the Justice Ministry. He was insane and penniless when he was finally released.

Thanks to Steven Maffeo for clarifying details of the Immortal Memory toast at Trafalgar Day banquets in British naval etiquette, and to the Weapons-Info group at Yahoo! for providing the perfect nineteenth-century blades.

Much of this book is set in Cairo and Constantinople during the twilight years of the Ottoman Empire. As if matters weren't complicated enough for an English-speaking author, the great Turkish leader Mustafa Kemal, known as Ataturk, led the conversion of Turkey's writing system and its language from Ottoman (i.e., extended Arabic) script to Roman. In other words, the names for the same characters and places have frequently changed over time and have multiple possible spellings in the Roman alphabet. I have therefore followed the examples of experts on translating them, while striving to maintain clarity and consistency.

Grab BEAST BEHAVING BADLY, the latest in the Pride
series from Shelly Laurenston, out now from Brava!

Bo shot through the goal crease and slammed the puck into the net.

"Morning!"

That voice cut through his focus and, without breaking his stride, Bo changed direction and skated over to the rink entrance. He stopped hard, ice spraying out from his skates, and stood in front of the wolfdog.

He stared down at her and she stared up at him. She kept smiling even when he didn't. Finally he asked, "What time did we agree on?"

"Seven," she replied with a cheery note that put his teeth on edge.

"And what time is it?"

"Uh . . ." She dug into her jeans and pulled out a cell phone. The fact that she still had on that damn, useless watch made his head want to explode. How did one function—as an adult anyway—without a goddamn watch?

Grinning so that he could see all those perfectly aligned teeth, she said, "Six-forty-five!"

"And what time did we agree on?"

She blinked and her smile faded. After a moment, "Seven."

"Is it seven?"

"No." When he only continued to stare at her, she softly asked, "Want to meet me at the track at seven?"

He continued to stare at her until she nodded and said, "Okay."

She walked out and Bo went back to work.

Fifteen minutes later, Bo walked into the small arena at seven a.m. Blayne, looking comfortable in dark blue leggings, sweatshirt, and skates, turned to face him. He expected her to be mad at him or, even worse, for her to get that wounded look he often got from people when he was blatantly direct. But having to deal with either of those scenarios was a price Bo was always willing to pay to ensure that the people in his life understood how he worked from the beginning. This way, there were no surprises later. It was called "boundaries" and he read about it in a book.

Yet when Blayne saw him, she grinned and held up a Starbucks cup. "Coffee," she said when he got close. "I got you the house brand because I had no idea what you would like. And they had cinnamon twists, so I got you a few of those."

He took the coffee, watching her close. Where was it? The anger? The resentment? Was she plotting something?

Blayne held the bag of sweets out for him and Bo took them. "Thank you," he said, still suspicious even as he sipped his perfectly brewed coffee.

"You're welcome." And there went that grin again. Big and brighter than the damn sun. "And I get it. Seven means seven. Eight means eight, etc., etc. Got it and I'm on it. It won't happen again." She said all that without a trace of bitterness and annoyance, dazzling Bo with her understanding more than she'd dazzled him with those legs.

"So," she put her hands on her hips, "what do you want me to do first?"

Marry me? Wait. No, no. Incorrect response. It'll just weird her out and make her run again. Normal. Be normal. You can do this. You're not just a great skater. You're a normal *great skater.*

When Bo knew he had his shit together, he said, "Let's work on your focus first. And, um, should I ask what happened to your face?" She had a bunch of cuts on her cheeks. Gouges. Like something small had pawed at her.

"Nope!" she chirped, pulling off her sweatshirt. She wore a worn blue T-shirt underneath with *B&G Plumbing* scrawled across it. With sweatshirt in hand, Blayne skated over to the bleachers, stopped, shook her head, skated over to another section of bleachers, stopped, looked at the sweatshirt, turned around, and skated over to the railing. "I should leave it here," she explained, "In case I get chilly."

It occurred to Bo he'd just lost two minutes of his life watching her try and figure out where to place a damn sweatshirt. Two minutes that he'd never get back.

"Woo-hoo!" she called out once she hit the track. "Let's go!"

She was skating backward as she urged him to join her with both hands.

He pointed behind her. "Watch the—"

"Ow!"

"—pole."

Christ, what had he gotten himself into?

Christ almighty, what had she gotten herself into?

Twenty minutes in and she wanted to smash the man's head against a wall. She wanted to go back in time and kick the shit out of Genghis Khan before turning on his brothers, Larry and Moe. Okay. That wasn't their names but she could barley remember Genghis's name on a good day, how the hell was she supposed to remember his brothers'. But whatever the Khan kin's names may be, Blayne wanted to hurt them all for cursing her world with this . . . this . . . Visigoth!

Even worse, she knew he didn't even take what she did seriously. He insisted on calling it a chick sport. If he were a sexist pig across the board, Blayne could overlook it as a mere flaw in his upbringing. But, she soon discovered, Novikov had a very high degree of respect for female athletes . . . as long as they were athletes and not just "hot chicks in cute outfits, roughing each other up. All you guys need is some hot oil or mud and you'd have a real moneymaker on your hands."

And yet, even while he didn't respect her sport as a sport, he still worked her like he was getting her ready for the Olympics.

After thirty minutes she wanted nothing more but to lie on her side and pant. She doubted the hybrid would let her get away with that, though.

Shooting around the track, Novikov stopped her in a way that she was finding extremely annoying—by grabbing her head with that big hand of his and holding her in place.

He shoved her back with one good push and Blayne fought not to fall on her ass at that speed. When someone shoved her like that, they were usually pissed. He wasn't.

"I need to see something," he said, still nursing that cup of coffee. He'd finished off the cinnamon twists in less than five minutes while she was warming up. "Come at me as hard as you can."

"Are you sure?" she asked, looking him over. He didn't have any of his protective gear on, somehow managing to change into sweatpants and T-shirt and still make it down to the track exactly at seven. "I don't want to hurt you," she told him honestly.

The laughter that followed, however, made her think she did want to hurt him. She wanted to hurt him a lot. When he realized she wasn't laughing with him—or, in this case, laughing at *herself* since he was obviously laughing *at* her—Novikov blinked and said, "Oh. You're not kidding."

"No. I'm not kidding."

"Oh. Oh! Um . . . I'll be fine. Hit me with your best shot."

"Like Pat Benatar?" she joked but when he only stared at her, she said, "Forget it."

Blayne sized up the behemoth in front of her and decided to move back a few more feet so she could get a really fast start. She got into position and took one more scrutinizing look. It was a skill her father had taught her. To size up weakness. Whether the weakness of a person or a building or whatever. Of course,

Blayne often used this skill for good, finding out someone's weakness and then working to help them overcome it. Her father, however, used it to destroy.

Lowering her body, Blayne took a breath, tightened her fists, and took off. She lost some speed on the turn but picked it up as she cut inside. As Blayne approached Novikov, she sized him up one more time as he stood there casually, sipping his coffee and watching her move around the track. Based on that last assessing look, she slightly adjusted her position and slammed into him with everything she had.

And, yeah, she knocked herself out cold, but it was totally worth it when the behemoth went down with her.

Don't miss Cynthia Eden's I'LL BE SLAYING YOU, out next month from Brava!

"Let me buy you a drink."

She'd ignored the men beside her. Greeted the few come-ons she'd gotten with silence. But that voice—

Dee glanced to the left. Tall, Dark, and Sexy was back.

And he was smiling down at her. A big, wide grin that showed off a weird little dint in his right cheek. Not a dimple, too hard for that. She hadn't noticed that last night, now with the hunt and kill—

Shit but he was hot.

Thanks to the spotlights over the bar, she could see him so much better tonight. No shadows to hide behind now.

Hard angles, strong jaw, sexy mouth.

She licked her lips. "Already got one." Dee held up her glass.

"Babe, that's water." He motioned to the bartender. "Let me get you something with bite."

She'd spent the night looking for a bite. Hadn't found it yet. Her fingers snagged his. "I'm working." Booze couldn't slow her down. Not with the one she hunted.

Black brows shot up. Then he leaned in close. So close that she caught the scent of his aftershave. "You gonna kill another woman tonight?" A whisper that blew against her.

Her lips tightened. "Vampire," she said quietly.

He blinked. Those eyes of his were kinda eerie. Like a smoky fog staring back at her.

"I hunted a vampire last night," Dee told him, keeping her voice hushed because in a place like this, you never knew who was listening. "And, technically, she'd already been killed once before I got to her."

His fingers locked around her upper arm. She'd yanked on a black T-shirt before heading out, and his fingertips skimmed her flesh. "Guess you're right," he murmured and leaned in even closer.

His lips were about two inches—maybe just one—away from hers.

What would he taste like?

It'd been too long since she'd had a lover, and this guy fit all of her criteria. Big, strong, sexy and aware of the score in the city.

"Wanna dance with me?" Such dark words. No accent at all underlined the whisper. Just a rich purr of sex.

Oh but she bet the guy was fantastic in the sack.

Find out. A not-so-weak challenge in her mind.

Why not? She wasn't seeing anyone. He seemed up for it and—

Dee brought her left hand up between them and pushed against his chest. "I don't dance." Especially not to that too fast, pounding music that made her head ache.

He didn't retreat. His eyes bored into hers. "Pity." His fingers skated down her arm and caught her wrist. He took her glass away, sat it on the bar top with a clink.

She cocked her head and studied him. "Are you following me?" Two nights. First, sure, that could have been coincidence. A coincidence she was grudgingly grateful for, but tonight—

The faintest curl hinted on his lips. "What if I am?"

His thighs brushed against her. Big, strong thighs. Thick with muscle.

Dee swallowed. So not the time.

But the man was tempting.

She couldn't afford a distraction. Not then. "Then you'd better be very, very careful." Dee shoved against him. Hard.

He stumbled back a step and his smile widened. "You keep playing hard to get, and I'm gonna start thinking you're not interested in me, Sandra Dee."

Who was this guy? Dee jumped off the bar stool. "You'd be thinking right, buddy."

He took her wrist again with strong, roughened fingers. The guy towered over her. Always the way of it. When you couldn't even skim five foot six with big-ass heels, most men towered over you. And since Dee had never worn heels in her life . . .

The guy bent toward her when he said, "I see the way you look at me."

What did that mean?

"Curious . . . but more. Like maybe you got a wild side lurking in you. A side that wants out."

Maybe she did. The guy sure looked like he could play. *After the case.*

"I don't know you, Chase," she finally told him, too aware of his touch on her skin. Too aware that her nipples were tightening and she was leaning toward him as her nostrils flared and she tried to suck up more of his scent. "I don't know—"

"I saved your life." A fallen angel's smile. "Doesn't that count for something?"

Donna Kauffman knows SOME LIKE IT SCOT, so go out and get her newest book today!

Just then he heard the loud reverberation of the chapel's pipe organ ring out the beginning of Mendelssohn's wedding march.

He sprinted back around to the front of the church and slipped inside behind her, just as she began her walk down the aisle. His heart sank, but he shook off the disconcerting feeling and edged as quietly as possible into the end of the last pew once she'd made her way down the aisle. All eyes were on the bride. No one noticed the man in the kilt. He pulled the now crumpled photo of Katie McAuley out of his sporran, and forced his gaze away from the bride and down to the picture in his hands. He needed to find her and start focusing on what he planned to do next.

He unfolded the photo . . . and frowned at the face smiling back at him, blonde tendrils were blowing wildly about her face, as were those of the brunette and redhead mates she was clutched between. All three women were laughing, smiling, as if enjoying a great lark. Or simply the company they were in, regardless of location or event. He couldn't fathom feeling so utterly carefree. Or so happy, for that matter. It was both an unsettling discovery, and a rather depressing one. He enjoyed the challenge of his work, but . . . was he happy? The carefree smiling kind of happy? He knew the answer to that. What he wanted to know was when, exactly, had he stopped having fun? He could hear Roan's voice ring through his consciousness, as if he were an angel—or more aptly, a devil—perched upon his tartaned shoulder. *"When did you ever start?"*

And then the pastor began intoning the marriage rites, and Graham's gaze was pulled intractably back to the woman standing in front of the altar. She turned to her betrothed and he lifted the veil. Graham felt himself drawn physically forward, the crumpled photo in his hands forgotten, as he shifted on his feet and tried his best to—finally—see her face. It was only natural, he told himself, to want to see what she looked like, after talking with her in the garden.

But why he was holding his breath, he had no earthly idea.

Then she turned her head, just slightly, and he could have sworn she looked directly at him. His heart squeezed. Hard. Then stuttered to a stop. Only this time he knew exactly why. He looked down at the picture in his hand, and forced himself to draw in air past the tightness in his chest. He distantly heard the pastor urge everyone to be seated. And one by one, everyone did.

Everyone, that was, except him.

He turned over the wedding program that had been handed to him as he'd entered the church. He looked at the lengthy name engraved on the front, then lifted his gaze to her. "It's you," he declared, his deep voice echoing loudly, reverberating around the soaring chapel ceiling. "Katherine Elizabeth Georgina Rosemary McAuley." Katie. The nickname that had stuck. He held up the photo, as if that would explain everything, while he stood there, acutely dumbfounded. His mind raced as fast as his heart, as everything suddenly made perfect sense. And no sense at all.

He lifted the photo higher, stabbing it forward, as if making a claim. And perhaps he was. He felt driven by something unknown, a force he could neither put name nor logic to. If he were honest, it had begun outside, in the garden. It was something both primal and primeval, driven by what could only be utter lunacy. Because clearly, he'd lost whatever he'd had left of his mind. Yet that didn't stop him from continuing. In fact, he barely paused to draw breath.

"You're meant to be mine," he declared, loudly, defiantly, to the collective gasp of every man, woman, and child lining each and every pew. He didn't care. Because he'd never meant anything more in his entire life. And he hadn't the remotest idea why. Yet it was truth; one he'd never been more certain of. It was as if all four hundred years of MacLeods willfully and intently binding themselves to McAuleys were pumping viscerally through his veins.

Clan curse, indeed.